A GREAT AND TERRIBLE DARKNESS

Center Point
Large Print

Also by Linda J. White and available from
Center Point Large Print:

All That I Dread
The Fear That Chases Me
When Evil Finds Us
My Darkest Night
Winter Flight

A GREAT AND TERRIBLE DARKNESS

K-9 SEARCH & RESCUE
BOOK 6

LINDA J. WHITE

CENTER POINT LARGE PRINT
THORNDIKE, MAINE

This Center Point Large Print edition
is published in the year 2025 by arrangement with
the author.

Copyright © 2024 Linda J. White.

All rights reserved.

The persons and events portrayed in this work of fiction are the creation of the author. Any resemblance to any person living or dead is purely coincidental.

Scripture quotations are from the ESV Bible (The Holy Bible, English Standard Version), copyright 2001 by Crossway, a publishing ministry of Good News Publishing. Used by permission. All rights reserved.

The text of this Large Print edition is unabridged.
In other aspects, this book may vary
from the original edition.
Printed in the United States of America
on permanent paper sourced using
environmentally responsible foresting methods.
Set in 16-point Times New Roman type.

ISBN: 979-8-89164-507-3

The Library of Congress has cataloged this record
under Library of Congress Control Number: 2024951719

For Kim and Drew
who persevere with courage and faith
on their own long journey.

He will swallow up death forever; and the Lord God will wipe away tears from all faces.

—Isaiah 26:8a

A GREAT AND TERRIBLE DARKNESS

1

I've been a street cop. A homicide detective. A hardboiled private investigator. But I had never sat across the table from someone as tough as this guy.

"No risky behavior," he said.

"Define 'risky,' " I responded.

"Potentially hazardous to life or limb." My husband's blue eyes narrowed.

"Okay, so you've just eliminated driving, handling knives in the kitchen, and riding your beloved horses." I pushed my chair back in frustration. "You're being unreasonable!"

"And you're being stubborn."

Scott and I were "discussing" what he considered proper activities during the remaining six months of my pregnancy. We had already covered my activities as a private investigator, during which he nixed domestic assault-related investigations and bitter custody battles. Now we were moving on to my work as a search and rescue volunteer. Apparently, he thought rock climbing, jumping into farm ponds, and scaling down cliffs barehanded, all of which I'd done in the recent past, were inappropriate behaviors for the mother of his unborn child.

In retaliation, I had objected to the father of

said child, namely him, doing the things which resulted in him being shot in the hip and later, in the shoulder, as well as nearly dying from hypothermia.

To be fair, he was rescuing his daughter from traffickers in the first case and was double-crossed by a depressed law-enforcement officer in the second. His injuries were hardly attributable to his risk-taking, but doggone it, I needed something to add to his side of the ledger.

Scott sat across from me at our well-worn farm table, his dark hair slightly graying at the temples—a development he blamed on me. His arm rested in a sling. He'd had shoulder surgery three days after Christmas, repairing the damage done to him by the bullet fired by the depressed deputy. Scott is impossibly handsome, and I had to fight myself to keep from giving in just for the embrace that would follow.

He took a deep breath. "All right, Jess. What *are* you willing to give up?"

I raised my chin. "Rock climbing. Rappelling. Swift-water rescues. Any searches that involve hazardous materials. Fires. Searching dangerous structures." I kept my gaze steady as I ticked off my concessions.

"How about searches, period." He said it as a statement, not a question.

"No. I'm not giving up SAR until I have to."

"You need your rest."

"Luke needs the work."

"How about put the baby before the dog?"

I stood up. "Oh, for crying out loud. I'm not fragile! Women have been carrying babies while they worked for generations."

There was a long pause. "I'm sorry," he said, adopting a gentle tone.

I sat back down. "I'll know when it's time to stop searching." I could tell by his face he didn't like that answer but he wasn't going to fight me about it.

"All right. I'll put down rock climbing, rappelling . . ." Scott jotted notes on a legal pad.

"What about you? What will you give up? This baby needs a father, too."

He shrugged. "I'm okay."

"You're not! You've just been shot for the second time in what . . . three years?"

"I'm fine! I'm on medical leave. The bureau doesn't expect me to respond to a tactical situation."

"Yet I've seen you out back practicing with your Glock." FBI agents are supposed to be on duty 24/7. They're also required to shoot accurately with both "strong" and "weak" hands. Even before his surgery, with his right arm in a sling, Scott had set up straw bales and a target and had been practicing smoothly drawing his gun and shooting with his left hand.

"That's for you, not the FBI!" he protested. "I

have to know I can protect you." He ran his hand through his hair then looked at me. "I promise you, my biggest hazard in the next few months will be eyestrain." Scott planned to use his recovery time finalizing his dissertation for his PhD.

I paused, frustrated, then crossed my arms and said, "Well, I don't think you should be riding. Horses are dangerous."

His face colored. "Ace is totally reliable."

I knew he was right. The chances of him falling off that horse were practically zero. Scott was so strong, I'd seen him ride bareback, no reins. But I couldn't think of anything else to make him give up.

Scott must have realized my dilemma. "Tell you what," he said, "I promise I won't intentionally get into dangerous situations. I won't ride bareback, and I won't climb ladders or go on the roof until my arm is healed."

"Or up in the loft," I said, desperate to balance our ledgers.

"Okay. No loft."

"And you'll let Ethan plow the driveway if it snows. And cut the grass in the spring."

A slight smile crossed his face. "Sure." He paused. "So, do we have a deal?" He held out his hand.

I pressed my lips together, but then I shook on it. "Deal. Hand me the pad."

Scott pushed the legal pad toward me, and I

wrote down what he had promised. "Done!" I said.

He stood up, came around the table, and wrapped his arm around me. As he enveloped me in his familiar strength, his chest warm, his breath soft in my ear, my battle armor melted.

No one ever told me how emotional pregnant women can be. One day, I stood on the front porch watching my German shepherd, Luke, race joyfully through the three inches of snow that had fallen overnight. Then a cardinal flew from the hitching post in the front yard over to my Jeep. As I stood there thinking about how pretty he looked against the white snow and the white Jeep, I realized something. The Jeep, which had been modified for search and rescue, had no back seat! No place for a baby's car seat. I was going to have to get rid of it!

Tears streamed down my face. *My Jeep!* It was part of me. I couldn't give it up.

But it had no space for the baby. And I could not stop crying.

I went back inside to get a tissue and ran headlong into Scott. "Hey, hey! What's wrong?" he asked me. "Why are you crying?"

I told him. To his credit he didn't laugh. Instead, he thought about it for a minute and said, "We can keep the Jeep."

"It's expensive to keep extra cars!"

He shrugged. "It's not a bad idea to have a spare car out here in the country. It's paid for and it's four-wheel drive, both good things. I think we should keep it and buy you something else, an SUV. Maybe even a mom van." He grinned.

A mom van? I tried to picture me in a minivan. "It has to have room for Luke."

"Luke and the baby. And maybe even me."

That made me laugh. "I don't know why I got so upset."

A few days later I got a book on what to expect during pregnancy. Scott had ordered it for me. I guess I should have thought of that, but honestly, he's more of a book person.

For a week after it came, I devoured that book. I had no idea having babies was so complicated. Then I panicked. We had barely made any progress on updating the old farmhouse we'd bought a couple of years before. Things kept interrupting our plans, things like investigations and hijacked school buses. School shootings. You know, the normal stuff.

Now we had a deadline: July 20. How in the world were we going to get everything done?

So I developed a plan. A very detailed plan.

Our jobs included transforming the small bedroom nearest ours into a nursery, converting one of the bigger bedrooms into workspace for both Scott and me, redoing the kitchen, stripping the wallpaper from the downstairs center hall, having the downstairs floors sanded and refinished, and painting all the walls.

Scott got the idea we should grab some space from the office/bedroom and create a laundry center upstairs. I thought that was a waste of time and money, but he said, "You have no idea how much laundry you'll be doing! You're going to get tired of running down to the basement."

"What? Baby clothes are small!" I countered naively. In the end, we compromised. We'd ask a builder about putting a laundry room on the first floor, maybe using part of the small back porch.

Meanwhile, Scott's friend Mike Perez, another agent, was bent on taking what used to be a smokehouse out back and turning it into a small gym. "Scott's got to rehab his arm," he told me. "He can either do it here or drive an hour. You all live in the middle of nowhere!"

I just rolled my eyes. I'd let the two guys wrestle that one out. But I did *not* put it on the project list.

On a whiteboard posted in the kitchen, I catalogued every job, the time allotted for it, the start and end dates, and the estimated cost. We would begin working through the list in two weeks, and the baby nursery was first up. Our friends, Nate and Mike, agreed to help Scott with the construction. I said I'd start by packing up my office stuff and moving what I could to the new workspace.

I was less than an hour into that project when I

got a phone call. Quickly, I changed into my SAR clothes and trotted downstairs. "I got a callout about a missing person police need some help with," I told Scott, as I walked into the kitchen. Luke danced around me, tail wagging. He knew what those clothes meant.

Scott looked up from his laptop. "What police? Where?"

"Harrisonburg." I pulled out the empty chair beside him at the kitchen table and began putting on my boots. "I didn't get all the details. It's a young woman from the university. I'm taking Luke, but it sounds like we'll mostly be working in the office."

"Who else is going?"

"Just me. One of the detectives attended my seminar. They're paying me as a consultant." I finished tying my boots, leaned over, and kissed him. "I'll probably be home for dinner."

I stood and he rose as well, wrapping his arm around me and kissing me goodbye. "No rappelling?"

"No rappelling. Or hazardous structures. Or farm ponds or swift water rescues and so on. I'm just a consultant."

"Okay. Be safe." He glanced down. "Your pants still fit?"

"One notch looser on the belt," I said, grinning. So far, Baby Cooper was still mostly our little secret.

2

The January sky looked like cotton batting overhead, thick and gray on the drive over to Harrisonburg. Around me the fields lay bare, corn stubble poking up like the Earth's five o'clock shadow. Off to the right, Angus cattle dotted the foothills rippling toward the Blue Ridge Mountains. Some stood in clumps around round bales of hay, chewing peacefully. Seeing them I remembered I wanted to buy a quarter of a steer from our neighbors the next time they had some. I made a mental note to add that to the whiteboard.

I turned onto Route 33, heading straight toward the mountains. The winter-bare trees of the Shenandoah National Park stood gray and silent in the still air, like millions of spears standing ready. Here and there stands of pines and cedars broke up the pattern. Jagged rock faces interrupted the landscape even further.

I heard Luke move in his crate. I'd brought him and my pack in case we needed to do some field work. But my impression was the police wanted my advice more than anything.

I went over in my mind what I knew about Harrisonburg as I drove. The mid-sized city lay in the central Shenandoah Valley right along

Interstate 81, a major north-south route. Home to James Madison University, my impression was that Harrisonburg was a relatively quiet place. Eastern Mennonite University and nearby Bridgewater College brought more young people to the area, and many stayed. I could imagine they would be attracted to the beautiful mountains and rivers, the small-city feel, and the outdoor activities.

I stopped to give Luke some exercise, then made my way to the glass-bedecked police station, parked, and went inside with Luke trotting behind me. I thought I remembered Detective Robert Porter from the seminar I'd done, and one look at him confirmed that. An African-American in his early forties, he stood about six feet tall. His broad shoulders stretched his blue shirt tight and his hand, when he shook mine, felt strong, like he'd thrown a football or two in his day. "Welcome, welcome," he said. "Thanks for coming."

After greeting Luke, Detective Porter led me back through the maze of offices to a small conference room, where he and a uniformed officer named Jason Black began walking me through the case. "Heather Burgess, twenty-one, was with a bunch of friends downtown in this area," he drew a circle on a blowup of a map, "on Tuesday night, her birthday. She hasn't been seen since."

"She was with a large group, at least eight people," Jason said, "and they'd all been drinking. Point last seen was here." He indicated an intersection in the downtown area just off Main Street. "Heather said she was going to throw up and went around the corner. They kept moving and never saw her again."

"When did they report her missing?"

"Thursday night."

"Why'd they wait so long?"

"They weren't thinking clearly, any of 'em. Not long after that, the group broke up into smaller groups. Some kept going to bars, others went home. They all thought Heather was with someone else."

"Her roommate didn't notice she was gone?"

Officer Black shrugged. "Apparently, it wasn't unusual for any of them to crash with a friend."

"Is there a boyfriend?"

"No."

I paused, trying on different scenarios in my head. Nothing fit. "You have a pretty low crime rate, don't you?"

Detective Porter blew out a breath. "One murder last year. And that was a domestic. The kids at JMU, they party, but not like some other schools."

When I was a Fairfax County homicide detective we used to joke about applying for a job in Harrisonburg because it would be like a year-round paid vacation. "Rapes?"

"We get forty or fifty reports a year," the

detective responded. "Most of 'em college kids who either don't understand the word no or are clinging to morning-after rationalizations."

I flinched internally. It was hard for a woman to stand up and say, "I was raped." Hard to undergo the forensic exam, the questioning. I suspected the number of false accusations from "morning-after rationalizations" was pretty low. It was much easier to just hide in shame. "What's this area?" I pointed to a green space on the map not far from the point last seen.

"That's a park. Creek running through it."

"Woods?"

"Yes."

"You got eyes on it?"

Porter shook his head. "No cameras in or around the park. And that alley is the point last seen. Full of dumpsters basically. No cameras there either." He paused. "And yes, we've checked the dumpsters."

I took a deep breath. "Okay. I'd like to get a visual of that area."

Porter nodded. "Jason, you keep canvassing the neighborhood. See if there's any video we overlooked, anybody who just happened to be there late." He looked at me. "I've got officers at the college working the dorms and going back over the bars. The chief is waiting on a phone call from the parents. They're traveling in Europe." He shook his head. "The way I'm looking at it, if we don't find her soon, we'll be in recovery mode, looking for a body."

I agreed with Porter, I thought, as I followed him in my Jeep to an area not far from the police station. We parked on a side street. I got out, my breath streaming out like smoke. I zipped up my North Face jacket, wondering if I'd make it through winter without needing a bigger size.

I let Luke out of the back and leashed him up, then followed Porter to Main Street, the cold air nipping at my ears. The air smelled good, fresh. Porter wore a nice black wool topcoat over his navy blue suit. I noticed for the first time he was wearing classy Italian leather shoes. I wondered where he was from. I doubted it was Harrisonburg, not originally anyway. This was more of a boots-and-parkas kind of place.

"There are drinking establishments here and here," Porter said, turning and pointing as we reached Main Street. The buildings were old, mostly brick, and they looked like they'd recently been renovated. "There's another one on the next street over. Let's go around back."

He led us to an alley that ran behind the cluster of businesses facing Main Street. It was, like most alleys, full of dumpsters and grimy back doors, paper trash, and the occasional wadded up rag or T-shirt. For Luke, it was a smorgasbord of interesting smells, and he tugged at the leash.

"The kids think this is where she went to throw up," Porter said.

"They think?"

"One of them was pretty sure they were walking up this street toward Main when she left them. But they said they couldn't be sure. It was dark."

"Right." It was dark and they were drunk. "I'm going to let my dog sniff around." I unclipped Luke's leash, although I gave him no command. We both began exploring the alley, peeking around dumpsters and trying to imagine Heather's actions that night. Luke used his nose, of course. "You checked all these?" I asked, gesturing toward the dumpsters.

"Yes."

If I were going into this alley to puke in the dark, I thought, *I wouldn't go far.* So I poked around the first couple of dumpsters looking for any evidence Heather had been there. Looking for puke, even. When I raised my head, I saw Luke had moved much farther down the alley. He was taking a special interest in the green dumpster behind a Chinese carry-out place. I hoped he didn't smell a rat. I was about to call him back, when he moved on, walking nose to the ground.

Porter was behind me talking on his phone. I flipped over some trash on the ground with my foot. The next time I looked up, I saw Luke had returned to the green dumpster. I walked toward him as he circled the thing. An employee emerged from the business with two large bags of trash. He saw Luke and cursed.

"He won't hurt you," I yelled, picking up my pace.

The young man hesitated, apparently trying to decide if he believed me, then approached the dumpster, lifted the lid, and dumped the bags, keeping one eye fixed on Luke.

"Were you working Monday night?" I asked, slightly out of breath.

"You a cop?"

"No, just a searcher."

"For that girl?"

I nodded.

"I wasn't working and wasn't down here," he said. He shook his head. "I didn't see her."

"Okay, thanks."

He went back inside. That's when I noticed Luke was really focusing on a corner of the dumpster, his nose working hard, like he smelled a hot dog.

I thought that was probably what it was. Some food product. But I bent down to look closely and there, under a bent corner of the dumpster, I saw something. "Detective?" I called out.

Porter looked up, clicked off his phone, and jogged toward me.

I pointed down. "There's something under

there." I pointed my cell phone flashlight toward it, catching a glint of metal.

He looked, removed gloves from his pocket, and retrieved a small silver earring from under the corner of the dumpster. He held it up. It was a tiny Tree of Life.

3

Detective Porter placed the earring on the ground next to a ruler. He took a picture. So did I, just for my own records. Then he put the earring in a clear evidence bag. "I'm sending that picture to investigators working the dorm where Heather lived. See if we can identify it as hers." He gestured toward Luke. "How did he know to alert on that?"

"He didn't," I responded. "Not really. He's trained to sniff out human remains or live people. I hadn't asked him to do either. But that earring was out of place, and he knew it, and it drew his attention, which drew mine."

"Amazing. So if we get a positive ID on that earring, it places her in the alley. That's not much, but it is something."

"If you have your evidence team pull everything out and lay it on a tarp, I can ask Luke to check it for the scent of human remains," I suggested.

"Sounds good. They're going to be thrilled to climb through that dumpster again." Porter grinned.

"In the meantime, I think we'll go check out that park," I said, pointing toward the ribbon of trees nearby.

The park, according to the topographical map

I carried, was a strip of green with a thread of blue in the middle—a small stream. As I walked toward it, I wondered if I should ask Luke to "seek" out any live person, or "find" evidence of human remains. Was Heather Burgess alive?

It would have been easy for her to lose an earring throwing up in the alley. She naturally would have bent over and pushed her long hair back to keep vomit out of it, dislodging the earring as she did. Visualizing that scenario, I decided to take the positive approach. She was probably alive, just missing. As we stepped onto the paved path through the park, I told Luke to "seek," to search for a live person.

He took off down the path, muscles rippling under his black and gold coat. He swung left, then right, "quartering" to try and catch a scent in the still wind. He dropped down into the creek, ran along it for a while, then came back up to the path. His pace never slowed.

We walked upstream until the creek disappeared into a small pipe running under some buildings, then we turned and walked downstream. The whole park was only about a mile long, so within forty minutes we had covered the whole thing. He sniffed but didn't alert on anything. When we reached the end, I saw a young man with a backpack. Luke "found" him, raced back and pulled the tug on my belt, and I played ball with him. He'd found a human. Good dog.

I clipped on Luke's leash, and we walked back to the alley. Detective Porter stood watching as two white-uniformed evidence techs passed the last bit of material out of the dumpster and laid it on the blue tarp spread out on the alley. He looked up as Luke and I approached. "You're just in time."

I nodded and scanned the material on the ground. Food boxes, empty cans, paper trash—a veritable buffet of smells and a scent-discrimination challenge for my dog.

"Can he tell if she was in there? With all that?" Porter gestured toward the debris on the ground. "He's not going to eat the leftover Kung Pao chicken, is he?" Porter grinned at me.

"He's looking for a higher reward," I said, joking.

That was a line Nate often used. *You got to want the higher reward,* he'd say when I expressed frustration over some failure or habit I couldn't break. *How do I do that?* I'd respond. *You got to ask God to help you want him more than what's temptin' you. That's the gospel way.*

Oh, Nate. One eye on Jesus, always.

I brought my attention back to the job at hand. "Luke is cross-trained to detect human remains," I explained to Porter. "I use a different command. Also, because of the circumstances, he knows what I'm asking him to do. And he will, or at least should, ignore the other enticing smells."

The detective gestured toward the pile. "Have at it."

The two evidence techs, still dressed in their white coveralls, stood by, their eyes fixed on us. Few people have seen SAR dogs working, especially up close. I positioned Luke at the end of the tarp, made him sit at the heel position, and then gestured toward the garbage before us. "Find it, Luke. Go find."

When Luke is air-scenting, he usually moves fast, sweeping widely through a field or forest. Searching for human remains can be a more delicate task. Human remains detection dogs may be asked to find a body, or where a body has been, or the dust of a decomposed body. They may search for a body buried in the ground or in the rubble of a collapsed building or one that is under-water. It's really pretty amazing they can do that.

Luke stepped onto the tarp, his nose down, and began sniffing through the debris. I heard the evidence techs joking, taking bets on whether he'd go for the orange chicken or the pork fried rice first. Maybe the leftover spring rolls. Honestly, it kind of irritated me. It was like they were making fun of my dog, doubting his dedication and training. I shot them a look but decided not to say anything. Let them have their games. Luke would show them.

And he did. He went over the whole tarp without so much as a lick on the food. Although he hesitated once or twice, he never gave his indication that he'd found the scent of human remains. When he was done, he looked at me, his deep brown eyes announcing the tarp was clear. I told him he was a good dog and looked straight at the evidence techs. "So who won the bet?" They murmured a sheepish response. Then I pulled a small tug toy out of my pocket and played with my dog.

Just to be sure, I guided Luke around every other dumpster in that alley, this time asking him to "find it." If Heather Burgess had been placed in any one of them, Luke would have told us.

"It's all clear," I announced to Detective Porter.

"How sure can we be of that?"

"Ninety-nine percent. My dog's pretty good."

He paused, frowning. "You have time to come back to the office?"

I checked my watch. "Sure."

We made our way back to the conference room in his office. I got Luke some water, which he slurped noisily. Detective Porter and I began going over the facts of Heather's disappearance. I was a little surprised at how open he was and how many questions he asked on topics well beyond the scope of SAR. Finally, my curiosity got the better of me. "You don't have a lot of these cases out here," I suggested.

He snorted softly and shook his head. "Thank God. I mean, a few kids every year disappear for a while. A handful commit suicide. But this feels like more than the usual case. I'm new here, their first black detective, and I want to get it right." He rubbed his jaw. "I called Fairfax for advice."

I felt a tightening in my back.

"The chief of detectives thought you lived out this way and recommended you, and not just for the search aspects."

"The chief of detectives?"

"Right."

My old boss.

"He suggested I pick your brain. Said you're the best that'd come through his shop."

I felt my face grow hot. I'd left the Fairfax police under less than ideal circumstances.

"So help me out." Porter grinned at me. "Pretend I've never done this before. Because I haven't. At least, not in Harrisonburg."

So I told him how I would investigate the disappearance of Heather Burgess, the people I'd interview, the cameras I'd check, the financials, phone records, and online posts I'd review. "Talk to her professors," I suggested. "Everybody in the dorm. Her high school friends. Her parents. Find out if she could be suicidal. If there's been recent drama in her life."

"And what about more widespread searches? With dogs?"

"I'd do that sooner rather than later." I told him how to get in touch with the Virginia Department of Emergency Management and, looking down at the map on the table, I outlined some places I'd search.

I caught the look in his eyes. "Look, if the girl turns up okay, the worst thing that will have happened is that you've wasted a bunch of people's time. Trust me. SAR people would rather waste time," I said, using air quotes, "than miss a chance to help."

Porter straightened up. "I'll check with the chief and recommend what you've suggested. If the state calls out SAR, will you be back?"

"That's up to VDEM and the search group I belong to, Battlefield. But I will be happy to help if we are activated. And if you need me to come back and consult again, I can do that too."

I loaded Luke in my Jeep and drove back over the mountains toward home. The clouds had darkened, threatening snow or at least a cold rain. I hoped Heather Burgess was somewhere warm and dry, somewhere safe, and that she would show up again on her own. Maybe she'd had a fight with one of her friends. Maybe she was embarrassed about getting drunk. Maybe she'd ended up in a compromising situation and didn't want to admit it.

Maybe she just wanted to be alone.

The house was dark when I pulled up, except for a small lamp in one window that we always left lit. That's when I remembered it was Thursday and Scott was taking his daughter out to dinner. He'd made a practice of that recently, trying once again to grow their relationship with these once-a-week dates. So far, Amanda was going along with it, but he was always waiting for her to balk. I gave him credit. He hadn't given up.

I parked and let Luke out of the back. He raced around sniffing and watering the bushes. I grabbed my pack and went inside, knowing Luke would run down and check out the horses, do a perimeter search around the property, and then bark when he was ready to come in. Inside I found a note from Scott, saying he'd be home about nine.

I went upstairs, showered, and put on my comfy sweats. I heard Luke bark at the door and went back down to let him in. I noticed it was beginning to rain. "C'mon, buddy. Are you hungry?" Leading him to the kitchen, I poured kibble into his dish.

As I listened to Luke chomp his food, I kept thinking about Heather Burgess, the missing woman. Curious, I used my iPhone and accessed the Virginia State Police missing persons list. It contained two hundred forty names. Heather would be Number 241, once her case was added. As I scrolled through, I was struck by how diverse the list was. Black, white, Hispanic, and all ages, including forty- and fifty-year-olds.

Lots of people listed as "needs medication." And people in wheelchairs! How do people in wheelchairs go missing?

What about their families? How do the families of all these people live not knowing what happened to them? In Virginia, a missing person is presumed dead after seven years, but many families refuse to give up on them. I couldn't blame them. If there was a wisp of a chance my father was alive, I'd search until I was dead looking for him. But there was no question. He was gone, crushed under the falling South Tower of the World Trade Center, an NYPD 9/11 hero.

Automatically, I touched my belly. *You're probably the safest you'll ever be, little one.* I shivered just thinking about it.

4

A few minutes later, my phone rang. Nate. Nathan Tanner. My friend and mentor in all things related to dogs and God.

"Y'all havin' dinner?"

"No. Scott's out with Amanda."

"Have you eaten?"

"No."

"How 'bout I pick up some barbeque and we come by."

"Both of you?"

"Yep. You okay with that?"

"That sounds great."

"See you in about forty minutes."

I clicked off my phone, curious about what prompted the call. In normal times, Nate and Laura dropping by would be no big deal, but I'd had a blowup with Nate's wife. I'd accidentally discovered that a young woman I'd met in Highland County was Laura's long-lost daughter, given up for adoption when Laura was a teenager. Shocked that her secret had been revealed, Laura had taken her anger out on me. That hurt—and ticked me off. It had taken a while to get past that. Our relationship was just beginning to thaw.

I checked my watch. They'd be here around six, which gave me forty minutes to prop my feet up, something my obstetrician told me to do as often as possible.

I walked into the living room and settled into Scott's brown leather recliner. Before I knew it I'd dropped off to sleep. Luke's barking woke me up.

"Jess?" Nate called out.

"Come on in!" Groggy, I lurched to my feet, blinking hard to wake up. I slid into my moccasins and walked out to greet them. Nate and Laura were laying out food on the kitchen table. "Welcome!" I said. "What can I get you to drink?"

Nate gave me a hug. "We got everything we need, including a bottle of water for you."

"Laura, how are you," I said, giving her a hug. Her body felt stiff.

"I'm okay," she said. "Thanks for letting us come on such short notice."

"Of course!"

Nate said grace and we started to eat. Nate knew what I liked—a messy pulled pork sandwich. In our area, that meant topped with coleslaw. I was starving. Nate asked me what I'd been up to, and I told him about my trip to Harrisonburg and the missing young woman. As we talked I noticed Laura barely ate. I turned the conversation away from me. "Laura, how have you been?" I asked.

She swallowed, hard. A woman in her late forties, she was trim, with dark, wavy hair and blue eyes, a pretty woman who loved Nate but was sometimes standoffish with me.

"That . . . that's why we came. I want to apologize for getting so angry about my daughter. I never in a million years expected to see her." Nate put his hand over hers as tears flooded Laura's eyes. "I was very mean to you and I'm sorry about that."

"I didn't mean to embarrass you, Laura. I had no idea—"

"I should never have treated you like that. You didn't do anything wrong. I'm sorry, Jess."

"I forgive you, Laura. I won't lie. Your anger really hurt. But I'm sorry I embarrassed you, and I forgive you," I said. I rose, leaned over, and hugged her. "I love you," I said.

Those words don't come easily to me. I came from a very non-expressive family. But I knew I needed to say them. It wasn't that long ago that part of my past that I was deeply ashamed of emerged from the shadows. Then, it was Nate who helped me regain my balance, patiently loving me as a friend. I'd learned the truth of something I'd read: *When someone sees your scars and loves you anyway, the scars almost disappear over time.*

I sat back down. Laura played with her napkin, folding and refolding it. "I had a lot of shame built up inside," she said. "It's taken awhile for me to see that I didn't need to carry it anymore."

"Jesus took our shame," Nate said softly. "Bore it for us on the cross so we could be forgiven and free." That's what he had told me, too, back in the day.

Laura remained perfectly still, silent, staring straight ahead at the kitschy little sugar bowl in the shape of a fat puppy in the center of the table. I didn't know what to do. Express more sympathy? Ask a question? I glanced at Nate for a cue. His hand gave me the subtle equivalent of a 'stay' command.

After a time, Laura began to speak again, her voice as distant as the story she recounted. "My friends and I all thought he was the coolest guy in the school, a dark-haired football player with a grin that could sell toothpaste." She closed her eyes, remembering. "And then he started noticing me. I was only fourteen, but he chose me out of all my friends. Me. He'd wait by my locker before school. Walk me to class. He said I was beautiful. One day, behind the gym, he kissed me, and I felt things I'd never felt before. It was so exciting."

Laura shook her head. "I was so naïve back then. I didn't know a thing. Very little about sex, nothing about protecting myself emotionally. Before long, I was sneaking out to see him, meeting him in the woods, lying to my mother about where I was going. I didn't even know what was happening when he . . . when he did it. Afterward, I was shocked. I knew it was wrong. Still, I wanted it again, wanted *him* again. I wanted to be wanted, to belong to someone. I wanted to belong to him.

"We kept meeting in the woods, in an old barn, once even in my bedroom when my parents weren't home. It was thrilling. Exciting. And at the same time, scary and wrong. I knew I should stop, but I was terrified of losing him, losing the one person who wanted me."

"This went on for a month, and then he just disappeared like morning mist. He stopped asking me to meet him. I'd see him at school, and he'd look past me. Every day, I hoped he'd be by my locker, but he wasn't. He quit walking me to class. I wanted to ask him why, but he avoided me. Then, when I saw him walking with another girl, carrying her books, I was crushed. The rock I'd stood on had turned to sand. Quicksand. I was nobody again. A used nobody. And I wanted to die." She wiped her eyes with her napkin.

I jumped up, grabbed the box of tissues off the counter and placed them on the table. She pulled one out, blew her nose, and then continued. "When I missed my period, I just ignored it. I told myself it was a fluke. I missed another one. Same thing. Eventually, I couldn't ignore my growing belly, or my aching breasts, or the fact I could barely stay awake in class. I finally told my best friend. She made me tell my mom. It was the hardest thing, even though it was the right thing to do.

"A week later, my stepfather drove me to a home for unwed mothers over in West Virginia, and that's where I spent the next four and a half months. Didn't know anybody. Didn't know anything. They took care of me," she said, using air quotes, "but there was no counseling, no help with my emotions, no guidance.

"The social worker, a man, was the one kind person in that place. He came to speak to me about adoption. There was never any question that I'd give the baby up," Laura said, continuing. "My stepfather told me that's what would happen on the drive up and I didn't question it. The one thing I asked was that my baby be placed with Christian parents. And the social worker said he'd try.

"Basically, I spent the whole time I was there trying not to feel. But I *did* feel. I felt sad and lonely and scared and ashamed. I had no one to talk to, so I'd talk to my baby, and I'd talk to Jesus."

Laura looked at Nate, then me. "Despite what I'd done, my sin, I somehow knew to seek out Jesus. I felt like I was in the middle of a tug of war. My guilt and grief made me want to die, and yet I kept reaching for Jesus to live. Back and forth, back and forth.

"Finally, the day came for my baby to be

born. Six hours of labor, more pain than I'd ever experienced, my body out of control—it was terrifying. But then," her voice softened, "there she was, a perfect little dark-haired girl, pink skin, sweet little mouth. Holding her, I was in love. What a rush! This was my baby, *my* baby, and I felt bonded to her. Her tiny hands, her perfect face, that little nose. She was beautiful and I whispered, 'I love you' over and over.

"I had fifteen minutes with her. Fifteen minutes. Then the nurse came in and took her. And I never saw my baby again."

My head spun at Laura's words. I instinctively put my hand on my belly, cradling my unborn child. I had not even felt my baby move yet but I could already feel the bond. I couldn't imagine carrying her for nine months, feeling kicks and hiccups, having our very blood intermingle, and then having her abruptly taken away and given to a stranger.

Tension wrapped around me. Hot tears filled my eyes. I plucked two tissues out of the box. I wanted to speak but words would not come out. My throat was too tight.

"The day of her birth, the nice social worker came back. He saw how upset I was, and he was so kind and gentle. Like Nate." She looked at her husband, love flowing in her lingering gaze. "He gave me a clipboard and, tears streaming down my face, I signed the adoption papers, signed my baby away. What else could I do?"

"Nothing," I whispered.

"Two days later, my parents came to get me. They didn't say anything to me on the way home. Not one thing. I got the message. *We are not talking about your shame.* I locked my feelings away deep inside me, until—"

"Until I accidentally found your daughter." My words were almost a confession. Laura sobbed, and I rose and held her. "I'm so sorry," I whispered. As I held her I thought about all the stories behind the people we meet, all the reasons for their standoffishness or foolishness that we just can't see. All the grace we all need.

I sat back down. I started to say I was sorry again, but Nate cleared his throat and held up his hand. "Findin' Kathryn weren't no mistake, Jess. And it weren't no accident either. It was God-ordained." His jaw shifted. "When I lost my leg and you went and searched out Laura, my long-lost love, you were doin' it to help me heal. To bless me. What you didn't know was that Laura needed healin' too. All that shame inside was like an infection needin' to be drained. Jesus knew it were poisoning her. He put us together, usin' you to do it. Laura helped me get over losin' my leg, and I helped her with this. Now, here we are, limpin' home together, by his grace." Nate's eyes glistened.

I measured my next words, my heart pounding with the power of her story, *their* story. Would Laura resist what I was about to say? Be angry? Feel more guilty? I took a deep breath. "Kathryn is a wonderful person, Laura. A lot like you. Loving, kind, gentle."

Laura stayed still for a minute. I held my breath. Then she looked at me, her eyes red-rimmed. "Do you think," she said, "do you think she would ever forgive me?"

My heart jumped. "I'm sure she would." I reached out and touched her hand. "She told me she's not angry with you. She said you don't owe her anything. She's had a wonderful life. She doesn't know the details of why she was put up for adoption, but she doesn't blame you. I think she'd love to get to know you!"

Tears flowed again down Laura's face.

"Think you could set that up?" Nate said.

"Absolutely. Give me some dates and I'll see what works for her. I'll invite her down here." Laura looked up in alarm. "Don't worry. I'll tell her why so she'll be prepared. This is awesome!" *Praise God.*

That night, I went to bed feeling like I was in the middle of a miracle.

5

I was asleep by the time Scott got in at about ten. I vaguely recalled him sliding into bed, his body warm and comforting, the scent of his soap infusing my dreams. We were cuddling like spoons when, at six-thirty the next morning, I got the callout for Heather Burgess, the missing woman from Harrisonburg. I slipped out of bed.

"A callout?" he asked me as I clicked off the phone. His eyes were full of sleep.

I leaned over and kissed him. "Yes. And I'm going. It's for the young woman I consulted on yesterday. Stay in bed. I'll grab my stuff and go."

Scott lurched out of bed, wincing as his shoulder moved. He was so stubborn about painkillers. He wouldn't take opioids and the ulcers in his gut, which were hopefully healing, made taking ibuprofen out of the question. That left Tylenol, which he took when he had to. "I'll make you breakfast. What do you want?"

"Something light. Yogurt. Fruit if we have it."

"Got it."

I began pulling on my blue SAR pants. Luke rose from where he'd been sleeping on the floor, stretching his big body. "Hey, buddy!" I stroked the side of his face. "We've got a job to do." His tail wagged in response.

I finished dressing, went downstairs, and let Luke out. I'd left my SAR pack in the front hall closet. I scooped it up to make sure I had snacks left. At this point in my pregnancy, half the time I was nauseated and the other half of the time I was starving, so I always had to have something available.

"Here you go," Scott said, placing a bowl of yogurt and blueberries on the table. He added a steaming cup of lemon and ginger herb tea. "I filled the thermos, too."

"You are the best," I gave him a quick kiss. "How'd your dinner go?"

His eyes tightened momentarily. "I'll tell you some other time. It's too much to go into now."

Poor guy. His daughter Amanda was not easy. "At least she went to dinner with you."

"There is that."

Luke barked at the door. "I'll get him," Scott said. He let Luke in and asked me, "A light meal for him?"

"Yes. One and a half scoops." I heard the sound of kibble hitting the bowl and then crunching as Luke tore through it. He was finished in less than a minute.

I polished off my yogurt and took a few more sips of tea. "Gotta run. I'll be back later." I stood and hugged my husband.

"Take care of yourself. You have the Garmin inReach?"

I patted my right cargo pocket. "Got it." I kissed Scott goodbye, grabbed my parka and my pack, and started to leave.

"Is Nate going?" Scott called after me.

"Not sure. I'll let you know."

I whistled for Luke. We left and I was three miles down the road when I realized I hadn't told Scott about my trip to Harrisonburg, or Nate and Laura's visit, or about her apology, or inviting Kathryn down and the potential reconciliation. And I hadn't heard why he was so negative about dinner with Amanda.

So many things left unsaid.

Luke and I spent the rest of the day searching a large park near Harrisonburg, looking for Heather Burgess along with three other teams from Battlefield SAR. Nate hadn't responded, but my friend Emily was there, along with Tom, Carol, and one other guy, plus their dogs. Tom, the incident commander, split the park up into searchable segments. Volunteers would serve as our walkers. I stood waiting for instructions, my breath a frosty stream. The temperature was twenty-seven degrees, but the sun was shining and there was very little wind, so really, for early January, it was a beautiful day.

A young man named Dirk from JMU was my walker. I explained what I needed him to do, and we set off. The park was wooded and included some pretty steep places. Tom had given me a segment that was relatively easy, and we covered it in about three hours. We were the first ones back to the command post, where Tom told me that Emily's Border collie, Flash, had alerted on a few locations but not given a full-fledged indication. He asked me if I'd go over those parts with Luke.

"Of course," I responded. "Give me the map."

Dirk and I set off again, following Luke through a forested area full of rocks and briars. Tom had marked the spots Flash had hesitated on and I watched Luke carefully in those areas. But at the end of two hours, he didn't find anything worth telling me about.

"I think it's clear," I told Tom when we'd covered the route. And that was the response of all the searchers. We'd worked hard but found no trace of the missing woman, and I know I was not the only one who drove home tired, a heaviness settling in my gut like an undigested meal.

As I wound my way through the mountains toward home, I wondered, would the Burgesses rather know Heather was dead than wonder where she was and what had happened to her? Would the mystery of her disappearance—wondering whether she'd been abducted, lost, or if she'd run away—would that be harder to deal with than the finality of her death?

Scott would call this a "dark conundrum," a

riddle with no good answer, and I resolved to stop thinking about it. We'd done our job, found nothing, and that was that.

But my body kept telegraphing a different message. Tension had stiffened my neck. I was gripping the steering wheel so tightly my hands began to cramp. I was getting a headache.

I don't like open-ended stories. I can deal with tragedy, just don't give me uncertainty. Don't leave me hanging!

But that was only part of the reason for my stress. It wasn't the whole story. The truth was, for the first time in my life, I was feeling like a mother. Give me twenty years and the Burgess's dark conundrum could be mine. What would I say then? How would I cope?

Scott was in the barn when I got home. I let Luke out of his crate, put my pack on the front porch, and walked down to see him. He had his sling on to protect his shoulder. I'd bought him some button-front shirts that were a little bigger than what he normally wore to make it easier to get them on and off. He had one on now—a red, white, and blue-checked western shirt. I could see the collar under his barn coat.

He stood just outside Ace's stall. The black horse had his head out over the door. He nudged Scott like Luke nudges me.

Scott's eyes lit up as I drew closer. "I'm glad

you're home," he said, taking me in his one good arm. "How'd it go?" He bent down and kissed me.

"We didn't find her," I said. I nestled my head on his shoulder and tried hard to keep the disappointment out of my voice. The feeling of his body next to mine calmed me. "It was a good day to search. Not too cold. I felt strong. And we had four teams turn out."

He gave me a gentle, one-armed squeeze. "Four teams isn't much for the whole Harrisonburg area."

"Four teams from Battlefield to cover just one park! We did the whole thing in just under five hours. They've got other groups and hundreds of searchers looking in other places. As far as I know, no one has found a trace of her." I pulled back. "What have you been up to?"

"Grooming Ace, fixing a few things around here. Just fooling around, really."

I kissed his cheek. "The barn is your happy place."

"Yes, it is." He let go of me and pulled his work glove off. "How about I take you to dinner? We've got some catching up to do. Or are you too tired?"

"Tired? No. Give me half an hour. I want a shower first."

That half an hour turned into almost two hours. When Scott came upstairs, he found I'd showered and then fallen asleep. Despite my assertion that I wasn't tired, clearly I was. Denial was becoming a habit.

When I woke up, he had dinner ready. He'd pulled salmon from the freezer and baked it, along with a salad and some bread. "We can talk here just as well," he said, and I agreed.

Over dinner he asked me about the missing young woman, but I went for positive news first. I had to tell him about Nate and Laura.

"That's great!" he responded.

"I think it's a miracle. I mean, Scott, I could almost see the chains falling off. The guilt, the shame."

"It may still be rough for a while," he warned.

"I know, but still, I'm so excited."

"I'm proud of you."

"For what? I didn't do anything! I just accidentally found Kathryn."

"But you were patient with Laura after she got angry with you, and you've welcomed Kathryn every time she's come down here. You've been an agent of healing, Jess."

I shrugged.

"Now tell me about this search."

So I went through the whole thing, beginning with my solo trip to Harrisonburg, consulting with Detective Porter, and Luke finding the earring. Scott found that amazing. "It held the scent of human but was out of place," I explained. "Not all SAR dogs would trigger on that. He didn't use his indication, but he was curious. That caught my attention and so we found it."

"You're a good team."

Then I told him about the callout and our search that morning. "It was a walk in the park, literally, and that's all," I said. I felt disappointment again in my gut.

"What percentage of your searches find the subject?"

I had to think about that. "Certainly fewer than 50 percent. Maybe 30, 35." Put into cold statistical terms, that seemed a low success rate for the time we put into SAR. But we loved working with our dogs and being outside. And when we did find the subject of our search, the thrill made it all worthwhile.

"So you did your best," Scott affirmed.

I guess I did.

After dinner I called Kathryn. She was excited that Laura wanted to meet. So excited. We set it up for a week from Saturday, the day the guys were going to start working on the nursery, but we decided everyone being here wasn't a bad thing. "Maybe you and Laura can take the horses out," I suggested. "I can't ride, now that I'm pregnant, and Scott's not riding as much. They're getting a little antsy. That would give you time alone."

"Doing something we both love," Kathryn said.

"Yes."
"Together."
I could hardly wait for that day to come.
I could never have foreseen what was ahead.

6

I busied myself waiting for Laura's big reunion by cleaning out what I could from the nursery-to-be and working my PI cases, most of which were boring. I kept tabs on the Heather Burgess investigation and fielded a couple of calls from Detective Porter. The young woman was still missing but a new clue had popped up. A young man had come forward and admitted he'd followed Heather into the alley, and that after she finished throwing up, they'd walked together through that ribbon park Luke and I had searched. They'd had sex in the bushes, he passed out, and when he woke up, she was gone.

"How cold was it that night?" I asked Detective Porter when he told me this.

"Approaching midnight? About 36 degrees. A light snow had begun to fall and, drunk as they were, these two kids thought making love with snow falling would be romantic," he said.

"So he wakes up, finds her gone, and then just goes back to his dorm?"

"Yes," Detective Porter affirmed, "and went to class the next day like nothing had happened. Didn't even bother checking to see if she was okay."

"So is he now a person of interest?"

"I don't think he killed her."

"Why not?"

Porter sighed. "Some of these kids have the morals of a rabbit. They'll sleep with anyone anywhere. But this kid's killer instinct is about rabbit level, too. He's even a vegetarian."

Cop humor.

Over the next week, I planned for Saturday like it was a party. Not that I was used to giving parties. Or even going to them. But I wanted our friends to feel welcome and at ease and I wanted to celebrate the reunion of Laura and Kathryn. Plus I felt excited about finally getting started on the nursery.

So I made a lot of food—pulled pork, sliced turkey, coleslaw, potato salad, and a wonderful, scoopable dip made of beans, corn, tomatoes, and avocado. I bought chips and drinks and made German chocolate cheesecake and a fruit salad.

Everything was ready to go, so on Thursday, when Nate called and asked if I could come help him the next afternoon, I was able to say yes. Actually I was excited to. I wanted to gauge Laura's mood. Was she excited? Nervous? Scared? Reticent? I wanted to be prepared for anything, but I was hoping for the best.

Nate needed help with Ember, his solid black German shepherd. She was still young, and she'd suddenly balked at navigating the seesaw we used for training. Something about it was throwing her off. Nate thought maybe I'd be able to figure it out, or maybe watching Luke do it would motivate Ember to try again.

Nate and I both had agility equipment set up permanently in our yards. We used them nearly every day to keep the dogs, and us, in practice. Mine included a tunnel, jumps, a ladder, an A-frame, a high plank, an unstable bridge, and the seesaw. For the seesaw, the dog had to run up the ramp, balance at the pivot, and maintain his balance on the downhill as the seesaw tipped forward. Ember, Nate told me, was jumping off at the pivot.

I pulled into Nate's lane at about 2 p.m. He'd taken a couple hours off work so we could do this. Gravel crunching under my tires, I wound my way through the woods, across the small creek, and up toward the log house Nate and his friends had built. In a way, it always felt like coming home.

I backed into a parking space next to Laura's new car, a cute little red Kia. I hadn't seen it before, but Nate had told me she'd bought it.

The day was sunny and bright, the temperature about 40 degrees, which is pretty typical for our area of Virginia in winter. I decided to leave Luke in my Jeep at first, so I could watch Ember work without distraction. Nate came out of the house, Ember at his side. I gave him a quick hug and petted the dog. "You ready?" I asked.

"Yeah." His tone was low.

"Tough day at work?"

A short shake of the head told me that wasn't the problem. "Laura, she's nervous."

I rubbed his upper arm. "I get that."

"Cain't figure out how to retrain her, so I figured I'd work on the dog."

I laughed. "My K-9 techniques don't work on Scott either. Why don't you play with Ember a little bit to loosen her up?"

Nate pulled a tennis ball out of his pocket and threw it for her. Ember was three years old, still young and limber, but I watched her closely for any evidence of pain. A lot of times when a weird behavior pops up in a dog or a horse, Scott would say that there was an underlying physical reason. After a few throws, I didn't see anything, so I said, "You want to try her?"

"Sure."

We walked over to his agility equipment. "Is it always set up this way?" I asked.

"I do move it around some."

Right now, the seesaw was the second to last obstacle. I positioned myself in the middle of the ring like a judge would, and I watched as Nate ran the course with Ember. It was a little painful watching him hobble to try to keep up with the dog, but they did fine, until Ember went up on the seesaw. She hesitated at the pivot and jumped off. Nate shook his head.

"Hmm," I said. "Let's do that again, and I'll video it."

So Nate ran Ember through that routine again and she ditched the seesaw same as last time. This time, though, I thought I saw something. I looked at the video and confirmed it. "Check this out, Nate," I said, showing him my phone. It was barely perceptible, but right at the apex of the seesaw Ember glanced toward Nate. Then she jumped off.

He frowned. "What?"

"She gave you a side-eye."

"Let me see it again."

I showed it to him once more.

"Dang."

"Think back," I said, "to when she first started ditching the seesaw. How were the obstacles arranged?"

Nate frowned and stared at the ground, struggling to recall. "About ten days ago. It was cold, I remember." He looked up. "The seesaw and the A-frame were switched." He walked that direction, then retraced his steps, looking down. "I fell right about here." He looked at me. "I fell as she was doin' the seesaw. Tripped right here and fell hard and yelled pretty loud."

I grinned. "And now every time she does the seesaw, she looks to see if you're going to fall. And yell."

"Ember, you little pea-brain," Nate said,

laughing and rubbing his dog. "You didn't make me fall!" The black shepherd looked at him adoringly.

"Let's try walking her through it," I suggested, "on leash."

At first Ember hesitated at the pivot point, but after four or five tries and lots of encouragement, she walked the whole length of the obstacle, balancing on the downhill. Nate rewarded her each time.

Then we decided to let Luke show Ember how to do it fast. I got him out of the car, let the two dogs meet, then I ran him through the obstacles. I made a big deal of it when he did the seesaw. Ember got super excited. Then we tried her on it, with me running beside her. She performed like a champ. Within fifteen minutes, she and Nate were running a flawless obstacle course, seesaw included.

"Girl, you fixed us!" Nate said, giving me a hug.

"Just like you've fixed me so many times."

I heard the back door of Nate's house open. Laura came out, her purse on her shoulder. "She's got an appointment in town," Nate said.

"Wow, late on a Friday afternoon." I looked at my watch. Four-thirty.

We walked toward her. "Hey, Laura," I said.

"I'm sorry I have to run," she responded, but she took the time to give me a hug. "Thank you in advance for tomorrow. I'm looking forward to it."

"Me, too!" I said. "Kathryn said she'd be at our house around nine. So come whenever you can!"

"We will." She kissed Nate goodbye, and he told her he loved her, then she got into her Kia and started it up.

"I like her new car."

"That woman," Nate said, watching Laura go down the driveway. "She loves that thing. Insisted on buyin' it. Said she didn't like puttin' miles on her truck. Said she'd get better gas mileage." He shook his head. "Gave me all the arguments. I barely fit in it. It's like a toy. But if it makes her happy . . ."

He let his voice trail off, then turned to me. Beyond him I saw the Kia disappear into the woods. "Let's try Ember a couple more times and call it a day. It'll be gettin' dark soon anyways."

We gathered up the dogs from where they were wrestling with each other. "You go ahead and send Luke," Nate said.

I was just about to do that when we heard tires squealing, a sickening crash from beyond the trees, the sound of metal-on-metal crunch, followed by a thud.

Nate looked at me, eyes wide. "Laura!"

7

Nate took off running, hobbling really, down the driveway toward the sound of the crash.

"My Jeep!" I yelled. "Get in my Jeep." I called the dogs, put them in the house, slammed the door, and raced to my Jeep. I jumped in the driver's seat and sped down the driveway, gravel pelting the Jeep's frame, Nate gripping the dashboard, the tension so thick I could barely breathe.

"Which way?" I asked as we reached the road.

"Right." Nate gestured.

I turned, went around the curve, and there it was, Laura's little red car slammed up against an oak tree. Next to it, crushing it, was a full-size black Ford pickup. It apparently had run the stop sign across the road.

Nate jumped out before I'd come to a complete stop. He raced toward the Kia, fell, got up, and slid down a small ditch, calling Laura's name. I grabbed my EMT bag and followed him, calling 911 as I ran. The driver of the pickup, a six-foot-tall man, stumbled out of the truck covered in airbag dust. At first I thought he was stunned by the crash. When I drew closer, the smell of alcohol nearly knocked me over.

I bypassed him. I could smell gasoline and hot

metal. Nate was trying to break the back window of the Kia with his foot. "Nate, stop!" I dropped my bag and found the glass breaker in an outside pocket, along with thick gloves. "Move!" I said, tugging at his shoulder. He pulled back, and I used the device to break the window, pulling the shattered glass away with my gloved hands. Nate couldn't wait. He clawed at it as well, oblivious to the cuts he was getting. The moment the opening was big enough, he dove inside.

There really wasn't room for both of us in that little car, but as a certified EMT, I wanted to get in there. I snapped on gloves and squeezed in beside my friend, who was draped over the front passenger seat.

The little car had folded like a soda can under the impact of the pickup. The left side of Laura's body was trapped by crushed metal. The airbags were no match for the giant truck just outside. Her neck tilted to the right. I felt it and found a weak, thready pulse. I felt around some more, searching for arterial bleeding. I didn't find any, but the hair on the left side of her head felt sticky. *Blood.* Her respiration was jagged, her eyes closed.

She was alive, but just barely. I couldn't properly assess her, not in that tight box, and not from that angle. I suspected she had a fractured skull and possibly broken bones and internal bleeding.

Sirens. The rescue crew would have the extrication tools I didn't have. We needed to get out of their way. There was nothing we could do for Laura at this moment, nothing anyone could do. I started to crawl out of the car through the back window then realized I'd never get Nate out if I left him. "Nate, come on. We need to get out so they can extricate her."

He spoke softly to his wife, using her name, encouraging her, his voice amazingly calm.

"Nate, come on!" I tugged at his sleeve. He ignored me. "Nate!"

"I ain't leavin' her."

"Nate, you have to." I tempered my voice. "Listen. They'll need the space to get her out. We want her out, Nate, before the car catches on fire." I had no idea if that was a possibility. I just had to use whatever I could to motivate him.

Fire got his attention. "Go on. I'll follow."

I crawled out of the back window, snagging and ripping my jeans as I did. "Come on, Nate."

Getting a hundred-and-sixty-pound man with an artificial leg out of the back window of a crashed Kia is no mean feat. He tried turning around in the car but couldn't make it. He tried to back out and got stuck until I helped him by lifting his artificial leg out of the window. We both came out covered with airbag dust and bloody from the shards of glass still attached to the frame.

I identified myself to the medics and briefed

them as I removed my gloves. They began taking the car apart, their equipment screaming worse than a dentist's drill. I quickly texted Scott, then stood next to Nate, my arm around him. Waves of trembling passed through him like ocean waves crashing on the shore, one after the other. I knew everything in him wanted to get back in that car. "I'm praying," I said in a moment of quiet.

"It ain't good."

The air chilled rapidly as the sun went down. I pictured life draining out of the day and Laura at the same time. I couldn't stop shaking.

Medics finally got Laura out and placed her in the ambulance. Nate climbed up to ride with her. "I'll see you there!" I called to him. He gave me a small nod in response, his face grim.

I checked my watch. We were forty minutes into the Golden Hour, the optimum window for lifesaving trauma care after an accident.

I turned toward my car and saw Scott running toward me. "Scott!" I said. He grabbed me in a hug.

"I couldn't get closer. The road is blocked." He was breathing hard. "Is that her car?"

"Yes. I think the guy in that truck ran the stop sign."

"How bad?"

I shook my head and pressed my lips together, trying not to cry. "I need to go. To the hospital."

"Let's do it!"

• • •

The antiseptic smell at the trauma center made me feel nauseated. No wonder. Just stepping into the place brought back multiple memories.

Scott was trying to talk us past the front desk when I spotted a nurse who'd treated him just a few months before. "Aren't you—" she asked.

"Yes!" I responded, pointing to Scott's sling.

"Who is it this time?"

I told her. Her facial expression changed. "Come on," she said, moving quickly.

In Trauma Bay 5, Nate stood by his wife. He held her hand, his eyes full of tears. Scott put his hands on my shoulders and moved past me. He put his arm around Nate, then said something to him in a low voice. I didn't try to hear it. I didn't need to. My eyes were on the monitor above Laura's bed. The numbers told a sad story.

My head spun. I took in a deep breath and let it out slowly. "Can we pray?" I asked.

Nate looked at me, his eyes completely blank. He was in shock.

"Yes," Scott said.

I put my hand on the white sheet covering Laura's leg and reached for Scott's belt, under his sling. He put his left hand on Nate's shoulder, and we prayed. Two of us prayed. Nate remained silent.

I want to say I felt God's presence, that his Holy

Spirit comforted us, that the "peace that passes understanding" filled the room. But honestly, I felt nothing like that. Instead, I was walking on a tightrope, trying to stay in balance, trying not to fall into the abyss of fear and grief that gaped like the mouth of hell beneath me.

Laura was dying. My friend's great love. His wife.

We said "Amen," and opened our eyes. I heard an alarm. I looked at the monitor. Flatline. Laura's heart had stopped.

Grief escaped Nate's throat in a deep groan. The intercom announced a code. Nurses, interns, and doctors rushed in. Scott and I stepped out of their way. Nate stayed. They brought the crash cart, tried CPR and the paddles and all kinds of other things until Nate stepped up with all the authority of Moses and put his hand on the doctor's hand and stopped them. Laura was gone. He knew it. "Leave her be," he said.

The finality of it made my head spin. Scott wrapped his arm around me and held me tight. I think I would have dropped to the floor otherwise.

The code team slowly wrapped up their equipment and left. Nate stood next to the bed, his hand holding Laura's, tears dripping onto the sheets. Scott and I joined him. I could barely see for the tears in my own eyes.

Scott found me a chair. I sat while he helped Nate with papers he had to sign and questions from the patient advocate. What medical insurance? Who was the next of kin? Which funeral home? On and on she went until there were no more questions.

I knew it would be hard for Nate to walk out of that room, to leave the woman he'd loved lying there alone. The trauma center is a busy place. They were kind. They gave Nate half an hour, but then gently let us know it was time to leave. They needed the space. Nate nodded, slipped Laura's rings off, kissed her cheek, and with shoulders sagging, walked out.

He seemed older. Bent over. Limping hard. At one point he stopped, as if he could not go one step further. He looked down, closed his eyes, and covered his face with his hand. I put my hand on his arm. "Come on, Nate. We'll take you home."

He looked at me. "Why?"

In that one word, he summarized everything. Why go home? Home was gone. Killed by a drunk driver on a cold January afternoon.

We rode to Nate's house in silence, the three of us processing what had just happened. We all had experienced grief before. We all knew the dread of death. The finality of it. I still had a lot of questions about it. Now was not the time to ask them.

"You want to sit for a while or shower?" Scott

asked Nate when we walked into his house. Nate didn't respond, so Scott continued. "How 'bout a shower? You've got dust all over you. I'll help you."

"I'll take care of the dogs," I said.

I stepped outside into the dark night. The dogs, oblivious to what had happened, ran around sniffing. I raised my head. The night sky looked like a black bowl pricked by tiny dots of light. I started asking my questions. I heard no answers.

Ten minutes later, I went back in and fed the dogs.

Scott helped Nate, dressed in fresh clothes, out to his recliner. Nate's thirteen-year-old dog, Sprite, danced around his chair. I lifted her into his lap. A small springer spaniel, Sprite had been his companion and SAR dog all her life. Arthritic now, she was still his heart-dog. She settled in his lap and soon Nate's hand was stroking her rhythmically, his head bowed.

"I'm going to go help Scott with the horses," I said. "I'll be back in a few minutes."

Out in the barn while we worked together to feed and water the horses and clean the stalls, Scott and I strategized. "We need to make a list of the things to do, the people to call. We need to get somebody to take care of our horses. We need to figure out the things Nate will need."

"Kathryn. We need to let her know and we need to be sensitive when we tell her."

"For sure," Scott said. "Amanda. I'll call her. Maybe she and Ethan can take care of our horses. And what about that little girl who came here to ride? What's her name?"

"Harper."

"Yes, her dad's the one to call, so he can break it to her gently. Can we find their number?"

"Nate has it, I'm sure. I'll get his phone. I'll call the SAR people. And Nate's pastor. He ought to be an early contact," I said. "I think I have his number. If not, it's in Nate's phone."

Scott checked his watch. "It's only eight o'clock. If we split this up, we should be able to get everybody before nine."

"I'll spend the night."

"We'll both stay. I want you to be able to sleep if you can."

"Food," I said. "You haven't eaten."

"We all need food."

"I'll check the fridge and see what's in there."

"Can you get pizza delivery out here?" Scott asked.

"Not the last time I stayed here."

"We'll figure something out."

"Okay, look," I said, "I'll call Nate's pastor, then go back inside, check on Nate, and see what food is around. You call Amanda."

"Who's going to call Kathryn?"

"Would you?" Tears came to my eyes. I looked away quickly.

"Of course." Scott kissed my forehead. "Let me finish up here and I'll start calling people. She'll be the first."

"Thank you."

Nate had helped me in so many ways. Now, I would be there for him. I'd help Nate get through this grief if it was the last thing I did.

8

I moved through the next few hours stiff as a porcelain doll prone to shattering. Everything had emotional significance. I looked through the fridge for food I could make for us. I found the remains of a casserole I was sure Laura had made, cans of the sparkling water she liked to drink, and Nate's favorite dessert, a recipe of hers.

Death is so strange, so final. A person is here, full of life, full of quirks and joys and irritating habits, full of stories and jokes. Full of love. And then, they're not. They're gone. And what's left behind is a half-eaten casserole, two cans of black-cherry-flavored sparkling water, and some apple crumble. I stared at these things in the cold, white light of the refrigerator until the door alarm went off.

I went out into the living room and asked Nate what he'd like to eat. He shook his head. "I ain't hungry."

To be honest, neither was I.

Scott came in and motioned for me to come in the kitchen. "I couldn't reach Amanda or Ethan, so I'm going home to feed our horses. Then I'll come back. You'll be okay here alone with him?"

"Sure."

"Text me what you need me to bring back for you. Oh, Kathryn's coming. She'll be here early in the morning. I told her not to drive tonight."

"Good."

Scott left and I made two mugs of tea with sugar, lemon-ginger for me and Irish breakfast tea for Nate. I carried them into the living room and set them on the end table between us.

Nate sat rocked back in the recliner. He'd rested his head and closed his eyes, but he wasn't asleep, I could tell. I sat down near him on the couch and texted Scott a list of things I wanted from our house: Luke's bowls and some food. Two changes of clothes for me. My prenatal vitamins. Some of that food I cooked for the next day.

I turned to Nate. "Do you want some music on?" I asked.

He shook his head.

"Want me to read something to you? The Bible? John maybe?"

"No."

The steam from his tea rose like incense between us. How many cups of tea had I shared with him? With Laura? He reached over and took my hand.

After about ten minutes, I said, "The tea is probably cool enough."

At first, he just opened his eyes and stared at me, but after a minute, he took the mug and drained it. When he was finished, he rested his head back again. A few minutes later, his eyes popped open. "Kathryn!" He started to get up.

I put my hand out to stop him. "Scott called her."

Nate sagged back. He looked at me, tears in his eyes. "The last thing Laura said to me was, 'Katie. Take care of Katie.' That's what she called her baby. Katie."

"When was this, Nate? When did she say that?"

"In the car." Tears streamed down his face. "I didn't want to leave her."

"I know. I know you didn't. But we had to." I rubbed his arm, the arm with the anchor tattoo. I put the box of Kleenex closer. "She was thinking of her child right up to the end."

He nodded.

"You can tell Kathryn that when she gets here."

"She's coming?"

"First thing in the morning."

He took my hand, laid his head back, and closed his eyes again. We stayed that way for what must have been an hour. Nate had often talked to me about the power of the "ministry of presence," the practice of simply sitting with someone in their grief. Now, here we were.

At last, Nate spoke. "You should go home. Get some rest."

"I'm staying here tonight. With you. So is Scott."

He nodded and closed his eyes again.

Where does the proprietor of the Tanner House of Healing go when he's the one in pain?

I leaned my head back and stared at the books on the shelves on either side of the fireplace. Most were theology related—commentaries, Bible studies, Christian living, old books written by Puritans, new books written by freshly minted PhD's, catechisms, history, C.S. Lewis, J.I. Packer, Jerry Bridges . . .

For a guy with no degree who talks like a hick, Nate reads pretty deeply. When I first met him, I underestimated him. He called himself "the dog man." It took me a while to discern the depth of his soul and the breadth of his heart, to discover his talents, from tracking lost people to reading a dog's behavior to playing the banjo to carpentry and gardening. To find that he is the most tenacious friend a person could have and the most faithful, sincere Christian I'd ever met.

Yeah, look where that got him.

Guilt flooded me. Ugh. How could I be so cynical? "I'm sorry, God," I whispered, squeezing my eyes shut momentarily as if I could blink my sin away.

Luke came over and nudged my hand. I swear that dog can read my soul. I reached down and hugged him as he licked my ear.

After a while, my stomach growled. I didn't feel like eating but Baby Cooper was complaining.

"I'll be right back," I said to Nate, squeezing his hand.

I stared again at the leftovers in the fridge, then finally found a can of chicken noodle soup in the pantry, a comfort food if there ever was one. My mother was not a cook, but even she knew how to heat up a can of Campbell's Chicken Noodle Soup when I was sick.

"Want some chicken noodle soup, Nate?" I called out. "I'm heating some up."

He started to say no, then changed his mind. "Okay. A little."

"Okay!"

I put the soup in a large mug and carried it out to him. A cup of tea and some soup. It was a start.

We slept that night, Nate in the recliner and me on the couch, until Scott got back and made me move to the guest room. I still had the clothes on I'd been wearing at the accident scene, so I stripped them off and took a shower before crawling into bed. Baby Cooper and I were exhausted. We had no trouble getting back to sleep.

Scott slept on the couch, so he'd be there if Nate needed something. He told me later the sun streaming in the front windows woke them both up at about seven. Nate pushed the recliner upright, looked at Scott, and said, "How can it be so bright, so beautiful, when the whole world is empty?"

Kathryn arrived just after eight. By then, I was up. She came in dressed in slacks and a beautiful, cream- and light-blue Fair Isle sweater, a walking, living, younger version of Laura, and Nate broke down when he saw her. He struggled to get up on his one leg and they held each other, locked in a long embrace, until Nate couldn't stand any more. They sat down, tears flowing, and began to talk.

Scott and I retreated to give them privacy. We sat at the kitchen table, my husband with his little black Moleskine notebook and me with mine, going over what had been done, what needed to be done, and who would do what. The dogs moved around us, restless, so when we got to a stopping point I slid into my coat and boots and took them out into the cold, fresh morning, wondering if God's mercies were new this day, too.

Ethan arrived, then Amanda, tears fresh on her face. They spoke to Nate and Kathryn, then left to go see the horses.

Other folks started showing up around nine. Neighbors. Friends. Battlefield SAR members. People from church. Old Marine Corps buddies. Word gets around. Some dropped off food, others stood around talking, a few volunteered to help. Each person murmured something to Nate, sitting in the recliner, then most drifted away, unsure of what to say beyond "I'm sorry."

After a while, Nate gestured to Scott, who helped him into the wheelchair and followed him back to the bedroom. "Is all this too much for him?" I asked Kathryn, who'd been sitting near him.

"He said he wanted to put his leg on. He's tired of sitting." She paused. "He really loved her."

"Yes, he did." I sagged down onto the couch.

"He told me how you brought them together after all those years."

"It was a sweet moment." *And what was the point?* I thought. Back in those days, I never would have thought God was "leading" me to find Laura, to reunite these two sweethearts. I did it because . . . because I wanted to help Nate. He'd just lost a leg!

Nate is the one who, later, told me bringing Laura to him was a God-thing, "a blessing from the Lord," as he put it.

But why? Just to have her get killed a few years later?

I put my hand on my forehead, like I wanted to pull the answer out of my brain.

"Are you okay?" Kathryn asked.

"Yes, fine," I said quickly. "I'm fine. Just still a little stunned."

"He's quite a reader." She nodded toward his bookshelves.

"A reader, a musician, carpenter, landscaper. But most of all, a friend." I put my hand on hers, which was resting on the couch between us. "I'm so sorry you didn't get to know your mom. She was so kind, so gentle." I went on to tell her about Harper Lee, the little foster child who'd stopped talking. "Your mom thought being around horses might get through to her, might help her trust again, enough to talk. She was so sweet to her, and you know what? It worked. It was amazing."

Kathryn smiled.

"She loved kids."

Her eyes were blue like Laura's and right then they were shining. Amanda came in and plopped down in Nate's recliner. "So tell me what happened!" she said to me.

I looked at Kathryn. How much did she want to hear?

She saw me looking at her and nodded. "Yes, I'd like to hear it again, too."

So I recited the story, the horrible crash we heard, racing to the site, crawling into the car, and then the hospital. I found my heart beating hard as I told it. Felt a shiver run through me. Instinctively I touched my belly, as if to protect my baby. Suddenly, looking at Kathryn, I said, "Did Nate tell you? About the last thing she said?"

Tears fell. Kathryn nodded.

"What?" Amanda demanded.

"She told Nate to take care of Katie. Katie is what she called her baby."

"Katie? That's cool. So close to your name,"

Amanda said to Kathryn. "That's like Karma or something." She stood up. "I'm starving. Is there food?"

Nate came out of the bedroom, walking with a cane. "Will you come with me?" he said to Kathryn. "I'd like to show you something. You can come, too, Jess, if you want. You'll need your coats."

"Amanda says she's hungry," I said to Scott. "Want to point her to the food?"

The dogs came with us as we followed Nate outside. He headed toward the barn, telling Kathryn how Laura sold her house to build the barn, that when they got married, she made it clear her horse was part of the deal. "She were so attached to that mare," he said, "I doubt she would have married me if she couldn't bring her along."

Abby, Laura's horse, and Nate's quarter horse, Chief, were in their stalls. The smell of hay and horse greeted us as we entered the barn, and it felt like comfort to me—a warm, earthy comfort. The horse scene was growing on me, I guessed.

"This here's your mother's horse, Abby." Nate stroked the chestnut mare. "She's a good one."

Kathryn let Abby smell her hand, then gently stroked her face and neck. "She's beautiful."

"Your mom, she did barrel racing back in the day. Got pretty good. Quit competin' but she still played at it after she moved here. Abby'll kick up some dust, she will." Nate checked his phone. "It's warm enough. Let's let them out in the field. You okay to help with that?"

"Sure."

I watched as Nate handed Kathryn a lead line clipped to Abby's halter. "Whoa, mare," she said as she opened the stall door. I walked toward the pasture gate.

"You go first, Kathryn," Nate called out. "That mare's the boss."

So Kathryn led Abby out of the barn and into the field. She stroked the horse, talking to her as Nate brought Chief out. "Okay, let 'er go," he called out after I closed the gate.

Kathryn unclipped the lead and the beautiful chestnut took off, followed by Chief, racing down the hill toward the bottom land, manes and tails flying, happy to be free. "Gorgeous," Kathryn said.

"You kin ride her later on if you want. Somebody got to."

We heard a noise, and the three of us turned to see a Virginia State Police car driving up to the house. Nate stared at it. "Back to reality."

Two state troopers got out and walked toward us. One was older, his gray hair poking out from under his hat. His partner was a fresh-faced kid, tall and lanky. Learning the trade, I guessed.

"Mr. Tanner?" the older one began.

"That's me," Nate said.

"I'm Sergeant Blake and this is Trooper Clarkson. We're here about the accident, sir."

Nate nodded.

"Can we talk?"

"Here's fine."

"Would you like to sit down, sir?"

"Jus' git on with it."

"The driver of the pickup . . ."

"What's his name?"

Sergeant Blake paused. "Joshua Cranmer, age 36. His blood alcohol level was 0.20, almost three times the legal limit."

At four-thirty in the afternoon, I thought. Four-thirty! I saw Nate's hand tighten into a fist.

"He's been charged with DUI and vehicular homicide, sir. It's his third offense."

Nate's head jerked. "Third offense!"

"Yessir, a felony. He's looking at serious jail time and loss of driving privileges."

"One wreck too late." The tendon in Nate's jaw flexed. "I'll bet he has a good lawyer."

The trooper shifted on his feet. "Virginia's DUI laws are among the stiffest in the nation, sir," he said. "It depends on the judge, but I don't believe the courts will go easy on him. You'll be invited to give a victim impact statement if you'd like to."

He kept on talking but as I watched, my neck tight, I began to feel dizzy. I was there but not there. In my mind I saw another officer. He had on an NYPD uniform, and he was standing in our living room telling my mother that my father, who had last been seen helping others out of the South Tower of the World Trade Center, was missing and presumed dead.

My head began to swim. My mouth went dry. I closed my eyes. Luke bumped my leg with his nose. Then I felt an arm slip around my waist.

"Jess?" Scott said.

My eyes flew open.

"You okay?"

I couldn't respond. Nate turned to look at me.

"Come on," Scott said in a soft voice.

9

"What have you eaten?" Scott asked when we got to the kitchen. Luke padded behind us.

"Nothing since last night." I sat at the table, Laura's table, trying to force myself to drink the water Scott had poured me. My dog laid down next to me, resting his head on my shoe.

Scott started pulling things out of the fridge and the next thing I knew scrambled eggs and toast with butter and honey appeared before me. I stared at the food.

"It's not for you," he said.

Surprised, I looked at him.

"It's for Little Coop."

I smiled. "Thank you." I picked up a fork and started eating tiny bites.

He sat down next to me. "Hey, Kathryn told me she's going to stay for a few days. How about we go home?"

"We can't just abandon him!"

"We're not. We'll be available for whatever he needs. But if we go home—"

"I can get some rest, I know." I sighed. I knew he was right. But there was so much to do, a funeral to plan, Laura's things to go through.

Just at that moment, Nate and Kathryn came in. "Can I make you some eggs?" Scott asked.

Nate shook his head and Kathryn said she'd eaten at home. Nate sat down next to me. He took my hand. "I need you to go home." I started to protest. He shut that down with a look. "You been here for me, and I appreciate it. But now, I need you to go home."

"Nate, why? There's so much to do."

He squeezed my hand. "When's the last time you planned a funeral?"

Like never. I shook my head.

"Kathryn here, she's done it, and she's volunteerin' to do it again. And since it's her mother, I'm gonna let her."

A lizard of jealousy slithered into my soul. "But Nate . . ."

He held up his hand. "I love ya, you know that. I need to know you're okay, and you need to rest and de-stress to make that happen." He paused. "Do you know how bad I'd feel if anythin' happened to your little one because you were all wrapped up in my worries? Now save me from that. Go home. I'll call you when I need somethin' I promise."

I gave in. What else could I do? He was kicking me out.

Scott and I made our way home, him in his car and me in mine, my vision blurred by tears. Laura was dead. Dead! And my friend Nate was alone again. *Oh, God, I don't understand you!*

. . .

I walked through the next week in a daze, robotically moving from task to task. Get up, take a shower, let Luke out, feed Luke, make my own breakfast, stare at it, do laundry, repack my SAR bag. I couldn't pray, couldn't even think about God. I was Mary and Martha, questioning why he didn't show up before their brother died. I'd forgotten everything I'd learned from Job. I was lost in my hurt for Nate.

I didn't even go to Scott for comfort. He was around, staying busy with his dissertation and the horses and his physical therapy for his shoulder. It's important, apparently, to keep a shoulder moving so it doesn't "freeze."

But how do you keep emotions from freezing? From locking up your insides, keeping you in an eternal loop of sorrow? I apparently had learned nothing from the time Luke was lost.

Instead, I kept hearing the sound of that crash in my head, kept seeing the shock on Nate's face. *Why? Why, God?*

When the pressure of that question became unbearable, I did not pick up my Bible. I did not put on worship music or read one of the books Nate had given me. I did not pray.

I just put on my running shoes and called my dog and let the rhythm of my feet try to chip away the iceberg my heart had become.

Late one night when I couldn't sleep I started

researching the guy who killed Laura. I tried to tell Scott about that the next day when we were driving to the store. "So, this Joshua Cranmer? The guy who killed Laura? I've been doing some research on him."

Scott shifted uncomfortably in the driver's seat of my Jeep. His jaw flexed. "Why?"

"I'm a PI! It's what I do."

"Who's your client?"

My face grew hot. His question was a criticism. Basically, he was saying I had no business doing that.

I didn't respond.

"So, what'd you find out?" He knew I was dying to tell him.

"He has priors, not only for drunken driving, but domestic assault as well. He's in the middle of a divorce. And it looks like they've assigned a prosecutor to the case that I don't like. She's too soft."

"How do you know her?"

"Other cases I've worked. She never goes for the jugular. Nate's never going to get justice if she tries the case."

"Is that what he wants? Justice?"

"That's what everybody wants when a loved one is killed. Justice. You know that."

Scott's sister had been murdered when he was young.

He gave his head a little half-shake. Or maybe

he was just looking before he made a turn. "Do me one favor," he said.

"What?"

"Don't tell Nate all this."

"Why?"

"Nate knows what you do. If he wants you to look into this guy he'll ask you. I think bringing all this up," he said, gesturing, "I think it might get him more torn up than he is already."

So I kept my mouth shut, but just barely.

The funeral was on Saturday, eight days after Laura had died. That morning, I tried slipping on my one black dress and found it didn't fit. It seemed like my belly had popped out in one short week. So I put on black pants with a forgiving waistband, a soft white sweater studded with pearls, and a long black cardigan. It was time to look for maternity clothes.

Kathryn had stayed with Nate all week. She'd helped him pick out a casket and work out the order for the funeral. Together they'd found Scripture passages and picked out music. She'd arranged for a reception at the church afterward and helped him gather pictures and memorabilia for a display. Later she told me helping Nate that week was one of the most profound, deeply emotional experiences of her life. I believed her.

I stood in that church on that day, right behind Nate and Kathryn, holding hands with my husband and singing songs that praised God and affirmed our faith, even though I couldn't feel anything. A crowd of about two hundred stood behind us. The associate pastor gave a short message, and a few people spoke about Laura—the director of the women's center where Laura had worked, the head librarian who was her boss before that, and some friends.

Then, surprisingly, Charles Lee, the father of the little girl who Laura helped regain her speech, stood up and walked to the front. In his rough, country manner, with his little girl by his side, he spoke about the effect Laura had had on his daughter. "She loved Harper when I couldn't," he said, his voice catching, "and then she done give her back t' me."

Nate ducked his head, tears in his eyes. As Charles moved back toward his seat, his daughter broke away, ran to Nate, and hugged him. He nearly lost it.

Somehow I got through the noisy reception after the funeral, everyone chattering like kids just let out of school. The burial, up near Clear Spring where Laura grew up, was private, but Scott and I were invited. Kathryn drove Nate up, her Subaru following the hearse, and Scott and I followed her in Scott's Suburban. We'd drive Nate home afterward as Kathryn had to return to her teaching job on Monday.

At one point on the long drive I turned to Scott

and asked, "Hey, where was Mike? I didn't see him." Mike and Kathryn had been dating/not dating for several months. "Does he know about Laura?"

Scott shifted his grip on the steering wheel. "I told him. I let him know about the funeral. He said 'Yeah, that's not my thing.'"

I pressed the point. "Didn't he imagine Kathryn might need him?"

Scott shrugged. I could tell he was disappointed with his friend but didn't want to say anything against him. My husband is kinder than I am.

Up in the mountains the day had turned cold, with a light snow falling. Nate remained stone-faced, stoic, as Laura's coffin was placed over the grave. He laid a single white rose on it, his hand lingering in a last goodbye, his eyes closed, his lips moving in what I knew was a prayer. Then he turned and embraced each of us without speaking. We left quietly. As we drove away, I looked back and saw the cemetery grounds crew gathering to lower the coffin into the earth.

Ashes to ashes, dust to dust. A mist that appears for a little time. That's all we are.

I slept in the next day. When I woke up, I could hear voices. Amanda and Ethan, I realized. I forced myself out of bed and got dressed.

Luke was not in our bedroom. He'd been left at home a lot the day before and I'm sure was looking for any action he could get involved in. Maybe Scott had taken him out.

I checked my phone and found I had a message from Detective Porter. Had they found Heather Burgess? I listened as I walked downstairs, a frown forming on my face as I processed what I was hearing.

"Good morning!" Scott said, moving to give me a quick kiss.

I greeted Amanda and Ethan with hugs.

"What's up?" Scott asked, nodding toward the phone still in my hand.

"The Harrisonburg case."

"What's that?" Amanda asked. She was chewing on a piece of toast, which made me realize how hungry I was. Tall and lanky, her pregnancy showed less than mine, although she was about a month ahead of me.

I outlined the Heather Burgess case, realizing halfway through it mimicked Amanda's situation—the night of drinking that ended up with her pregnant. She was raped by a virtual stranger.

"Yeah, he raped her," she declared when I mentioned Bobby had admitted they'd had sex.

I raised my eyebrows. "They were friends."

"Doesn't matter. Drunk sex is not consensual. If you're drunk, you don't have the capacity to consent."

"But they knew each other. They were drinking together, celebrating her birthday with a whole group. Then they paired off. College kids mix sex and alcohol all the time."

"All of that may be true, but if she was drunk enough to be throwing up, he shouldn't have had sex with her."

I looked to Scott to see if he agreed. He was beaming at her.

I slid my phone into my back pocket and moved to get myself some toast and yogurt. Scott looked at me. "So, did they find her?"

"No. I got a voicemail from the detective. Heather's parents want to hire me privately to investigate her disappearance." I put the toast in and turned to the fridge.

"How do you feel about that?"

"I'm not sure yet." I pulled a carton of strawberry yogurt out and took off the lid. Then I grabbed a spoon from the drawer and began eating.

The room was quiet for a minute, then Amanda spoke up. "After that happened to me, I felt so stupid. Then, when I found out I was pregnant, I felt so ashamed. How could I be so dumb!" She paused. "Honestly, I wanted to kill myself, but the way you guys and Ethan responded stopped me." She took his hand. Ethan drew her into an embrace.

"We love you," Scott said, "and we've all made mistakes, too."

My toast popped up. I turned, took out a plate for

it. I buttered it and dripped a thin thread of honey over it. With my back to the others, I thought about shame and what Nate taught me about it. How evil uses it to divide us and draw us into sin. How Jesus took our shame on the cross and we don't need to carry it anymore. I wanted to say that to Amanda, but I knew she'd reject the idea.

Having physical work to do on a project I cared about—the nursery—did help get my mind off Laura's death. We removed the desk and other furniture in the room and cleaned it well. The oak floors could use sanding and polishing but we opted not to do that.

Around midmorning, I texted Nate. This was his first day alone and I wanted him to know I was thinking about him. Nate didn't respond.

Moving on to paint, we put down drop cloths and taped the room. Scott had asked me to choose the color, and I'd picked a light blue that was repeated in a western-scene art print—blue skies, mountains, a valley, a ranch, horses and cattle. That was for Scott.

"You two should get out of the house until the paint smell dissipates," Scott said when the room was prepared. He pulled out his wallet and removed a credit card. "Go buy something that makes you feel beautiful. Because you are." He hugged Amanda and kissed me. "I love you both."

I don't deserve that man.

• • •

I had yet to buy a single piece of maternity wear, but Amanda knew all the places to go—Target, Old Navy, and "baby and me" type stores. We ended up driving to Fredericksburg, because she said we'd find more there. By the end of the day, I had a nice dress, three pairs of jeans, some tops, bras and underwear, and two pairs of dress pants. Everything but SAR clothes. "Check online," Amanda told me, and I said I would.

Amanda had insisted on driving and that was fine with me. I yawned on the way back and asked, "How long does this fatigue last? Are you through it yet?"

"Mostly. My doctor says pregnancy is a journey in three parts. A mountain, a valley, and another mountain. First trimester, second trimester, third. I'm in the valley part right now, so I'm good."

A journey in three parts. I realized I was either resisting the idea that my body was different or wanting to race through to the end.

She glanced at me. "Want to pick up dinner on the way home? Take it to the guys?"

"Sounds like a plan." I mentioned a Chinese place on the way. She nixed it. "Too much sodium," she said.

I tried a few other ideas, but we settled on barbeque. Not sandwiches, though. Brisket this time, and ribs, slaw, and corn, plus country-style green beans and gingered applesauce. A feast. I called it in and said we'd pick it up in half an hour, then texted the guys and told them.

"How have you been feeling?" I asked her after I clicked off my phone.

"Pretty good. My hips are hurting, and I still get tired at night. School starts back up next week, and I'm hoping all the walking won't kill me."

"Have you decided what you're going to do?" I meant in regard to keeping the baby or arranging an adoption, but she went a different direction.

"Law school, for sure, if I can get in. After that, I'd either like to work for a nonprofit helping sexual assault victims or," she paused, "don't tell Dad, but I'm thinking about the FBI."

I grinned. "He'd be over the moon if he knew that."

"He'd be insufferable," she retorted, "handing me advice every 2.5 seconds. Encouraging me until I was sick of it."

I looked over at her, relieved to see she was smiling.

"What about you? Are you gonna help those parents?"

"I will at least go talk to them. And if I think I can help, I'll take the job."

10

I did call Heather Burgess's parents Sunday evening, and we arranged to meet in Harrisonburg at their hotel at eleven the next day.

Kevin and Carol Burgess looked to be in their early fifties. Tall and slender, his blond hair flecked with gray, Kevin looked me up and down with his smoky blue eyes as I walked in the room. I had the strong feeling talking to me was not his idea.

Carol was short and slim, with dark hair cut short and red-framed glasses. She had on black slacks and a black-and-white sweater. She was barely holding back tears.

I knew immediately I was going to have to use some of Scott's techniques with them, techniques he'd taught me after I'd asked him what made him so good at interviews. Things like mirroring and curiosity, tone of voice, and labeling emotions. He made me practice with him using made-up scenarios to be sure I got them right. It got hilarious at times, but I learned a lot.

I took a deep breath. "Hi, I'm Jessica Cooper," I said, smiling. I put my attaché case down on the large walnut table.

"What's that for?" Kevin gestured toward Luke.

"This is Luke. He's my partner. A search-and-rescue dog."

A look of disgust passed over his face and he swore again.

"Luke, the one who found what we think may be your daughter's earring." I kept irritation, anger, and defensiveness out of my voice, turning on my best calm, soothing tone.

My comment about the earring registered. Kevin shot another look at my dog, then sat down, gesturing for me to do the same.

We had arranged to meet in a private conference room at their hotel, one of the nicest in Harrisonburg. Someone had provided a pitcher of water and glasses, and I was grateful for that. I still missed my morning coffee. "Anyone like some water?" I said, pouring a glass.

"No," Kevin said definitively. "Look, Miss Cooper. Porter recommended you. I don't know why I listened to him. He can't find our daughter and I'm angry."

"I can understand you being angry."

"And I don't want to waste my money on some second-class PI friend of his. I think this was a mistake."

He rattled on about his perceptions of my inadequacy. It wasn't taking long for me to decide I really didn't like this man.

"Of course you don't want to waste your money," I said, "or your time. I understand that.

You don't have to hire me." I quickly went through my credentials, including my time as a Fairfax County homicide detective, some of the missing persons cases I'd solved as a PI, and my search-and-rescue background. "I may not be the private investigator you're looking for, but as long as I'm here, and since I'm interested in finding Heather anyway, why don't you let me ask a few questions and see if we can make some progress?"

"That's what I want!" he said, exploding. "Progress."

"Yes, progress. Absolutely! You want to find your daughter. So let's talk. If at the end of an hour you don't want to use me, okay. But let's at least talk."

He grumbled something and looked toward his wife. A look passed between them that I read as hostile.

"What can you tell me about your daughter?"

He shrugged. "She's just a normal kid, a normal twenty-one-year-old. Majoring in sociology."

"English," his wife said. "She switched."

He rolled his eyes.

Mrs. Burgess took over. "Heather is a very naïve young woman. Never had a boyfriend, never ran around with the in-crowd."

"Never played sports," Mr. Burgess grumbled.

"Was she prone to drinking?"

They looked at each other. "I don't think so," Mrs. Burgess finally concluded.

"Any siblings?"

"Her brother is five years older. Top student. Law school. Played lacrosse at Maryland. The whole package," Mr. Burgess said.

Ah, yes. The golden child. "His name?"

"Kevin R. Burgess, Junior."

Of course. "He sounds very accomplished." I drew us back to the main subject. "When is the last time you saw Heather?"

"New Year's Day, right before we left for Europe." Mrs. Burgess tapped her expensive manicured forefinger on the table. "We had Christmas together, the four of us, plus Kevin's girlfriend. We celebrated his new job."

"Top DC law firm," Mr. Burgess interjected.

"Kevin and Macie went back to their house, and Heather stayed until New Year's Day."

"She lives off campus?"

"Yes, in an apartment with two other students, a guy and a girl."

"Names?"

They looked at each other. "Brandon and Alice, but I don't know their last names," Mrs. Burgess said.

"It's hard to keep up with college kids' friends, isn't it?" I said soothingly. "Why did Heather choose JMU? You live in Maryland, right?"

"Bethesda, just outside of DC. She didn't want to follow her brother to the University of

Maryland for some reason. We couldn't figure out why she chose JMU."

"Did she seem happy at the school? I mean, she's in her third year, right?"

"Happy? I don't know if Heather has ever been happy. She's a Debbie Downer if there ever was one." Mr. Burgess could barely keep the disgust off his face.

"She has depression!" Mrs. Burgess said, her eyes flaring as she stared at him.

I stayed calm. Sympathetic. "Was she on medication?"

"Always," Mr. Burgess said.

"Had she ever mentioned suicide?"

"No!" Mrs. Burgess said, quickly. "Never suicide."

Mr. Burgess grimaced. "Her father committed suicide." He tipped his head toward his wife. "I think it's in the genes."

Mrs. Burgess stood up quickly. "Oh, shut up!" she said, and left the room.

Okay, Scott, what's your technique for this? His interview subjects usually couldn't leave the room. They were prisoners. I was on my own.

"Do you want to take a break?" I asked Mr. Burgess.

He gestured. "She's overly emotional. Just like Heather."

I'm going to lose it with this man. I took a deep breath, channeled my inner Special Agent

Cooper, and kept asking questions. At the end of the hour, Kevin Burgess Sr. hired me. I collected the Burgesses' full contact information, had him sign my standard contract, and collected my thousand-dollar retainer fee.

Then I shook hands with Mr. Burgess, promised him frequent updates, gathered up my dog, and left. *Holy moly, what a couple!*

Why did I take the job? I felt sorry for Heather Burgess.

Plus, now I was curious. Had Heather committed suicide? Was she still alive? Had she run away from her dismal life? Had she been abducted? Murdered?

I called Scott, vented about the Burgesses, and then told him I'd have to stay in Harrisonburg for a few days.

"I expected that," he responded. "Let me know where you land."

By that he meant where I ended up staying. Part of me wanted to stay in the ritzy hotel, just to catch glimpses of the Burgesses. Part of me wanted to get as far away as possible. My decision was made easier by the text I got after I hung up with Scott. The Burgesses were going home. Praise God.

There's a chain of hotels I like to use when I'm traveling, and I was able to get a room in the Harrisonburg location for Luke and me. It was not a dog-friendly chain, but I'd used them enough in some pretty prominent searches that they'd made an exception for Luke, as long as he was crated when left alone in the room.

First things first. After checking in at the hotel, I texted Scott the location and room number, changed clothes, and took Luke out for a run. Thank goodness for elastic waistbands on my running pants. After that, I was starving, so I ordered a stacked turkey sandwich and a salad, had it delivered to my room, and ate it while strategizing. Who did I need to talk to? What locations did I need to investigate? What information did I want from the police reports?

Then I started calling people, beginning with Detective Porter. He was awesome, sharing all the information I needed right away and suggesting we meet for dinner to cover the rest.

Fine with me. We set a time and a place. Then I started calling the young people I wanted to interview: first of all, the boy who'd confessed to having sex with Heather. After that, her roommates.

The young man's name was Bobby Morganthal and he seemed eager to talk to me when I called him. We met off campus at a park. I took Luke with me. I've often found having a dog on the scene helps. Most people relate to dogs. They lower their defenses and forget to hide their secrets. I'd recommended the technique to Scott, but he seemed to think the FBI wasn't going to start issuing puppies any time soon.

"I'm Bobby," the young man said as we shook hands. He was tall and thin and looked bookish. Clean-shaven, glasses, short-cropped hair. He had the long fingers of a pianist and in fact, he told me he was a music major and was from Springfield, in Northern Virginia, near where I grew up.

"Tell me about that night," I said, keeping my voice soft, "the night Heather disappeared."

He swallowed hard and looked down, struggling for composure. "I've gone over and over it so many times. We were just out to have a good time, you know? Then things got out of hand."

"Was drinking like that the norm for your group?"

"No, ma'am. Not for me anyway. And I . . . I haven't had a drink since."

"How did you know Heather?"

"We had classes together, English and music. We were . . . are friends."

"But not lovers."

His face reddened and he shook his head. "No."

"So, step-by-step, you're out drinking, she says she's going to throw up, and you . . ."

"I followed her into the alley. I held her hair back. I felt bad for her!"

"And then what? You suggested you take a walk?"

"No! No, that was her idea."

"Her idea to walk down that path."

"Yes. She was tired. Didn't want to go to another bar. She asked me to walk with her."

"So you did and then . . ."

He shrugged. "It started to snow. She took my hand. I kissed her and then." He shook his head. "We started fooling around and, well, one thing led to the other."

"She was drunk."

"We were both drunk."

I paused. "And then . . ."

"I must have passed out. When I woke up, I was freezing, and she was gone."

"How long were you passed out?"

"Ten minutes? Fifteen maybe? Not long."

But long enough.

"Did you look for her?"

"Yes! I looked and called for her. I couldn't find her, so I walked home."

"Where's home?" I jotted down the address he gave me. "How far is that from her apartment?"

"Half a mile? Maybe more?"

"Did you go to her apartment and see if she was there?"

He shook his head. "And I didn't check on her the next day. I was embarrassed. I'd never done anything like that before. I felt awkward. So I did the easiest thing."

"Which was nothing."

"Right."

At that point, Bobby began weeping. I pulled a pack of tissues out of my bag and handed it to him. "I'm sorry, so sorry. But I didn't kill her. I swear, I did not kill her."

"Would you remember if you did?" I asked gently.

He could not respond.

I was able to meet Heather's roommates next, Alicia Thomas and Brandon Newcastle. They said the three of them were just friends and roommates, and yes, they'd been in the group that had celebrated Heather's birthday but didn't see her go off with Bobby.

The trio lived in a three-bedroom, cottage-style apartment on a hill just off campus. It struck me as pretty luxurious. I saw a community room with couches and billiards and some old-school pinball machines on the way in to their building. Behind it was a beautiful swimming pool. Inside the two-level apartment was a large living room/kitchen area, and each bedroom had its own bathroom. Not exactly the way I lived in college.

The roommates let me go through Heather's room and belongings. "Are her parents still gonna pay the rent?" Alicia asked as I slipped on gloves and began to rummage.

"You'll have to check with them on that."

The police had seized her computer, as I

expected. I went over her room with a fine-tooth comb, including behind the drawers in her desk and under her bed. An English major's got to have a journal, right?

Eventually I hit paydirt, finding a small diary between her mattress and the mattress cover. Skimming through it I found no mention of suicide or even dark despair—just a lot of normal young-adult angst. I took the diary anyway. I'd give it to Detective Porter at dinner after I'd read it more closely.

While I went through the room, Luke stayed in the living room, charming the roommates. I could hear them talking to him while I went through Heather's bathroom. I found her prescription drugs for depression along with some over-the-counter remedies. I wondered, if she was intending to disappear wouldn't she have taken the antidepressants with her?

Returning to the living room, I found Luke sprawled indecently on the floor while Alicia rubbed his tummy. "Terrifying, isn't he?" I said, taking off my gloves.

"Aw, he's a sweetie," Alicia crooned.

I took advantage of the relaxed attitude. "So, tell me about Heather. What's she like?"

"I mean, I like her and all that. She studies a lot. We had to talk her into going out for her birthday."

"So she isn't usually a big drinker."

"No way!"

Brandon chimed in. "She keeps to herself." He looked at Alicia. "Even here, at the apartment."

"So she doesn't hang out with you in the community room or at the pool?"

He blew out a sharp breath. "Are you kidding? No."

"I don't know what she does besides study," Alicia said.

"How'd you all end up rooming together?"

"There's an app for finding roommates."

"Okay, how about drugs? Did you ever see her using them?" I asked.

Brandon burst out laughing. "Not even a joint."

"We tried to get her to, you know, loosen up."

"Lost cause," Brandon said.

So what had happened to this quiet, studious, sad girl? I was more determined than ever to find out. I handed each of the two roommates my business card and asked them to call me if they thought of anything else.

11

After a nap and a quick text to Nate, which he didn't answer, I read over Heather's diary again. Page after page of roommate problems, professor problems, and parent problems. I thought that was it, until I happened to notice a neatly hidden pocket on the inside back cover. I slipped my finger under the edge and withdrew a small piece of paper with the word "Jaime" written on it and a bunch of random numbers.

None of her friends, as far as I knew, bore that name. Puzzled, I took Luke out for a quick run. Then I took a shower, put on some nice pants and a pretty sweater, and got in my car to meet Detective Porter at Seared, a steak restaurant in Harrisonburg. I was starving and ready for good beef. Detective Porter, or "Robert" as he asked me to call him, recommended the New York strip, so that's what I ordered, along with salad and creamy mashed potatoes.

In the small talk that followed, I found out that his wife had died two years before of cancer, and that he had a little girl, age eight. "I'm hoping she'll remember her mom," he said. "I took this job so I could raise her away from the big city. My mother has stepped up to help. She's moved in to care for her when I'm working." He smiled.

"I had to promise to bring her a steak dinner after I told her where we were meeting."

I laughed.

"You been married long?" he asked.

I went through my history with Scott, leaving out how obnoxious we both were in the beginning and the part about his drinking and my resistance to him. Instead, I focused on how our mutual friend Nate had brought us together. When I mentioned Nate, I got a little choked up. So I told Robert about Laura.

He shook his head. "I had a long, difficult run-up to losing my wife. All those CT scans, PET scans, appointments, chemo, radiation." He shook his head like he was trying to dislodge those thoughts. "It was hard, but I think your friend's road, losing his wife suddenly like that, is even harder. I imagine he's still in shock."

"Yes," I said, resolving to call Nate later.

"Grief is a journey," Robert went on to say. "It's different for everyone. There are twists and turns, advances and setbacks. You think you're getting better when *bam!* It hits you again."

I know I wanted to say. But I stayed silent.

Our food came and we talked about Heather. I shared my reactions to the Burgesses, and then what I'd learned from Bobby, Alicia and Brandon. I gave him the diary I found. I'd looked at it in my hotel room and found nothing that, to me, would indicate Heather was suicidal or wanted to run away. I'd handled the diary with gloves on and afterward, I'd slid it into a zip-closure bag marked with where I'd found it, the date and time. It was standard evidentiary practice, but Robert appreciated the care I'd taken, I could tell.

We spent the rest of the meal batting around scenarios, and the best we could come up with was she either got lost and came to some sad end or had been abducted. Neither of us could see any evidence she'd run away or was suicidal.

"Except for one thing," I said, raising a cautionary hand. "If she sobered up, realized what she'd done, and been filled with shame, suicide might be an option."

Robert nodded.

"Just in case, Luke and I will cover all the trails within walking distance of the place she was last seen."

"We've done that," Porter said. "And the dogs covered them, too."

I shrugged. "It's not unusual for people or even dogs to miss something. I have to exercise him anyway. I might as well do it there."

"How long will you be up here?"

"I want to talk to her professors and some people in her class. So a few more days."

I got back to my hotel room and called Nate. Again, he didn't answer so I left a voicemail. It was 8:30 p.m. Where was he?

Then I called Scott, who picked up. I could hear he was in the car. "Where are you off to?" I asked.

"Just coming back. I took Nate some dinner."

"Without me?" I felt a rush of anger.

"I looked around, but you weren't here!" He laughed. "I looked everywhere! Honest."

I forced myself to calm down. "How is he?"

"He's okay. About what you'd expect."

What did that mean? Sad? Depressed? Lonely? In shock? Suicidal?

Scott continued. "Today was his first day back to work."

"Work?"

"Part time. Four or so hours a day. Said he'd rather do that than sit at home."

"So, is he depressed?"

"Just grieving. It takes time, Jess." Scott paused. I heard sirens go past him. "Nate said to tell you he got your texts and to tell you he's okay. He's just not much for talking right now."

I blew out a breath.

"Look, I've got to go. There's an accident up ahead and I've got to sort my way through it. I love you, Jess!"

"Love you, too." I hung up and tossed my phone on the bed, irritated. Luke looked up at me, apparently surprised by my action. "He went to see Nate without me!"

He wagged his tail, but I knew it was just because I said "Nate."

I had intended to go to bed, but after talking with Scott my adrenaline wouldn't let me. I changed back into my sweats and running shoes, put my room key in my pocket, and grabbed Luke's leash. I left my phone on the bed. Intentionally.

With Luke on leash, I took the elevator down to the first floor, walked through the lobby, and stepped into the dark night. I took a right, jogged to the far edge of the parking lot, and let him off leash near the tree line so he could water the bushes.

The sky had been swept clean of clouds. The stars, brilliant against the black sky, formed a thousand points of light. I took a deep breath and tried to focus on the beauty, inhaling the crisp, cold air as if it would cleanse me inside.

But I knew only God could do that.

The hotel was on a small road leading into Harrisonburg on about fifteen acres of relatively flat land that rose to become a hill in the back. As I stood waiting for Luke to do his thing, I stared into the woods, wondering how a person like Heather would possibly find her way through such a place if they were blind drunk. The smart thing to do would be to follow a path or, if you couldn't find a path, a stream. But then, being drunk doesn't make anyone particularly smart.

Luke nudged my leg, and I leashed him up again. I didn't want to run on the road in front of the hotel. It was too dark and there was virtually no shoulder. The parking lot was lit. That seemed boring, but also the most doable, so I took off. At nine-fifteen, cars were still pulling in and one or two left, their headlights sweeping over us as they moved through the lot. Luke and I jogged on, my breath a frosty stream, his pads a rhythmic whisper on my left. My goal was to give my anger something to chew on besides my gut.

We ran the "U" of the parking lot and reached the front of the hotel three times. Then, impulsively, I decided to run around the building, through the parking lot in the back. It was darker back there. Not as many lights. I saw a gravel path take off from the parking lot to the right. Curious, I took it. That's when I realized I didn't have my headlamp.

I should have turned around. I didn't. I kept on that path. The woods closed around me like a shroud. I felt a check in my gut. I ignored it, my jaw set, willing my eyes to adjust to the dark.

Then suddenly Luke came to a dead stop. My shoes scuffed on the gravel as I stopped my run. "What?" I asked him. He growled. Then he stepped in front of me, blocking my path. I peered into the night, looking with my inadequate eyes, listened with my puny human ears, and even tried smelling with my stub of a nose. Nothing.

Luke growled again, his hackles up. *What is he sensing?*

My Apple watch vibrated, indicating a call.

I looked. Scott. I clicked it off. My mouth dry, I began backing up, moving toward the hotel while staring into that black night, watching for whatever Luke had alerted me to.

I stumbled, nearly falling. Panic jolted me. My fear took over. I turned around and ran, ran hard down that path, back toward the hotel, listening for footsteps behind me, braced for a hand on my shoulder. My breath came hard, my heart beat harder.

I heard a limb fall. A twig snap. I ran faster. Black tree branches seemed to reach out to grab me. I caught my foot on something and almost fell. Underbrush scraped my arm.

Finally, I glimpsed the lights of the parking lot.

I put on extra speed and raced toward the lights. I didn't stop once I was under them. My fear forced me around to the front of the hotel. More lights. People.

I thought my heart was going to hammer out of my chest. I paced up and down the sidewalk in front of the hotel, refusing to leave the light, trying to regain my breath. Luke stood still, panting, staring hard at the corner of the hotel. He was guarding me, I realized.

My watch indicated another call. Scott. Again.

I was too out of breath. I couldn't answer. So I clicked it off.

Fifteen minutes of pacing and walking finally brought my heart rate down. "Let's go inside, buddy," I said. We entered the front door and walked past the front desk. I hesitated. "Where does that gravel path behind the hotel go?" I asked the desk clerk.

He looked at me quizzically. "What?"

I said it again.

"Oh, that goes back to a utility shed where we keep equipment. Why?"

"Just wondering. Good night," I said, and Luke and I walked toward the elevator.

Once upstairs, it still took me a few minutes to calm down enough to call Scott.

"Well there you are," he said when he picked up my call. "Did I catch you in the shower?"

"No. I just couldn't answer." *I was outside being stupid.*

"Okay. Sorry I had to cut our phone call short. I just called to say goodnight. I miss you."

"I miss you, too, Scott." I hugged a pillow to my chest.

"Is Luke in the room with you?"

"Yes."

"Good."

I shook off my self-focus. "How'd your PT go today?"

"Oh, it's getting real. Got a whole new set of exercises. But I like that guy."

"Good." I kept the small talk going, then I said, "I'm sorry I got irritated you went to see Nate without me."

"It's okay. I get it. You're concerned about him."

"Yes."

"And he's worried about you, getting stressed out."

Who me? "Right. I'm fine."

"He doesn't want you worrying about him."

"I'm not." *That was a lie.* "Look, I've got to get to bed. Love you."

"Love you, too," he said.

I clicked off the phone and squeezed my eyes shut as tears began to fall. I'd been angry with Scott for no good reason. Put myself and Baby Cooper at risk by being stupid and running that path in the dark, by myself. Unarmed, I might add, since I'd left my weapon at home. And just now, I'd lied to my husband. What was wrong with me?

Discouraged, I took a shower and went to bed.

His mercies are new every morning. That was the first thought that ran through my head when I opened my eyes the next day. Nate's voice. It was something he'd said to me a lot. I grabbed my phone and texted Scott. *I'm sorry. I lied. I am worried about Nate.*

He texted back. *I know. It's okay. I love you.*

And as I lay there in bed, thinking about how lucky I was to have Scott, I felt a kick. A *baby kick*. In my belly. My first one! I lay perfectly still, trying to feel it again. But Baby Cooper didn't cooperate. *That's normal,* I thought.

It's amazing I could feel him at all. According to my book, he was only about the size of a mango.

I texted Scott. He was excited. My pregnancy journey had advanced several paces.

My plan for that day was to run a couple of trails near where Heather had disappeared. But first I was going to see if I could catch up with a couple of her professors.

Luke and Baby Cooper required breakfast. I took my dog outside briefly, then came back in, fed him, and scooted down to the breakfast bar to snag some protein. I found scrambled eggs and yogurt, fruit, and cereal bars. I ate the eggs and kept the other stuff for a mid-morning snack, all the while smelling coffee and wondering if just a little would hurt.

Who was I kidding? If I breached that wall, there would be no stopping me. I love my coffee.

Detective Porter had handed me a sheaf of papers at dinner. Among them was Heather's schedule. JMU has a big campus, and of course, her classes were all over the place. I found two that were clustered, however, and a third nearby, so I headed there.

Neither her English Romantic Poets nor her Chaucer professors had much to say about Heather. She was one of about thirty in each class. Her writing was pedestrian and her thinking simplistic, one of them said. "Unremarkable," said the other.

The last instructor was a little more positive. As a teaching assistant in the big Psych 101 class, he had had more contact with her. "She's super interested in psychology, and I found her insights into family dynamics very interesting. I encouraged her to pursue it," Jason Fields said.

"She's an English major."

"Students change majors all the time," he said, shrugging.

In their third year? I thought about all the additional credits she'd have to earn, and I wondered if her father would put up with that.

Another question popped into my head. "She use drugs, do you know?"

He looked at me oddly.

"I'm not law enforcement. I'm just trying to understand what happened to her."

He took a deep breath. "We had a long talk about whether psychoactive drugs that our society classifies as 'illegal' might actually be helpful in ameliorating conditions like depression or anxiety. Maybe even other illnesses."

I kept my face neutral and simply nodded. "I understand she was depressed."

"Most of them are," he said, gesturing. "Who wouldn't be with the world they've been handed. But did she use drugs? Not that I know of, except prescription medications. She did tell me she was taking antidepressants." He laughed softly. "We shared personal reviews of the various kinds. In the end, I told her a simple joint beats them all."

Oh, really? The jury was still out on cannabis. Some studies found short-term use helped depression but that continual use exacerbated it. Other studies found it just worsened depression. What's more, I found the discussion he related was very immature for someone who was supposed to be a role model.

But, maintaining my neutral expression, I smiled at Mr. Fields and thanked him for talking to me. Then I gave him my business card and invited him to contact me if anything else occurred to him.

12

The ticking of the clock, Laura's grandfather clock, seemed to echo throughout the house. *Ask not for whom the clock ticks, it ticks for thee.*

Nate took a deep breath, closed his eyes, and summoned up the image from a famous sermon he'd read way back in school. He was hanging over a deep black hole, like a spider on a thin thread, darkness all around him. Darkness in him. No way to get a foothold. Just hanging there, with nothing but blackness all around. "Lord," he whispered, "that there's exactly how I feel."

He sat at his kitchen table, a plateful of food in front of him. Food he'd heated up. Food he didn't want to eat.

"Evenin's are the worst and being it's almost February, evenin's start afore five o'clock," Nate said out loud. "That's a long time to be sittin' in this house by myself. A long time to hear nothin' but my own heartbeat. God, I don't think I can do it!

"The worst of it is, I cain't feel you! Cain't find you. Cain't see you in this. God, why have you left me?"

Despair threatened to clip the thin thread holding him, dropping him into the pit. He shoved back from the table and forced himself to his feet. His young German shepherd, Ember, jumped up, while his old springer spaniel, Sprite, waited to see what he would do.

Ember shoved her nose into his leg. He reached down and rubbed her behind her ears with both hands. "I been thinkin' maybe I should give you away. Find you a young family, kids to play with. I been thinkin' you don't need to be here with an old man." Ember wagged her tail, her deep brown eyes fixed on his face.

Sighing, he straightened up and made himself walk into the living room. He stared at the bookshelves flanking the fireplace, shelves he'd built himself. They were filled with books he loved, books he'd feasted on long before Laura had ever reentered his life. Now, their messages of hope and joy, sovereign grace and love mocked him.

He strode over, grabbed an armful, and threw them into the fire, yelling as he did. He watched, tears in his eyes, as the bright yellow flames licked their pages and darkened their covers.

"C'mon, dogs," he said, and he walked to the back door, grabbed his jacket off the peg, and went outside into the dark night, a mirror of his soul.

He didn't bother bringing a flashlight. He knew this property like he knew his own body. Knew the dips in the ground, the places the gravel had pooled. Knew the rough spots in the path.

What he didn't know was how to get over the death of his wife.

He walked into the barn. Abby, Laura's horse, nickered as he came in. Nate stroked the chestnut's nose and cupped his hand around her jaw, the way he'd seen Laura do. "I imagine you're missing her, too."

He still remembered that day, lying in a hospital bed, trying to imagine life with one leg. And who came walking in the door behind Jess and Scott? Laura. His long-lost love. The woman whose picture was still in his wallet after more than twenty years.

They married pretty quickly. He felt like he'd been waiting for most of his life and couldn't see a reason to keep waiting. And now, just five short years later, God had taken her.

The weight of that thought made him sit down, hard, on the straw bale across from the stalls. He leaned his head back against the rough wood of the barn wall. Sprite jumped up next to him and rested her head on his leg. He stroked her head until his phone buzzed. A call. He looked at the screen. Jess. He clicked it off.

"A man's got to be alone sometimes," he said aloud to the animals. "There's some things you gotta go through by yourself."

Maybe that was it. Maybe God just meant for him to be alone.

He sat there talking to them for a long time

with Ember nestled at his feet and Sprite next to him, her silken head soft under his hand. He talked about Laura, and how she'd brought so much into his life. Married, committed love, her passion for horses, her tender but tough spirit. She'd awakened in him a deeper purpose. Loving her, protecting her, providing for her, sharing his faith with her, worshipping together. A richness to his life that had nourished him.

Now, like a snuffed-out candle, like a letter tossed into the fire, she was gone. Poof. And there was nothing he could do about it, nothing he could have done to prevent it. God just took her.

"There's some would say it was just an accident," he told the animals. "That God had nothing to do with it. God would never do something so . . . hard," he said. "But I think different. The Bible says that he knew her when she was yet unborn, that all the days of her life were written afore there were any of 'em.

"God knew this was comin'. He ordained it or at least he allowed it. He is God! I jus' cain't figure out why he left me alive. Why he's walked away from me."

Nate stretched his legs out and leaned back again. The cold was seeping into his body, chilling him. He thought about the fireplace inside the house. He should go in. Warm up.

He didn't want to. He just didn't care.

13

I spent two more days in Harrisonburg. I interviewed a dozen more students, stalking them outside Heather's classrooms and approaching them as class let out. I randomly walked up to a few kids I saw around campus who seemed her "type." Not real flashy, not jocks, sort of bookish-looking.

Of the fifteen kids I'd interviewed, eight of them knew who Heather was. Three knew she was missing. I guess college kids don't watch the evening news, because the story had been on nearly every night. But I got more information about Heather's personality and habits, and it squared with what I'd found before. She studied a lot. Was quiet. One described her as "mousy." Didn't drink regularly or do drugs.

I stumbled on something almost by accident. I asked Porter if he'd run her credit cards for the last two months. He had. He texted me the printout, and as I studied it, I saw she had charged coffee at a particular coffeehouse almost every day at 4:45 p.m. So leaving Luke at my hotel room, I went there. I smelled the coffee but bought herbal tea—yuck. And, while pretending to read, I studied the people in there. Mostly students, I guessed, based on clothes and the books they were carrying.

The second day I did that, I saw someone come in and look around, like he was looking for someone. He was Hispanic and wore the clothes of a construction worker, work boots and all.

I watched him for a minute, and then something made me jump up. "Are you looking for someone?" I asked him. He had beautiful brown eyes and dark skin. He stood maybe five foot seven and a hundred sixty pounds.

He looked away quickly when I spoke to him.

"I'm sorry, what I meant to say is that I am looking for someone. Have you seen this woman?" I showed him the picture of Heather.

I saw fear come into his face. His eyes darted around the room. "She's missing," I said, softly. "I'm worried about her. She came in here every day at this time. I'm guessing she was meeting someone. Do you know her? Have you seen her?"

He swallowed hard, his Adam's apple bobbing in his smooth neck.

I took the lead. "Let me grab my purse and let's talk."

As I suspected he would, he ran as soon as I turned to get my purse. But I had not spent years running in the mountains for nothing. I raced after him. A student coming the other direction saw me chasing him and stuck out a foot. The young Hispanic man fell.

I was over him before he could get up. "Stop. I just want to talk to you." I saw a campus cop headed in our direction. "Look, I'm guessing you're not a student. Walk with me if you don't want to answer a lot of questions from the cop that's coming this way."

He looked around quickly, confirmed the cop sighting, and nodded.

I helped him up and we began walking. "So what I'm looking for is someone to clean out the flower beds and turn over the garden to get them ready for planting. Can you do that?" I asked.

"Yes, ma'am. No problem."

The officer barely gave us a glance as he passed us.

"When do you think you could start?"

"Prob'ly next week," he replied.

I lowered my voice. "Why'd you run? Do you know her?"

He looked straight ahead and nodded.

"Are you seeing each other?"

He hesitated.

"I'm not a cop. I'm just trying to find her."

He took a breath. "We met there at the café. We can't see each other because of her father. She said he would kill her."

"Because . . ."

"Because I am Hispanic. A construction worker."

"And here illegally."

He nodded. Then he looked at me. "What am I supposed to do? My parents brought me here when I was two. This is the only home I have ever known. Some people want to send me back to El Salvador. I don't know anything about that country! This is where I belong. This is my home."

"Okay, I get that. When is the last time you saw Heather?"

He gave me a date. It was the day before her birthday. "I come every day, but she is not here. So now she is missing?"

I nodded. "Her parents have hired me to try to find her. Where else did you meet up with her."

He shook his head. "Only there, at the café."

"In your car? In your apartment? In her apartment?"

"No! I would not dishonor her." He ducked his head. "I love her."

"Did you ever take walks?"

He shook his head.

"Go drinking?"

He grimaced. "No, I told you. We talk at the café. That's all."

"How long have you been meeting?"

"Two months, maybe three."

"Every day."

"Nearly."

I paused. "Is your name Jamie?"

He nodded. "Jaime, actually," using the Hispanic pronunciation.

My heart thumped. This was the guy whose name Heather had in her diary. I took down his information, his full name and address and so on. "Look you're going to have a visit from the police. That can't be avoided. Don't panic. They don't care about your immigration status. They're just trying to gather information about Heather."

"Would it help if I go to them?"

I hesitated, taken aback by his wisdom. "I think that would help a lot." I gave him Detective Porter's card. "I'll call him and tell him you're coming," I said.

True to his word, Jaime Hernandez showed up at the police station. Detective Porter interviewed him for over an hour. "He's not a person of interest," Porter said. "I don't see that. He's brokenhearted."

"So, stranger abduction, suicide, accident. Is that what we're down to?" I asked, in my meeting with him.

"Looks like it."

He sat at his desk petting Luke, who sat beside him, soaking up the attention. Robert loved dogs, he told me, and had Milkbones in his desk drawer in case a K-9 officer wandered by. He gave Luke one every time we came in. "I'll keep my eye on these young men, both Bobby and Jaime," he said. "But it's looking more and more like she either encountered someone who abducted her, killed herself, or had an accident and died. She's sure not still out there in the woods alive.

She'd have made her way to somewhere by now."

"I agree." I rose to my feet and extended my hand. "Good working with you, Robert. I'm going to keep at this until we find her. I'll probably come back up next week, and in the meantime, I'll do what I can from home." I patted my leg. "C'mon, Luke."

My dog glanced at the drawer where Robert kept the Milkbones before he got up to follow me. So much for loyalty.

My mind bounced between Nate and Heather Burgess all the way home. I wanted to go see Nate as soon as possible. That would be tomorrow after my doctor's appointment, I guessed, since it was getting late today. I was already tired. I asked Siri to text Nate and ask if I could come by in the early afternoon. I didn't get a response. So frustrating.

I wound my way through the mountains. About two dozen wineries dotted the area, most built since the Virginia wine industry took off in the 1980s. I knew virtually nothing about wine, but I'd been told Virginia wines were high quality, the vineyards were beautiful, and wine tourism was a thing.

Not for me. I only had time for missing girls and grieving friends, a growing baby, my husband, and my dog.

Scott wasn't home when I got there, and I toyed

with the idea of driving to Nate's even though I hadn't heard from him. Then I got a text from my husband—he was picking up dinner and was on the way home.

There were flowers on the farm table when I got there, daisies, my favorite, and a little card noting Baby Cooper's first kick and the date. I smiled at that. When I went upstairs, I found Scott had put up the Western art in the nursery and assembled the crib and the dresser/changing table. A rush of gratitude went through me. I wondered, did he do all this one-handed? Who got up on the ladder?

I took a quick shower and changed into sweats. As I started to walk downstairs I heard him come home.

"Jess?"

"Coming!"

His face lit up when he saw me. "There's my girl!"

He wasn't wearing his sling. I kissed him, feeling the brush of his five o'clock shadow on my cheek. "Thank you, Scott! You've been busy."

"Let me put this down." He put his packages on the table and turned to embrace me with both arms. "I missed you!"

That hug felt so good. I laid my head against his chest and soaked in his presence. Then I lifted my head and kissed him again. He cupped my jaw in his hand and stroked my cheek with his thumb, a gesture so tender it brought tears to my eyes. *Who am I to deserve this love?*

"You hungry?" he asked.

I was starving. "Yes. What'd you bring me?"

"Greek salad and gyros."

"Perfect!"

"Good, let's eat."

He lit the candle at the center of the table and unpacked the food while I got us both water to drink. "Where'd you find a Greek restaurant?" I asked.

"Charlottesville. I had a meeting with my doctoral advisor."

"How'd it go?"

"I'd like to hear about your search first. Let's say grace."

We did, and then I launched into a review of my week. He listened carefully, appreciatively, and asked good questions. Then I said, "How have you been? Who helped you with the nursery?"

"Nate and I knocked most of it out one day and then I finished it."

"Nate? Came here? How is he?"

"Quieter than usual. Said he hates being alone in the evenings. So he was happy to help." Scott took another bite of his gyro. "His schedule at work is flexible right now. Not a lot of grass that needs cutting and he can switch around the other stuff."

"Is he depressed?" I asked, desperate to know. I mean, he'd just lost his love! He was alone. I wanted him to be okay. I needed him to be okay.

"He didn't talk a lot about himself."

"Well, what *did* you talk about?"

"Well," Scott began, "we've had an ongoing discussion about, you know, discipleship, and what it means to walk with God, prayer, and all that."

I stopped chewing. Nate was mentoring him, just like he had mentored me.

Scott abruptly changed the subject. "What time's your appointment tomorrow? Are you excited?"

I accepted the diversion without comment.

My ob/gyn appointment the next day went fine. Baby Cooper's heart was healthy and strong, my weight was good, my uterus was expanding as expected, and my blood pressure was normal. Scott came with me. He squeezed my hand as together we heard the baby's heartbeat, and he asked a couple of good questions. Then we went out to lunch.

"I want to see Nate tonight or tomorrow. How about if I take him dinner?" I asked over burgers and fries.

Scott nodded. "We could do that."

I hadn't said "we." I was afraid if we both went, Nate wouldn't share his heart. Before I could object, Scott pulled out his phone. "I'll text him," he said.

A beep signaled a response almost immediately. "He's got someone bringing dinner tonight, and he's sure he'll have leftovers for tomorrow," Scott reported.

"Then Sunday. I probably have to go back up to Harrisonburg next week, and I'd like to see Nate before I do."

"Are you worried about him?"

"Of course, I'm worried about him!" I exploded. I quickly checked myself. "I'm sorry. Yes, I am worried. I need to know he's okay."

"He's okay! Really," Scott said.

I gave him a look. "I need to see him."

"Okay, okay." He pulled his phone out. "I'm telling him we'll bring dinner by Sunday evening." Scott texted as he spoke.

I took a deep breath and accepted the partial victory.

"Oh, one more thing," Scott said as he finished. "I'd like to go church on Sunday morning."

"What? Why?"

Scott ducked his head. The man behind him glanced over his shoulder. Scott lowered his voice. "Nate said we need to find a good church."

"Why?" I asked, challenging him.

"He said there's no such thing as a Lone Ranger Christian. We're meant to be in community."

I crossed my arms in front of me. "Why now?"

Scott shrugged. "I thought with the baby coming, it was time. Nate gave me some names of churches he thought were pretty good. And he told me what to look for. So I checked out the websites for a bunch of them and I'd like to try this one about twenty minutes away." He pulled out a 3 x 5 card with the name of the church written on it.

I wouldn't look at it.

"He told me you'd resist."

My anger flared. "What? Nate told you that?"

Scott grinned. He reached for my hand, patiently waiting until I unfolded my arms and took his. "Let's just try. If we don't like it, we'll go somewhere else the next time." His face grew serious. "I think finding a church is something we need to do."

"Neither of us grew up in church," I said, implying we'd turned out okay.

"And how long did it take us to find God? To get the big picture of what life is all about? And how much sin did we pile up and how much damage did we do to ourselves and other people in all those years?"

I felt my face redden.

"When I was sitting out next to that mountain freezing to death, I was grateful I had God to pray to. Grateful I knew where I was going if I died." He paused and his eyes grew sad. "I am so sorry I didn't know about Jesus in time to teach Amanda the truth. Look at her!"

Amanda thought faith was a ridiculous fantasy.

The idea of a man dying two thousand years ago for her "sins" was absurd. She said church was full of hypocrites and homophobes. She wanted nothing to do with Christianity.

Instead, she drank too much and got pregnant from a drunken rape. Beautiful and brilliant, she had no anchor. She was a loose cannon.

"I don't want that for Baby Cooper," Scott said, squeezing my hand.

"Going to church is no guarantee your kids will believe."

"I know that. But it is one thing we can do. And I'd like to."

I knew he was right, but still I fought it. I couldn't see myself slipping on a little flowered dress every Sunday and leaving my dog at home to listen to a preacher tell me how to live. I mean, I trusted Nate and Scott but other men? Not so much. And what if I didn't fit in? What if all the other women were little homemakers who baked bread and made casseroles and thought dogs were dirty and didn't belong in the house?

But I looked at my handsome husband and those clear blue eyes, and I thought about how, just a few months ago, I'd found him deep into hypothermia, shot in the shoulder. How gray he was. How near death. And how grateful I'd been to God that I'd found him, and he lived.

So I gave in. But not gracefully.

14

On the drive over to Nate's on Sunday night I gave Scott a review of the church we'd visited that morning. The room was too dark, the music too loud, and the sermon was too short.

"Okay," he responded. "We'll try a different one next week."

We pulled into Nate's driveway and there, before the creek, was a gate. A new gate. "What's up with this?" I said, staring. It was at least twelve feet wide and four feet high, made out of pipe, and connected to a wire fence that ran to the trees on both sides.

"I'll get it," Scott responded. He got out of the Jeep, fiddled with something, and swung the gate open. He got back in the Jeep, moved forward, got out again, and closed the gate.

"When did that happen?"

"I helped him install it last week."

"Why'd he want a gate? He's never had a gate!"

"I don't know. He asked for my help, and I helped him. I didn't ask why he wanted to install it."

Was Nate getting paranoid? Had he been threatened? Was something else going on I didn't know about?

I stayed silent as Scott navigated the driveway.

It had more ruts and potholes in it than I remembered. We bounced up the hill, and I put my hand on my belly as if I could protect my baby from the rough road.

I can't protect her from any rough road. Not now. Not ever.

That was depressing.

Nate's dogs greeted us as we parked. "You get Luke, I'll get the food," Scott said.

I let Luke out of his crate in the back. The three dogs greeted each other in a swirl of energy. I waded through them and followed Scott up the ramp. He tapped on the back door, opened it, and yelled, "Nate?"

"C'mon in!"

We left the dogs outside and pushed into the house. Nate came limping into the kitchen. He gave Scott a hug then turned to me. "Hey, girl."

I hugged him as if I hadn't seen him in years. He kissed my head, as he always does. "How are you, Nate?" I said, pulling back so I could look in his face.

"I'm all right."

He didn't look all right. He looked older, grayer, and more wrinkled. "You're limping." I wanted to talk more, to get more out of him.

"My old leg's been rubbin', making my stump sore. But I'm workin' with my leg guy on a new one." He glanced at the food Scott had laid on the counter. "Did you eat?"

"We have more at home. This is all for you," Scott said.

"Well, thank you. It's a lot."

"I made that balsamic meatloaf you like, Nate, and mashed potatoes and green beans. Bread, too. Oh, and brownies."

"Thank you."

That's all he said. Just thank you. "What's up with the gate?" I asked.

He shrugged. "Been meanin' to do that for a long time."

Really? He'd never mentioned it to me. "You have time to talk?" I asked.

He checked his watch. "I ain't fed the horses."

"I can do that," Scott said.

"Let's all go," Nate responded.

He doesn't want to be alone with me.

"Let me close the screen on the fire."

"I'll do that!" I said. "Meet you at the barn."

I walked into the living room. As I passed Nate's chair I saw his pipe. I picked it up, more out of nostalgia than anything.

It was warm. The bowl of the pipe was warm.

In the five years I'd known Nate, I'd never seen him smoke. He told me he gave it up in Afghanistan. He carried the pipe and stuck it in his mouth sometimes, but it was always empty.

I laid the pipe back down where I found it. I

opened the drawer of the end table and found a pouch of tobacco and some matches.

Puzzled, I closed the drawer. *Why was Nate smoking?* I turned to the fireplace, found the chain for the screen, and pulled it shut. The fire was low, well-contained. Safe.

I stood to leave. My eyes fell on the bookshelf to the left of the fireplace. I saw a gap, a large gap. My heart thumped. Where were those books? Nate's shelves were always filled. We teased him about it. His shelves couldn't hold all the books he bought. His collection spilled over into the end tables, his office, the bedroom.

I touched the books on the partially empty shelf, fingering them, trying to figure out what was missing. *The Heidelberg Catechism.* One of my favorites! Where was that book?

I hurried after the guys, stepping into the cold, black evening, my senses prickling. I caught up to them at the barn. They were talking about the weather. "Nate!" I said, touching his arm. He turned to look at me. "Your books! What happened to your books?"

Scott frowned. Nate reddened and ducked his head.

"You have books missing!"

Nate turned and opened the grain bin. I heard the swish of the scoop as he measured it out, then the rattle of the grain going into the bucket.

These were normal sounds, comforting sounds, but I couldn't rest.

"Did you loan them out?"

"Nope."

"Then where are they?"

"I got plenty of books," Nate said, softly.

"But *The Heidelberg Catechism.* It's missing!" That book contains the truth that had meant so much to me. I said those words now, my voice barely above a whisper. "I am not my own, but belong—body and soul, in life and in death—to my faithful Savior Jesus Christ." My eyes searched Nate's face.

He turned and walked away.

I started to reach for him. Scott blocked me. Wordlessly, he told me to back off. I didn't want to.

On the way home, Scott asked me, "How'd you know books were missing?"

"There's a big gap on the shelf to the left of the fireplace. There's never a gap. The shelves are always full." I sat in the front passenger seat of the Jeep, my knee bouncing from nerves.

"Maybe he donated them."

"He was avoiding me. Something happened to those books, something he doesn't want to admit." I put my hand on my forehead. "It's not just that." I told him about the pipe.

My husband remained silent for a little while.

I know he was considering alternative responses. Finally he spoke. "Give him a little space, Jess. He's grieving. Dealing with some hard emotions. So give him some space."

Enough space to hang himself?

I didn't really think Nate was suicidal, but when Luke was missing, and I was in a deep pit of despair, Nate *wouldn't* leave me alone. He put a single rose on my nightstand every night. He'd sit there waiting for me to wake up, his empty pipe stuck in his mouth. He refused to abandon me to my grief.

I thought I should do the same. My husband disagreed.

When we got home that night, I told Scott I wasn't hungry, which was a bold-faced lie, and I went upstairs, leaving him to deal with our horses and my dog on his own. I felt like the guys were conspiring against me, an echo of my life as a woman in law enforcement. Only this time, I was trying to do something *for* them, for Nate anyway, not competing with them. I felt blocked. Stymied. Frustrated and angry. Even disrespected by the two people I loved most in the world.

I went into our new office space. We had arranged my desk, chair, and filing cabinet in a workable cluster. I'd found a pretty lamp at Target and added that to my desktop.

I sat down and opened my laptop. My plan was to focus on the Heather Burgess case, but in my email I found that I had three inquiries about my PI business. One was a cheating heart case, one a background check, and the last involved an inheritance.

I have an introductory form on my website I use for potential new clients. I need to know up front whether a case involves something I can deal with or not from a time and distance standpoint, my ever-fluctuating workload, and the agreement I'd made with Scott. Two of the three potential clients had filled out the form. The third, a lawyer in the inheritance case, had not.

That was typical. Lawyers often don't.

I figured I could knock out the background check quickly, so I sent that company my welcome letter, which included my hourly rate. I read the cheating heart sob story, noted there was no domestic violence involved, and sent that person, a man in this case, a letter with my rates and a proposal to meet in Charlottesville to discuss more about his concerns. I decided calling the lawyer's office in the morning was the most efficient way to deal with that case.

Scott stuck his head in the door at ten. "You about ready to come to bed?"

Of course I was. I could barely keep my eyes open after nine these days. "No, I've got some more work to do. I'll be in later."

He hesitated for a moment, then said, "Okay, good night, then."

Wise man. He didn't push me. He knew I was still irritated.

Luke had come upstairs with him. He looked at me, then Scott, like he didn't know which way to go, because certainly it was time for bed, but there I was at my desk. Then he pushed through the partially open door and plopped down next to me. Wise dog.

I turned to the Heather Burgess case. Robert Porter had given me reams of information, everything from her phone records to her driving record to her financials. I had pored over most of them once, but I picked them up again, intending to study them.

I didn't make it fifteen minutes before I began nodding off.

Half an hour later I finally gave up and went to bed. Luke padded into the bedroom with me and slumped down onto the floor. I slid into bed next to my sleeping husband. I laid there thinking about the evening and I realized something. What started out as concern for my friend Nate had turned into me feeling irritated and disrespected by both men. Somehow, I'd made the evening all about me.

Who can deliver me from this body of death?

Scott turned in his sleep and put his arm around me. He drew me near. And in his arms I finally fell asleep.

15

Nate stood out on his front porch watching the Jeep's taillights travel down his driveway as Scott and Jess left. He saw the Jeep stop, saw Scott pass in the front of the headlights to open the gate, saw the Jeep proceed, then saw it stop again on the other side as Scott closed the gate. *I need to get that automatic gate opener kit. The one with the keypad.*

"Lord," he said as the lights disappeared, "I don't know why I cain't talk to Jess. Maybe just her being a woman reminds me too much of what I had and what I don't have now. There's a curtain come down around my soul and a darkness black as this night fills it. Worse, I cain't even tell where you are in this. I cain't tell if you're hearin' me or not.

"Were you with my Laura in that car? Watchin' as that truck flew into her? Had you counted that man's drinks that day? Did ya know what was comin'?

"Then why didn't you stop her? Make her stand and talk to me here in the yard a while longer? Make her take her truck, my truck even, and not her little car? It wouldn't have taken much, and she'd still be with me."

Nate sat down on the top step, oblivious to the

cold. "I was all broke up from the war when my eyes was opened, and I saw you for the first time. I was awestruck, stunned at you, Jesus. Amazed you wanted to hang out with someone like me. You gave me a future. Hope. You became my anchor.

"We been together now, what? Twenty, twenty-five years? And I look at the black velvet sky and a thousand points of light poppin' out and I'm still in wonder at you.

"So why'd you have to take her? To wake me up? I'm awake, Lord, believe me. Awake all the time because I cain't sleep. Not in that bed we shared. Not even on the couch where we sat together."

He stomped his foot on the wood of the top porch stair. The dogs jumped. He went on. "Years ago you took my leg. You limited what I could do, searchin' and all. Climbin' these hills.

"But you gave me Laura. And it was good. Very good.

"God, there ain't nothin' you can give me now to make up for taking her. Not another wife. Not a passel of kids. So forget the thing you did with Job. I love Laura. I'll always love her. And God, I'll always miss her."

He wept. The dogs came, Sprite shoving her nose under his arm and Ember licking the tears off his face.

After a while he got up. He walked inside with

the dogs and put the food away without eating. He went into the living room and threw two more logs on the fire. He put a pillow and a quilt on the floor and laid down. And there he slept, the dogs beside him, all night long.

16

I paid for my stubborn refusal to eat the next morning. I was so hungry I felt nauseated. Baby Cooper's revenge. I'm sure Scott noticed me consuming everything in sight, but he didn't say anything. He gave me grace, like I was supposed to be giving Nate. The difference is, I was *worried* about Nate.

"Hey, I'm sorry I got mad," I said to my husband.

He hugged me. "I get it." He kissed me.

"He won't talk to me!"

"Men avoid talking about hard things. Especially in mixed company."

I reminded him of what Nate did when Luke got lost and I was so depressed. "So why is it okay for him to pursue me when I was depressed but not the other way around?"

"He was being a man, rescuing you."

"And I can't rescue a man?"

"Nope."

"Why not?"

"Because first he has to admit he needs rescuing."

The next week seemed to fly by. I worked on my PI cases, including Heather Burgess's, and Scott worked on his dissertation. When we had energy left, we worked on the house. But my to-do list on the whiteboard became dusty and smudged and I stopped even looking at it.

We saw Nate twice, and always together, and my concern for him, which I should have turned into prayer, sat like a pile of bricks in my heart. Sharp, heavy, cold, immovable.

I'd come up with a strategy to move the Heather Burgess investigation forward, so I drove to Harrisonburg to pitch it to Detective Porter. He loved the idea, which is how I found myself in the offices of the student newspaper.

"What I'm proposing is this," I said to the editor, a young man in jeans and a white dress shirt with his sleeves rolled up. To his right was a young woman, a reporter with a pixie haircut and a tiny nose ring. To his left, an older woman, maybe late twenties, with long brown hair. "Somebody out there knows something about Heather, some little snippet of information that could tell us what happened to her. We need to keep this story alive to jog peoples' memories. Somebody knows something they've forgotten to tell us."

"There's been no new leads in forever," the young woman said. "What do you want us to do? Just keep running the same story? Who's gonna read that?"

I nodded. "I get that. So here's my idea." I

handed each of them a sheet of paper. "These are people I've talked to who have some connection to Heather. Her professors. Her friends. Classmates. Some people she studied with. Her parents. A young man she'd been meeting at the coffee shop who no one but me knows about.

"I've given you contact information and some information about each of them. Why not run a human-interest story, a profile on each one, and on the impact Heather's disappearance has had on them?" The three journalists stared at the papers in their hands. "Humanize Heather's contacts. Bring her world to life. Make it real to the students and their parents. Make Finding Heather a puzzle that every person in the community can help put together."

"In fact," the editor, Jim Morris, said, "that can be our graphic." He held up his hands like a frame. "We've got a picture of Heather cut out like a jigsaw puzzle. Some of it has been put together, some of the pieces are scattered."

"That's awesome!" I said. "A great idea. Eye-catching."

"What's in it for these people?" the older woman, Eve, asked. "Why would they talk to us?"

"Because Heather is every parent's child, every young woman's roommate, every young man's girlfriend. If she was depressed, we need to know that. Abducted, we need to find the perpetrator. A victim of an accident, well, we need to figure out what students can do to protect their friends. We need to make it important to everyone to find out what happened to Heather so it won't happen to their own children, or their friends, or to them."

Guess what? They bought my idea. Got excited about it. Could see it playing out in ink for a long time.

I drove home that night hopeful. I'd texted Scott that I was on my way. I wound through the mountain road, thinking about how to get the stories the newspaper staff would write out to a larger audience. By the time I reached Route 29 a cold rain had begun to fall, the kind of cold, February rain that could freeze on the road and turn slick. I flipped on my wipers and dropped my speed a little.

Route 29 has two lanes, both ways, with a green divider in the middle, trees in some places, grass in others. It's normally a comfortable road to drive although it's dark out in the country, and I keep to a steady fifty-five because speed traps are common.

Scott and I did location-sharing, so I knew he wouldn't be surprised if it took me a little longer to get home. Traffic was light. I peered into the dark night and wished I'd changed out my wiper blades since the last time it had rained. They were smearing.

I was going down a long, dark hill. Up ahead,

I saw the bright lights of a police car flashing. A traffic stop. Pretty typical along 29, especially in this area.

Next to domestics, vehicle stops are the most dangerous thing a cop has to do. As I approached the flashing lights, I slowed down even more and moved over to the left lane. That's the law now in Virginia, but I always did it anyway, just to give the cop more room, especially at night. In my mind, I began rehearsing the normal scenario I expected to see: the cop car behind the vehicle, the cop in his car or at the driver's side window.

Sure enough, the deputy's car, its lights blazing, had stopped behind a black SUV, a Highlander. As I got closer, I could see movement around the vehicles, but I couldn't understand what I was seeing. Was the cop doing a road sobriety test?

And then I saw something that horrified me. The deputy and a man were wrestling! And my headlights caught the deputy's face, frozen in fear.

My heart pounded. They were fighting.

My reaction was instant. I jerked my Jeep over to the side, threw it into park, and reached in the console for my gun. I opened my door and ran back toward the men, who now were wrestling on the ground. "Police! Let me see your hands! Stop. Let me see your hands." I kept screaming. I couldn't get a clear shot. The men were tangled up! Then I saw the man pull the deputy's gun free. His hand flew up in the air. His body bladed toward me.

I fired. My gun roared. I pulled that trigger three, four times. I saw his arm jerk, the gun fall, and then the man collapsed. I raced forward, my heart in my throat. I kicked the gun out of range. "Police! Stay on the ground," I screamed. I saw the deputy's cuffs. I picked them up and cuffed that man, blood, bone, and all.

I gasped for air. Heard sirens. Help was coming. "Stay there," I commanded, holding him at gunpoint. The deputy lay nearby, on the ground, his chest heaving. "Officer, are you okay?" I yelled as I glanced toward him.

The deputy didn't respond, which worried me, but I looked longer and saw he was moving, trying to sit up, but clearly out of breath.

Lights. More sirens. A voice. "Put the gun down!" a woman screamed.

What? Me? She meant me! I raised my hands and slowly put the gun down as far away from the man as I could.

"Get on the ground!"

"Wait, I'm . . ."

"Get on the ground!" She raced forward as I sank to my knees and shoved me, hard. I fell forward, flat on my belly.

"Stop!" I said.

She didn't stop. She jerked my hands behind me and cuffed me. My cheek scraped a rock.

"I'm a private citizen with concealed carry. I saw your officer struggling . . ." I tried to explain.

"Shut up!" She kicked me, then grabbed my cuffed hands and tried to pull me up. "Get up." I struggled to my feet.

"Juanita hold up!" A man's voice said.

Out of the corner of my eye, I saw a male deputy talking to the deputy on the ground. I began shaking uncontrollably, my adrenaline spiking. I felt dizzy. The lights flashing, the radios squawking disoriented me. I looked down to get my bearings. I saw blood dripping on my left shoe.

Was I bleeding? Miscarrying? Had I killed Baby Cooper? *Oh, God!*

17

The male deputy spoke. "She's okay. Let her go. She saved him, saved Hatch."

I felt the cuffs release.

"Are you okay?" he asked me.

"I'm bleeding."

He put his flashlight on me. I saw blood on my hand, my pants. "It's your face. Your face is cut. Let's get you some help. Medic!"

Within minutes I was sitting in an ambulance and an EMT was cleaning up my face. "I'm pregnant," I said.

"Pregnant?"

"Yes."

"Do you want to go to the hospital and have a doctor check the baby?"

I was just about to answer when I saw Scott's face appear in the open door of the ambulance, his eyes wide. I was never so glad to see somebody.

"What happened?" he said.

"She saved his life. That's what happened." The EMT gestured toward Deputy Charles Hatchett lying behind me on the gurney getting oxygen.

"What?"

"The deputy. She saved his life."

Scott looked at me, his eyebrows raised.

"I need to go get checked," I said. I couldn't even say the word "baby." But he understood.

Scott arranged for a deputy to drive my Jeep home. He followed the ambulance in his car to the hospital. I looked at him, sitting at my bedside holding my hand. A PA had already cleaned and bandaged the cut on my face. "I'm scared," I whispered.

"Why?"

"I'm scared I hurt the baby when I got shoved to the ground. I haven't felt him kick."

He nodded and squeezed my hand. "He's still little and pretty protected."

What he said was true. I'd only felt Baby Cooper kick a couple of times. "How'd you know where I was?" I asked Scott.

"You were later than I expected. So I checked your location. You hadn't moved since the last time I'd checked. I thought maybe your car had broken down. I flipped on the scanner, and I heard what was going on. And somehow, I figured you'd be in the middle of it."

"I had to stop. When I saw what was happening, I couldn't just drive by."

He squeezed my hand. "I know. And I love you for it. Even if you do terrify me."

"Scott, what if . . . what if the baby's hurt? Because of me?"

"I love you, Jess. Let's not worry about that yet."

A few minutes later, a blonde woman walked in and introduced herself as an ob/gyn nurse practitioner.

"So tell me what happened tonight," she said.

I gave her a short version.

"And how many weeks along are you?"

"Nineteen."

"Almost halfway! Good for you. Shall I listen?"

"Please."

I uncovered my belly and she put her stethoscope to it, moving it around, searching for Baby Cooper. She was taking forever. What if she couldn't find a heartbeat? What if . . .

"Ba-bum, ba-bum, ba-bum, ba-bum," she said smiling. "Sounds perfect!"

And then Baby Cooper kicked me. Hard. Tears of gratitude sprang to my eyes. I looked at Scott. He squeezed my hand. "Thank you, God," I whispered.

Scott looked at me and smiled.

The nurse picked up my chart and checked the numbers on the monitor above me. "You had a pretty high heart rate for a while, but you're back to normal now. Your bloodwork looks fine." She flipped my chart closed. "Everything looks great. I think you're good to go."

I felt relief flood through me.

"You okay?" Scott asked, seeing me wipe a tear away.

"I was so scared I'd hurt him!"

He patted my arm. "You're okay. And so is he. Or she," he added quickly.

I smiled.

Scott and I were just about to leave when a uniformed officer walked in. "Cooper!" the man said. He was 50ish, gray hair, balding, and heavy-set.

"Jim, how are you!" Scott shook his hand. "This is my wife, Jessica."

"Your wife did this?" the sheriff said, staring at me. "Well, I'll be dang. Sheriff Jim Turner, ma'am. I wanted to stop by and thank you for saving my deputy. Not many folks would step in like you did."

I didn't bother to ask how Scott and the sheriff knew each other. I bump into the good ol' boy network every time I turn around. "I'm glad I was able to help."

"How is he? The deputy," Scott asked.

"He'll be fine. Got shook up and had some bruises and abrasions. Had a little heart flutter, so they're gonna keep him overnight. But he's okay." He hitched up his belt. "The suspect, he'll need surgery on that arm. He'll be charged with assault with intent to kill a law enforcement officer and assault on you, as well." He shook his head. "The Highlander he was driving was stolen, and it turns out he was fleeing a murder in North Carolina. You just never know who you're stopping out on the road."

"Yes, sir," I said.

"Jess is a former Fairfax County homicide detective," Scott told him. He was proud of that, obviously, but sometimes he forgot that I was not, because of the way I'd left.

The sheriff's eyes widened. "Well I'll be. If you ever want to get back into it, let me know. We probably got more package rustlin' than homicides out here, but you never know. We could use a good investigator."

"I've got a few other things going on, but thank you," I said. "I'm glad the deputy is okay."

"Y'all have a good night!"

The next day a young man delivered two dozen red roses to our house, a thank-you from the sheriff's office.

But that's not all. Nate called. "Are you okay?" he asked me.

"I'm fine. How'd you know?"

"Scott called me on the way to the hospital. Asked me to pray. What happened?"

I told him.

"You could've been killed," he said, a catch in his voice.

"Not my day," I said. "How are you?"

He ignored that. "Listen, I'll do that training on Saturday."

I was scheduled to run an exercise on human remains detection for our SAR group. "No, I can do it."

"You rest," he said firmly. "Let that adrenaline get out of your system." I started to protest but he interrupted me. "Jess, I cain't lose you, too!"

You've already lost me. You're not talking to me! I wanted to say. In a rare moment of discretion, I kept my mouth shut. "Okay, Nate," I said. "Thank you. I love you!"

"Love you, too," he said, and he hung up.

I stood staring at my phone. *What just happened?*

I looked up to see Scott watching me. "It took a lot for him to do that," he said. "He really does care about you."

"Then why—"

Scott's upraised hand stopped me.

"I know," I sighed. "Give him time."

He came over and wrapped his arms around me, both arms, because his shoulder was getting better. He kissed me and then said, "Sometimes when you're talking to someone who knows you really, really well, you get afraid that if you say what's really on your heart, you'll get upset, and you'll start crying, and you won't be able to stop. Ever."

I get that.

Scott switched topics. "Do you mind if Kathryn comes down this weekend?"

I cocked my head. "No. What's the occasion?"

"She's been coming down on weekends to help Nate, going through Laura's clothes and all that.

He's busy tomorrow so he suggested she come see us."

"He's going to do the HRD training that I was supposed to do. Is Mike coming?"

There was a long silence. "No."

"What? Why? Where's he been?"

"Mike took a TDY."

"Temporary duty assignment? To where?"

"South Dakota. He's doing some specialized training in Indian country investigations."

"For how long?"

"A couple of months."

I frowned. "Had he planned this?"

"It just came up. Somebody who'd been scheduled to go had to cancel and Mike grabbed the opportunity."

"Wait. A woman he's been seeing loses her mother like that and he immediately takes a TDY?"

Scott ducked his head. I thought he was going to close ranks, protect his brother-in-arms. But he fooled me. "I can't offer any excuses for him. When hard things happen, some people face it, some isolate, and some run away."

"That's so wrong!"

Scott's jaw shifted. "I'd trust Mike to have my back in a firefight in a heartbeat. But a fight is one thing, emotional situations are another." He sat down on one of the kitchen chairs. Luke went to him, and Scott started petting him, rubbing his thumbs on his head, behind his ears, like he was massaging out the tension he was feeling by petting my dog. "When my sister was murdered, I saw my father turn to stone. Just at the moment my mother needed him, he was hard as a brick. He thought he was being strong. He thought that's what she needed. He was wrong." He took a deep breath and looked up at me. "In actuality, he wasn't doing it for her. He was protecting himself."

I moved toward Scott, sitting down next to him. I put my hand on his knee. "Oh, Scott, I'm so sorry. I'm so glad you're not like that."

"I was for a long time."

"You're not now. Or I'd go crazy. Yes, let's have Kathryn come down. Anytime she wants. You two should take a ride. The horses could use it."

People think cops can't wait to throw their weight around. Shoot people. The fact is, the residuals of a shooting incident last a long, long time, even for the one who does the shooting. For the next few weeks I didn't sleep well. I'd jerk awake, heart pounding, reliving the crucial moments. I'd lie awake and go over the event, step-by-step, reminding myself I'd given the attacker opportunity after opportunity to surrender. During the day, if I saw a cop on the side of the road with a car pulled over, my heart would start beating hard. I tried to avoid driving at night by myself. And I had some legal stress. The fact that I was not a sworn officer gave Jayden Washington's attorney somewhere to shift the blame.

Still, I'd do the same thing all over again.

18

At five and a half months, I noticed I wasn't as tired. I didn't need naps as often and I wasn't nodding off at nine o'clock in the evening. Baby Cooper, my book said, was the size of a pomegranate. I definitely had a belly.

The student journalists had, true to their word, been running a series of articles called "Where's Heather?" They used the jigsaw puzzle motif and ran five-hundred-word profiles on Heather's friends and associates. They were running the articles on social media as well, and yes, tips were coming in. Robert Porter shared them freely with me, and I was spending an average of a day a week up in Harrisonburg chasing down leads.

One of those involved a man who'd come into town off the Appalachian Trail. Harrisonburg is about eighteen miles west of the AT, and hikers catch rides into town where they can take a break from the trail and get food or a good night's sleep.

The tipster, a cashier at a local convenience store, said the man, who had shaggy brown hair and a scar near his eye, "seemed creepy." When pressed, she said he couldn't take his eyes off the young woman stocking shelves, and after he left, they'd found a whole rack of beef jerky and a box of candy bars missing.

I called this tipster and asked more questions. No, the store didn't have security cameras in the aisles, just at the register. And she knew he was a hiker because of his clothing, boots, backpack, and "he smelled to high heaven."

The one problem I had with the story was the timing. Heather disappeared in January. I didn't think people would be hiking the AT at that time, unless they were just hiking a section. I decided to drive up to the Swift Run Gap entrance to the Shenandoah National Park and see what I could find out. If nothing else, Luke and I would take a walk in the woods.

So I drove east on Route 33 to Swift Run Gap. I found a place to park and talked to a ranger. She told me people hike all year on the trail, although thru-hikers, the ones who plan to travel the entire two-thousand-plus miles of the trail from Georgia to Maine, generally started in February or March. It took about five months, she said, to do the whole trail.

She told me a lot of other interesting things, too, like the fact that hikers usually adopted a nickname on the trail, that they signed logs along the way, sometimes leaving notes of interest or messages for other hikers. And that they discouraged hikers from bringing dogs, unless they were service animals. "How about search-and-rescue dogs in training?" I asked her. She allowed as how they'd probably get a pass, too.

"So, you'd expect if someone was hiking in January, it wouldn't be a thru-hiker, right? It would be a day hiker?"

"Or a section hiker," she said. "We've had a fairly mild winter—no deep snow, which is what would put off most hikers."

I asked her to show me how to find the AT and she did. I wanted to hike a little ways down it. So I put Luke's SAR vest on to make him look official. Making sure I had the Garmin inReach and my phone, as well as a bottle of water, I took off.

The AT is marked by white blazes, although sometimes they can be hard to see. They get weathered, or a tree falls, or rocks get disturbed, I was told. Still I picked up the trail at the backcountry registration area, where I checked the log. There'd been a handful of hikers since the first of the year, and I took pictures with my phone so I'd have their trail handles. Then Luke and I walked about a mile. I was used to running in the mountains and this seemed no different. The trail was narrow in some spots, wider in others, smooth in some places, rocky in others. On this beautiful forty-degree day, it was a pleasant walk. But then, I wasn't on Day 237 after having slept on the ground for three months, living on jerky and MREs or whatever hikers eat.

After about twenty minutes, Luke and I turned around. We'd seen no one else, so I let him off leash. Probably against the rules. Still, he needed to run. At least, at this time of year, I didn't need to worry about snakes.

I texted Scott and told him I was on my way home. He didn't respond but I figured he was busy. I listened to podcasts all the way. Some were sermons, some were true crimes. I tried to think ahead to what I might make for dinner and decided I could wing it.

When I pulled into the driveway, I could see why he hadn't texted back. Laura's truck and horse trailer were backed down beside our barn. What was happening?

I parked, got out of the car, and let Luke out. Then I walked toward the barn. Luke raced by me, barking happily. "Whoa, now. Steady," I heard Scott say. I walked past the horse trailer and saw why.

Scott was unloading Nate's horse, Chief, from the trailer. Luke had unnerved him. Scott stroked his neck, trying to calm him down.

"What's going on?" I asked.

"We have visitors."

"How can I help?"

Scott nodded. "Open the last stall." I walked through the barn and saw our two horses in their stalls and Abby in another. I opened the last stall and watched as Scott led the quarter horse through the barn and into it, my mind full of questions.

"Is Nate all right?" I asked as Scott closed the stall door.

"Yeah. Let me get them some hay and water. I'll tell you all about it when we go inside. I'm starving."

"I'll get dinner going."

Scott was actually a better cook than me, but both of us had mastered the art of quick, healthy meals. I pulled salmon burgers out of the freezer and dropped them into a pre-heated cast iron skillet with a little olive oil. Did we have hamburger buns? Yes, there were some whole wheat buns in the freezer, so I took them out and defrosted them. Then I steamed frozen broccoli and, to top off the meal, I found a jar of unsweetened applesauce and spooned some into two small bowls.

I could tell Scott was tired by the way he moved when he came in. He'd taken off his boots on the back porch. Sock-footed, he walked to the sink and washed his hands without saying a word.

We sat down at the table, and he took my hand and said grace, praying especially for Nate. "Father give him grace and peace for healing. Holy Spirit comfort him in his grief. Jesus, he has had such an impact on my life and on Jess's, sharing your gospel and your life, teaching us. Now he needs your help. I admit, I don't know what to say. I don't know how to help him right now. But you do. And I ask you to do it."

I blinked away tears as he said amen. "What's going on?" I asked softly.

He took a big bite of his salmon burger. He told me he was hungry. I should have waited to ask. But he gulped down two big bites and then he said, "Nate asked me if I could keep them for a while. He said it's just too much for him right now."

"Physically or emotionally?"

"Both. But especially emotionally."

"The horses were Laura's thing," I said while Scott continued to eat.

He nodded. "He said he'd go out to the barn and go through the motions, morning and evening, tears running down his cheeks. Felt like Abby was looking for Laura all the time. She's started picking on Chief. Bullying him."

"Because she's had trauma."

"Right." Scott took the last bite of his salmon burger. I hadn't even started mine. "Horses bond with people. When those people disappear, they feel it." He stabbed a piece of broccoli. "He was telling me all this, and I suggested maybe a change of scenery would be good. Give Abby something else to think about."

"So you suggested they come here for a while."

"Right. But Jess, I don't mean this to fall on you. Not at all. This is all on me. You've got enough going on."

I appreciated that. I also realized it was

unrealistic. I took Scott's hand. "We're in this together, buddy."

He smiled and thanked me. But I realized at that point there was more going on than just babysitting horses. I just didn't know what.

19

Nate walked into the stable alone, in the dark. He didn't bother turning on the lights. He stopped at Abby's empty stall and fingered the bridle that was still hanging there. "Lord," he said out loud, "I know we're not supposed to try to talk to the dead. And right now, I don't even know if I'm reachin' you. But if I am, and if you will, would you tell Laura I'm sorry I failed her. I failed her with the hoss. I couldn't keep Abby here. Every time I looked at that hoss, grief poured over me until I was drownin' again, drownin' in sorrow and emptiness."

He ran his hand over the rough wood of the stall door, inhaling the smell of horse that lingered there. "Comin' out here twice a day was mor'n I could bear after a while. Knowin' they ain't been ridden, seein' Abby grow restless and mean. It was just too much, too much for me. I thank you Lord that Scott was willin' to take them two, at least for a while.

"I miss my girl, Lord, miss her somethin' terrible. Worse than the first time I lost her. Tryin' to stay alive in war has a way of focusing your attention. And maybe that's what I need, another war."

He sat down hard on a bale of straw and leaned

his head back against the wood. Sprite jumped up next to him and put her head in his lap. He stroked her and wondered how long he'd have her. She was twelve, a right good age already, but the thought of losing her was too much to bear. "Stay healthy, little one," he murmured to her. "Stay with me." She nestled closer as if she understood.

Ember came into the barn, shoving her nose into Nate's leg, demanding his attention. She'd been doing her shepherd thing, running the perimeter, making sure the property was secure. It was. It always was. Almost always.

So why the gate? He asked himself that all the time. The best he could figure was that it was some weird psychological thing. Some retroactive impulse to keep Laura safe, even when that was no longer possible.

He stroked Ember with his right hand. She was still a young dog with lots of energy, bold, intelligent, and affectionate. He'd been toying with the idea of finding a young family to take her, a family with kids she could play with. He'd have to decide on that before too long, he figured. He'd hesitated because he'd asked himself what he would do, then, if he lost Sprite, too? He couldn't imagine being without a dog.

But then, two months ago he couldn't have imagined being without Laura either.

"Oh, Lord," he said, sitting up straight. "What are you doin' to me?"

He rose to his feet and walked out of the barn. Snow had begun to fall, big fluffy flakes like cotton balls dropped from above. He headed down the driveway, Sprite at his heel, Ember scampering about in front of him. His new leg was feeling good, thanks to Jeff, his new prosthetist. Jeff was a young man, athletic and strong, a hiker and a ridge runner like Jess. He was originally from Florida, but he loved living near the mountains and working for UVA Medical Center. He was good to talk to.

Laura always said hairdressers know everything because women find it easy to talk in that situation. You're up close and personal while they're working on you and then you leave the shop and don't see 'em for six weeks. Jeff was kind of like that too. Sort of a confessor. Easy to talk to. He knew about Laura. He knew what Nate was feeling. He understood about the horses.

For a young man, he had some depth. Wisdom. Nate appreciated that.

The snow began to gather on the ground. The temperature was perfect for a Virginia snow— about thirty degrees. The weather was coming from the south, which is where most of the big snows came from. The weathermen had predicted five to six inches, a right good snow.

Nate walked down the hill to the bottomland near the creek and stopped there, staring across the creek at the gate, now iced in white, and asking himself the question he asked nearly every day. Was it keeping strangers out? Or friends?

"C'mon, dogs," he said, and he turned and walked back up the hill, step-by-step moving closer to his empty house. "Yea, though I walk through the valley of the shadow of death," he said out loud, reciting Psalm 23 in the King James version he'd learned as a child. "I will fear no evil. For thou art with me. Thy rod and thy staff they comfort me."

"Lord, is it your rod or your staff that I'm feelin' now? Your discipline or your guidance? Did I make Laura an idol? Did you take her to punish me? Test me?

"I just don't get it. I don't understand where you are or what you're doin'. I don't even understand your heart right now."

He walked the rest of the way back to the house in silence. The cold, dark night and the beauty of the snow offered him no comfort. He walked up the ramp to his back door, opened it, and went in. He took off his boots but didn't bother wiping off the dogs' feet. He just didn't care.

He walked into the living room without turning on the lights. He threw another log on the fire and slumped down in the recliner. He sat there, staring at the flickering fire for a long time, hoping sleep would come.

It didn't. He kept thinking about his wife, about things he'd done or hadn't done, about trips he'd meant to take with her, about their dreams of growing old together, about fights they'd had and regrets he still carried. He replayed conversations in his head and reimagined the way it felt to hold her until, around midnight, he couldn't stand it anymore. He rose to his feet.

He opened his front door and stepped out on the porch, still in his sock feet. The snow had turned to small flakes, falling hard in the porch light. About three inches lay on the ground. Ember threw herself out into the storm, snuffling through the snow with her nose, then rolling in it joyfully.

Her delight was lost on Nate.

Sprite, on the other hand, walked slowly down the porch stairs and did her business like a lady, then climbed back up to rejoin Nate. He leaned against the porch post watching Ember, snow frosting her coal-black coat. When she was done, when she came back up on the porch and shook the snow off, they went back inside.

"Lord, somethin's got to change," Nate said.

20

Two days later, Nate asked us both to come over to his house. "Great! I'll bring dinner," I said.

I felt nervous as we drove to Nate's that evening. My husband was driving, the car was filled with the warm smell of chicken tetrazzini and hot bread, the roads were clear. And yet I felt anxious. I found myself resting my hand on my belly as if Baby Cooper could comfort me.

It had now been two months since Laura died, and I'd seen Nate only four times since the funeral. Before, seeing him four times in a week wasn't unusual. He had isolated himself, the very thing he always told me not to do. And I suspected this visit was not intended as an opportunity for him to confess and repent.

Since the last time I was there, Nate had installed an automatic gate opener. Scott keyed in the proper sequence of numbers and the gate swung open. "Laura's birthday," he said, looking over at me. He watched in his rearview mirror to make sure the gate closed. "It's on a timer," he explained.

Nate had heard us coming. He opened the back door and let the dogs out. Luke joined them and they began chasing each other and play fighting in the yard. "Come on in," Nate said, holding open the door. He didn't look either of us in the eye.

I stepped into his house and glanced right to the laundry/mudroom. It was full . . . stuff everywhere. I saw a large backpack and sleeping bag. What was going on? My stomach knotted.

"Jess," Nate said, drawing my eyes toward him. He hugged me. "You look beautiful."

"Thank you," I said. I pulled back, my eyes ranging over his face, trying to assess his mood. He looked away quickly. A dozen questions popped into my mind.

"Let's eat while this is hot," Scott said, unpacking the food we'd brought. Nate had set three places at the small table in the kitchen.

"I appreciate you all comin' and bringin' dinner," Nate said. "This sure smells good! Scott, would you say grace?"

He did, and for the next twenty minutes we ate, or pretended to eat, in my case. My nerves made consuming food impossible. The men talked about man-things—the weather, politics, the Super Bowl—and I wanted to scream.

One of the dogs barked at the door and Scott got up to let them in. They slurped water noisily, rotating between the two water bowls Nate had set out. Ember came over to greet Scott and me, and Luke sniffed Nate. I expected him to start petting Luke, or speak to him. Instead, Nate stood up and said, "Let's go sit by the fire."

"Can I load the dishwasher?" Scott said.

"Just leave the dishes. I'll do them later."

We put the leftovers away and moved to the living room, where I saw more boxes under the front window where Luke liked to lie. I looked at Scott, but he was lost in what he and Nate were talking about—the various grades of hay, if I recall.

Nate put another log on the fire, and we sat down, him in the recliner and Scott and I on the couch. Scott took my hand. I made up my mind if they didn't stop talking about trivia and bring up the real reason we'd been invited, I was going to force the conversation.

I was about to open my mouth when Nate took the lead. "Thank you for comin' and thank you for taking the hosses. That there's been a big help. So thank you." He shifted in his chair. "Now, I got another favor to ask." The silence in the room felt like a balloon about to pop.

Nate cleared his throat. "I wonder if you'd take Sprite for me for a while."

Scott cocked his head. "Sprite? Sure. How long?"

"Three, four months maybe."

"You going somewhere?"

"Yep. I'm goin' out on the AT."

"Wait. What? The Appalachian Trail?" I said, alarm bells ringing in my head. "You can't do that!"

"Why?"

"You've got one leg!" I said, stating the obvious.

"People do it."

"With one leg? That's crazy!" My heart was pounding. I unconsciously put my hand on my belly. "Who are you going with?" I demanded.

"Ember. I think Sprite's too old. That's why I want you to take her."

My alarm drove me to my feet. "Wait," I said, walking away then turning back. "You're going up on the Appalachian Trail with one leg and just a dog. Have you seen the trail? It's not just a walk in the woods, Nate. Some places are rocky, uneven. There are some scrambles. Slippery, muddy hills." I took a breath, but I didn't give either man a chance to respond.

"So what happens if you fall?" I said. "If you get hurt? If your stump gets infected? If you have an open wound? What happens then, Nate? Have you thought this out at all?" I have to admit I was practically yelling.

"I've talked this out with Jeff, my prosthetist. In fact, he's the one suggested it."

"He suggested it? Why? Does he want you dead?"

Nate gave a wry smile. "I hope that ain't it."

"Well what is it then, Nate?" He didn't answer right away so I went on. "You're not supposed to make any big changes for a year after you lose your spouse. You're not supposed to move, or remarry, sell your house . . ."

"I ain't doing any of that."

"But hiking the AT? By yourself? For *months?* That's big by any definition."

I caught the look on Scott's face, but I didn't stop. "And what about Miss Etta?" Laura's mom had been moved to a nursing home in December. Now, with Laura gone, Nate was her guardian and held her power of attorney.

"She's taken care of. Kathryn's backing me up."

I wasn't about to stop. "You know what you're doing?" I said, as if I'd had a sudden revelation. "You're running away. You've isolated yourself ever since . . . since January. You wouldn't answer my phone calls, my texts. You wouldn't talk to me! You're refusing to face reality. She's not coming back. You can't run from that."

"Sit down," Nate said. "Listen to me."

I stood, my fists clenched.

"Sit. Please."

I tried to resist, then reluctantly returned to the couch. Baby Cooper was kicking up a storm.

"I knew you'd react this way, which is why I ain't said nothin' afore this. Last thing I want to do is upset you. But I been thinking about this for a month, maybe more. And the more I think about it, the more I want to do it."

"Run away?"

Nate grimaced. "I ain't runnin' away. Listen,

Jess. Hear me out. I miss Laura somethin' fierce. I cain't stand to be in this house without her." Tears gathered in his eyes. "I walk in the bedroom and she's not there. I think of something I want to say to her, and she's gone." He hesitated. "I sit here at night. I cain't read, I cain't sleep. I keep playin' our lives together over and over in my head. What I said. What I should've said. What I didn't say.

"Truth is, I miss Laura, but that ain't the worst of it. The worst of it is that I've lost God, too. I cain't feel Jesus. Cain't hear him. Don't know why God took her and cain't figure out why he's left me." He ran his hands over his face. "I pray and get nothin'. Put on music, and cain't follow it. All the stuff in all these books," he gestured toward his bookshelves, "seems like a foreign language. The onliest thing I can figure out is that God wants me to be alone."

"He doesn't! He doesn't want you to be alone, Nate. He said he'll never leave you or forsake you, isn't that what you've always told me? Nothing can separate you from the love of God. Nothing. Where's your faith?"

"I don't know."

That admission went off like a bomb in my heart. "Nate! Listen! Listen. You may feel alone, but you don't have to be! You have friends who love you."

"I cain't stay in this house no more."

"So come stay with us."

"I got to do this. I got to do something big."

"But the AT? That's crazy!" I stood up again and paced away.

"I ain't doin' the whole thing. Just Virginia."

I gave him five reasons why his plan was a bad idea, beginning with his leg, ending with his heart. He didn't answer me. I got more frustrated. "Nate, I don't get you. You preach about Jesus to everyone. And now you're just walking away. Without a fight. Are you trying to kill yourself?" There, I'd said it. My worse fear.

"Jess . . ." Scott said.

I turned to him, my face hot. "Don't shush me! If you're not going to help me the least you could do is be quiet."

He raised his eyebrows. I had never said anything like that to Scott. Never.

Nate took a deep breath. "Jessica," he said softly. "Please listen." He paused to see if I would keep talking. I couldn't. Words could not get past the anger—and fear—in my heart.

So he continued. "I need a war."

"You *what?*"

"The onliest thing that got me over losing Laura the first time was tryin' to stay alive in Afghanistan. I need another war. I need to laser-focus on staying alive. Shed all the distractions. Walk and walk until I outwalk this grief. Until I find God again.

"I got it all planned out. I'm taking a leave

of absence from work as of April 1. I've got my gear. I been practicing climbing these hills around here on my new leg. It works great. I'm gonna be okay. Honest. I just need you to take care of Sprite. Now, will you do that? 'Cause the rest of it? It ain't open to debate." Those last words were spoken with final authority.

I stared at him speechless for a moment. My heart was about to explode. Then I walked out of the room. I grabbed my coat off the peg in the laundry room, pulled open the door, and left, tears of rage streaming down my face. Luke followed me but even his presence could not comfort me.

I jerked the handle on the Jeep door, intending to drive off. It was locked. Scott had the key.

Furious, I turned and began walking down the driveway. A cold March wind cut right through me. My head pounded like a war drum. I jammed my hands in my pockets. When I got to the creek, I forged straight ahead, the icy cold water seeping into my light boots. I got to the gate and fumbled with the keypad, trying to remember the code.

I heard an engine start up on the hill, then the crunch of gravel under tires. I didn't turn around. Luke whined and nudged my leg. I ignored him.

Scott stopped the car, got out, and came to me. "C'mon, Jess." I hesitated, then my will collapsed, and I allowed him to gently guide me back to the Jeep.

I fought tears all the way home.

21

What do you do when someone you love is doing something so foolish, so dangerous, that you can't stand it?

There wasn't anything I could do about it. Nate was a grown man. I had no control over him. I had "limited agency." Scott's words.

Control. That was the issue, I realized over the next few days. Control and fear. And anger. I wanted to be in control. I wasn't. God was. I was terrified of losing my close friend, like I'd lost my father on 9/11.

And I was angry. That took a little more working out. How did I know about the "one-year rule" for losing a spouse? Because my mother had married my stepfather months after my dad died. It was, in my eyes, a betrayal of my dad, one I had apparently not fully forgiven.

Reflexively, I did the one thing I knew to do, the one thing that, ironically, Nate had taught me to do. "Whatever happens, Jess, let it drive you to God," he'd told me.

Why didn't he do that himself?

I forced myself to let go of that question. I couldn't control him. I could only control me. I went back to the beginning of my spiritual walk. I went into our bedroom closet, found my box of treasures that I kept there. I opened it and took them out one by one—the order of worship for my father's funeral, his obituary, a copy of the eulogy his captain had given, his police badge, and then, his copy of the Gospel of John.

I felt the cover of the small black book. Opened it and ran my finger over my dad's signature, written on the day he'd become a believer, right before he was killed. And then I turned to John 1:1 and began reading. "In the beginning was the Word . . ."

I read and kept reading, and by the time Jesus had healed the man who'd been a cripple for thirty-eight years, by the time he'd matched wits with the scribes and Pharisees again, by the time he'd fed the five thousand, by the time he'd raised Lazarus from the dead, my heart had settled. Jesus was the way, the truth, and the life. The Bible was true. God was real.

"God," I said, clutching that book, "Nate is yours. I know he is. His faith is real. He's just lost in his grief right now. If it's your will, keep him from going on this ridiculous hike. And if that's not your will, protect him, Lord, I'm begging you. Protect my friend."

Three days after our dinner with Nate, I was finally able to talk about it with my husband. "Scott?" I said, walking into the kitchen where he was working at the table.

He looked up from his computer.

"I'm sorry," I said. "I should not have talked to you that way." I sat down in the chair next to him.

He leaned over, took my hand, and kissed me. "It's okay."

"He's being stupid. But I'm not God and I can't control him."

"No, you can't."

"I was angry because I wanted you to back me up."

I could tell he was thinking about that for a minute. "I understand your concerns about Nate hiking, I really do. But I thought if I echoed them, it would be ganging up on him. Two against one. And, honestly, I didn't think he could take that. You were pretty intense." My FBI tough-guy husband had a heart of compassion.

"When do we get Sprite?"

He raised his eyebrows. "Is it okay with you if we keep her?"

I shrugged. "I wouldn't want her to go anywhere else."

Scott clicked his phone over to the calendar and looked at it. "March 31. In the morning."

"He plans to leave then?"

Scott nodded. "Jeff will pick him up and drive him down to Damascus. He starts his hike on April 1."

"April Fool's Day."

He smiled. "Don't say it."

"I don't have to." I pulled my dad's Gospel of

John out of my back pocket. "Will you give this to him? Ask him to take it with him?"

"Are you sure?"

"Yes."

"It might get damaged on the trail."

"Take it to him."

"Okay." Scott took the book. Then he half-rose and kissed me. "You are a fierce warrior, girl. When you love somebody, you'll fight to protect them, even against themselves."

"For all the good it did," I said softly.

A "fierce warrior." I didn't feel fierce. I felt weak and tired and frustrated and scared. But whatever was going on with Nate, Baby Cooper reminded me I had a job to do, a baby to grow, and a missing young woman to find.

By now it was fairly certain Heather Burgess was dead. Unless she'd been kidnapped and trafficked, which I thought was unlikely, she'd either died in an accident, suicide, or she was murdered. I knew she had feelings for Jaime. I wondered if she felt so guilty about having sex with Bobby that she killed herself.

I stayed in frequent contact with Detective Robert Porter and Heather's father. I could hear the resignation in Mr. Burgess's voice. Still, he wanted me to keep looking.

My idea to run profiles on the people who knew Heather to keep her name in the press had generated hundreds of leads. Robert had assigned a uniformed officer to handle the ones they were getting. I pursued some of my own from home. Then, when I could, I'd drive up to Harrisonburg to pursue my own leads and consult with them. While I was there, I'd take Luke on a long walk on the trails around town. I'd stopped running. My belly was too big. I felt like I was bouncing Baby Cooper around too much.

My resolution at the beginning of my pregnancy was not to let it change my life. I quickly found out that was ridiculous. Halfway through my pregnancy my hips hurt, my breasts were sensitive, and I had to eat small meals to avoid heartburn. I felt awkward and emotional, as well as protective. The wonder of having this baby growing inside me colored everything I did. Soon, Scott and I would start labor-and-delivery classes. My life was about to change even more.

Still, I wanted to keep doing all that I could for as long as I could, including work the Heather Burgess case. By now, I knew so much about her and had invested so much that it had become personal.

April can be dicey in Virginia, especially the first few weeks. The weather can be chilly and cold and we'd even had a light snow before. Spring storms can be pretty violent. I wondered why Nate was leaving then.

Scott said he might be trying to finish his hike in time to be back for Baby Cooper's arrival in July.

Secretly, I hoped he was right. My burden for Nate still lay heavy on my heart. "Why don't we get him a Garmin inReach?" I said to Scott one day. We were in the barn, mucking and re-bedding stalls, Scott more so than me. The horses were getting along, and on good weather days, they were out in the pasture together. We'd had a string of sunny days, but rain was predicted, and Scott wanted the stalls ready. A March rain can chill a horse down in a heartbeat.

"I suggested a Garmin," he said, manipulating a shovel of horse poop into the wheelbarrow. "He won't carry it. In fact, he said he's going to have his phone off most of the time."

"Why would he do that?" Irritation colored my voice.

"No way to charge it. So he'll save it for emergencies."

"So he's going to be up on the AT for months without a cell phone. All alone." I stabbed a shovel into a pile of muck. "How is this going to work? How's he going to carry all the gear he needs for three or four months?"

"He's not." Scott stopped and leaned on his shovel. "Jeff, his prosthetist, apparently has done an AT thru-hike. All the way, Georgia to Maine. Twenty-two hundred miles. He's been coaching Nate. Jeff's going to drive him to his start point in southwest Virginia and drop him off. A few days later, he'll meet him at a crossroads, check his leg, and resupply his food. And they'll keep doing that until Nate gets up to Afton Mountain, near Charlottesville, then Kathryn's going to take over."

"Kathryn?"

"By that time, she'll be out of school, and she volunteered."

I felt slightly betrayed. She was helping Nate do this crazy hike. "I'll bet he won't make it that far," I said, setting my jaw.

"Honestly, Jess, he's really thought this out. Jeff gave him some special supplies to clean his stump. He's got his gear, trekking poles, his clothes, MREs, and this neat little stove. A water filter. Every once in a while he'll take what they call a zero day, no hiking. He'll stay in town at a motel, charge his phone, and rest. He's been practicing carrying thirty pounds, he told me, and Ember's been carrying water and her own food." Scott scooped up another shovelful of dirty straw. "He told me he used to camp out in the woods as a kid all the time. I think it was to get away from his father. And remember, he had to be pretty tough to get through Afghanistan twice. I think he's got this."

We'll see.

On the morning of March 31, the day we were supposed to go get Sprite, I got a call from Porter asking me to come up to Harrisonburg. Another young woman was missing.

This time it was a twenty-year-old. This time, I packed my gun.

Julia Whitaker's roommate had reported her missing at 2:30 a.m. The young women were both lacrosse players. Julia had gone out about eleven to pick up some ibuprofen. She wouldn't have stayed out all night, not with a game the next day.

Campus police found Whitaker's car parked on the side of the road near downtown.

"You don't mind me going?" I asked Scott.

"Of course not. Go help them. Just be careful, okay?"

Actually I was happy to have an excuse not to go to Nate's. I didn't want to face goodbye straight on. Plus I was afraid I'd rip into him again.

I flipped my hood over my head as I walked out to the Jeep. A chilly rain was falling. How miserable would this be to hike in, I thought, or worse, to sleep out in?

I forced my thoughts away from Nate and toward Harrisonburg and this missing young woman. I knew from experience the first twenty-four hours a person is missing is crucial. Witnesses' memories are fresh, evidence is undisturbed. That's when investigators can obtain the best leads.

By 8:00 a.m. I was on my way. Despite the wet roads I drove a little faster than normal and arrived at 9:10 a.m. I went straight to the location where Whitaker's car was found.

Detective Porter was there, along with Officer Jason Black, who I'd met before. "Thanks for coming," Robert said.

"Tell me what you've got."

He gestured toward the car, a silver Toyota Corolla. "No sign of a struggle there, no scuff marks or debris from the car. And the contents of the car appear to be undisturbed. There's athletic gear, a small bag containing a bottle of ibuprofen, a hairbrush, water bottle, some books."

"Purse?"

"Her roommate said she didn't carry a purse. Just stuck her wallet in her back pocket. Phone, too."

"She reported her missing quickly."

"As soon as she woke up and saw Julia's bed was undisturbed. She said 'that other girl's disappearance' had them all on high alert."

"Heather Burgess," I said.

"Right."

I took a deep breath. All those articles were doing some good anyway. "Have you had a dog run a track starting with the car?"

"A K-9 officer tried it but lost it about a quarter mile away."

"Along the road?"

He nodded.

"So maybe she ran out of gas, started walking, and got into another car?"

Robert shrugged. "Or maybe the dog just lost it."

I looked around. "How far are we from the area where Heather Burgess disappeared?"

"Close enough."

"If the women were on high alert from Heather's case, I doubt Julia would willingly get into another car, unless it was a police car."

"I agree."

"So, unless she tried cutting through the woods and got lost or injured, we are likely looking at a stranger abduction."

"That's what I'm worried about."

"Two in one year?" I said.

"Crazy, isn't it?"

22

Detective Porter and I mutually decided I would start by letting Luke have a sniff around the car. After that, I wanted to talk to the roommate.

I opened the back of the Jeep and let Luke out, guiding him over to the side of the road where he could water the bushes. Then I leashed him up and walked him to the driver's side door of Julia's car. He was used to ranging in front of me, off leash, when he was air scenting, but I needed him contained because of the road.

Luke's not a tracking dog, but like I said, he's pretty smart and, as Nate would say, this ain't his first rodeo. He walked all around the roadside gravel, his nose working. "Do you have her, buddy?" I asked him. "Do you smell her?" I wouldn't confuse him by giving either the "seek" command or the "find it." I wanted to see what he would do.

He kept his nose to the ground and started walking down the road. We were next to a wooded area, but about a mile away was a gas station. Julia would have seen those lights, I thought, and logically would walk toward them.

Luke picked up his pace. I hustled to keep up with him. Sure enough, we went about a quarter mile down the road and Luke stopped. He'd lost the trail. He turned around, found the trail again, and looked up at me. "All gone?" I said.

But he wasn't finished. The land sloped down to the right off the shoulder. Luke circled around and started moving down that bank, away from the road. The weeds over there were slippery, and I fell, landing on my bum. Baby Cooper kicked me. "Sorry!" I said.

"Are you okay?" Officer Jason Black had seen me fall and jogged to where I was.

"I think so," I said, pushing myself to my feet. I said a quick prayer and unleashed Luke. I had to be more careful.

Jason came down the slope and joined me. "Is he still on the track?"

"I think so." I shrugged. "Maybe a car pulled over, and Julia got spooked and ran away from the road."

"Could be."

We stood still and watched as Luke started quartering, zigzagging back and forth in search of a scent. Then I saw his pace change. He honed in on one area. Stood sniffing in a patch of weeds. Then looked up at me.

"Let's see what that's all about," I said.

Jason and I walked over there. He stayed close to me, ready to catch me if I started to trip or fall. The ground was uneven, the weeds were high and the brambles just right for tripping. "What do you have, buddy?" I asked my dog. "What'd you find?"

I couldn't see anything. Neither could Jason. Whatever Luke had smelled was beyond our understanding.

"Maybe just a rabbit," Jason said.

I acted surprised. "What? You think Luke is a dog?"

He looked confused for a moment, then he smiled. "Oh, I'm sure Luke is not just a dog. Oh, no. He's more than just a dog."

"Way more," I said, grinning. I started back up toward the road. I slipped again on the wet weeds.

"Hold on," Jason said, and he moved past me. Then he turned around and offered me a hand up.

"Whew, thanks," I said, out of breath.

"My wife's been pregnant twice. It ain't easy."

I smiled my appreciation.

We walked back up the road to where Detective Porter stood, his phone to his ear. He clicked it off as we approached.

"Got something?" I asked.

"A lot of leads."

"That's good."

"Unfortunately, spotting a twenty-year-old woman with long blonde hair in this town isn't a rare occurrence. I've got to get back to the office. You want to go talk to the roommate?"

"Yes."

"Jason, take her, will you? I'll see you both at the office after that."

Jason made a phone call and arranged for us to meet Lissa Anderton at the girls' apartment just off campus. Lissa was a year older than Julia. They'd met through lacrosse, had hit it off, and decided to room together, he told me.

A young man opened the door when we knocked. Lissa's boyfriend, we discovered, had come over to support her. We stepped into the living room. Lissa sat on a slightly battered blue couch. She'd been crying. Her eyes were red and her face puffy.

Jason introduced me. As I looked around, I noticed the apartment was similar in design to Heather's. Each girl had her own bedroom and adjoining bath. They shared the common area—a living room, kitchen, and a balcony.

"Okay if I look around?" I asked Lissa.

She nodded her assent.

"Julia's bedroom is on the right," Jason said.

I listened to him talking to Lissa and her boyfriend while I went through Julia's room. I was looking for anything that might indicate she'd had a secret affair going on or was out looking for drugs other than ibuprofen . . . anything that might indicate why she might be a victim of foul play.

What I found was a lot of athletic clothes,

lacrosse sticks, helmets, and balls, lacrosse magazines, textbooks, a little makeup, and a Bible.

That's right—a Bible. One with loads of notes and highlights.

Lissa came in about then. I looked up. "She's a Christian?"

"A Jesus follower," she replied. "That's what she calls herself."

"She have a boyfriend?"

"No. She was going with a guy, but he broke up with her."

"Why?"

She nodded toward the Bible. "It was too much for him. Her faith."

"Was he angry?"

"No."

I asked for his name and made a note to be sure Robert had checked him out. "Looks like she's really into lacrosse."

"She played in high school and did really well. So they invited her to try out."

"You have a game today?"

"Did. We did have a game. I got excused. I just . . . just couldn't go, not with her missing!"

"You called it in pretty quickly," I said.

Lissa sniffed. She grabbed a tissue off of the box on the dresser and blew her nose. "I fell asleep around eleven o'clock and woke up at two. I came in here to check on her. She'd hurt her knee two days ago and had run out of ibuprofen.

That's why she went out. To get some. When I saw she was gone and her bed was obviously not slept in, I got scared. I called the coach, then the cops. Because, you know, of that other girl."

"Heather Burgess."

"Right. It's still in the paper all the time. Posters everywhere. I can't believe they still haven't found her!"

"Heather? Or Julia?"

"Either one! It's creeping me out."

"I don't blame you. You did exactly the right thing, calling it in right away. We have a whole slew of people looking for Julia right now."

Jason and I left after about half an hour. The evidence response team had gone over the apartment and had grabbed Julia's computer. I didn't find anything else of interest. We drove back to the police station. I took Luke in with me.

More than two dozen people were manning phones and hunched over laptops in the bullpen outside Detective Porter's office. The police chief, Charles Dunning, was there, too, huddling with Detective Porter over a desk littered with paper. I put Luke on a down-stay inside Robert's office, then I joined him and the chief.

"Do you have a lead-tracking software?" I asked, staring at the innumerable slips of paper on the desk.

"Yeah, but they're coming in so fast we can't

keep up with it. Not everybody knows how to use the software, and we got everybody from secretaries to police cadets on the phones taking leads."

"The FBI's coming in," Chief Dunning said.

I raised my eyebrows. "Did you call them?"

"Yes. Because of the prior case and the circumstances. They're presuming an abduction. Their mobile command center will be here first thing in the morning. They've already set up a 1-800 number."

"They're coming from Charlottesville?"

"Right."

I could imagine once the bureau came in they'd be hinky about having me around. I wondered if I should call Scott and get his help in heading that off? "Well, in the meantime," I said, "I'll do any job you need. I can type, or I can analyze leads."

A few minutes later, two other employees and I sat down at desks and began tackling the mountain of leads. The software was intuitive, and similar to what we'd used in Fairfax. The problem was the volume. The campaign to keep Heather Burgess in the public's eye was paying off.

Except for a half-hour break around six o'clock, during which I scarfed down a pretty good steak-and-cheese sub, I worked until nine. Luke had a more active day. There was no shortage of people who, anxious for a short break from the tension, volunteered to take him outside and play ball with him.

Over the course of the evening the lead traffic slowed down. By nine o'clock our logging was up to date. I was willing to stay longer, but Robert insisted I go get some sleep. In fact, he'd had someone book a room for me at the hotel where Luke and I had stayed before. My obvious state of pregnancy was bringing out the protector in everybody.

I checked in to the hotel, then I took Luke on one more walk around the building. I stayed in the lighted area this time. When we got back upstairs, I called Scott. "Hey, hon. Hope I didn't call too late."

"No! How's it going?"

I filled him in on the missing woman and what we'd done so far to find her. "The whole community is all in. I have hope," I said. "By the way, Charlottesville will be here in the morning."

"The bureau?"

"Yes." I hesitated. "I think they might object to my presence. Could you head that off?" I knew Scott knew people in Charlottesville. He knew people everywhere.

"And what? Tell them to kick you out because I want you home?"

I could hear the teasing in his voice. "You know what I mean."

He laughed. "Yes. I'll call."

"Thank you." I changed the subject. "How's Sprite?"

"She's settling in. She's sleeping actually."

I smiled. Sprite thought she was a lap dog. "Where?"

"What?"

"Where is she sleeping?"

There was a long pause. "Actually, she's on the bed."

"What? The 'no-dogs-in-bed' guy has caved on the first night?" I said, laughing.

"Well, you're not here. So I'm letting her have your side."

"I'm telling Luke."

"He's a bit bigger."

"And hairier."

"When do you think you'll be home?" Scott asked.

I yawned. "Not sure. I'll let you know."

We talked a little more and said goodnight. I promised to call him the next day. I clicked off the phone, turned out the light, and prayed for Scott, for Julia, and of course, for Nate.

23

Nate sat in a rocking chair on the porch of the hostel in Damascus, Virginia, looking out at the mountains that surrounded the town. Ember, his black German shepherd, lay at his feet, her muzzle resting on her paws. *Feels like home,* Nate thought, and by *home* he meant the mountains where he'd grown up in western Virginia, where he'd met and dated Laura, the place he'd left when he'd joined the Marines at age eighteen. He'd never gone back.

Damascus, in the southwest corner of the state, calls itself The Friendliest Town on the Trail. "The Trail" is, most famously, the Appalachian Trail, although six other trails run nearby. The AT is a nearly 2,200-mile hike from Springer Mountain in Georgia to Katahdin, a mountain in Maine. Thousands of people set out to complete the approximately five-month trek every year. About a quarter of them actually make it.

Nate's goal was to hike the 550 miles of the AT that lies in Virginia by mid-July when Baby Cooper was due to make his or her arrival. No way did he want to miss that. To accomplish his mission, he figured he'd have to hike about eight miles a day six days a week. By AT hiker standards, that was a slow, easy pace, but then most AT hikers weren't hiking on one leg.

Jeff was confident the new artificial leg he'd made Nate would carry him the distance. It featured the latest advances in prosthetic technology, namely, a computer-controlled artificial knee. This allowed Nate to maintain better balance over uneven ground, walk up stairs step-over-step, and even walk backwards. In addition to giving him a more natural gait, the leg was weatherproof. Yes it was expensive, but between Nate's medical insurance and an unexpected life insurance check from Laura, Nate had decided he could afford it. "It'll open up a whole new range of activities for you," Jeff had told him. Like walking the AT.

Now, sitting on the porch of the hostel, Nate looked at the mountains, still slumbering in winter dress, with gray, leafless trees and subdued underbrush. Here and there a stand of pines broke up the landscape. In his mind he could see the hollows, the folds, and the vistas that lay ahead of him. He'd grown up in the mountains. He knew there'd be hard climbs, steep descents, rock scrambles, and creeks, all of which he'd face hiking by himself. On one leg. And in all weather.

This was his journey, his pilgrimage, his war. "I just got to stay alive for 550 miles," he told himself.

Jeff had picked him up at his house that

morning at six o'clock and had driven him four hours to Damascus. Along the way, he regaled Nate with more stories of his own AT thru-hike three years prior. The people he'd met. The sunrises, sunsets, and amazing night skies. The freedom of the trail.

He'd already helped Nate get the gear he'd need, had coached him on caring for his stump on the trail, and had promised to be his trail boss—resupplying him with food and supplies—for the first half of Nate's journey.

Grateful, Nate bought him breakfast, then lunch, and then gave him gas money.

What Jeff had given him was priceless.

For the first time since Laura died, Nate had a goal. A mission. A purpose. Focus. A reason to get up in the morning.

Now here he was, at the hostel, ready to begin his pilgrimage tomorrow morning at first light.

"Well, Lord," he whispered, quietly rocking, "the irony is, my hike starts in Damascus. Like Paul, I am blind. Cain't see you and I cain't hear you neither. Cain't feel you. I'm walkin' out of here blind and deaf, hoping to find you on the trail. It'll be jus' me and you now, Lord. Jus' me and you. Not countin' the dog."

According to the plan he and Jeff had worked out, he'd take short hikes the first few days, then walk eight miles on the fifth day, still a relatively easy pace. Jeff would meet him at Grayson

Highlands State Park to resupply his food and check his stump.

For this trip, Nate had bought a Gregory backpack, similar to the one he used for SAR, just newer and a little lighter. In or on it, he'd carry a tarp, a sleeping hammock, a Sawyer Squeeze for filtering water, a small Solo stove, a stove pot, paracord, extra clothes, rain gear, a small first aid kit, food for himself and Ember, and a packet of cotton balls with Vaseline as fire starters. In a side pocket of the pack in a waterproof box, he had his iPhone. In the other side pocket, a waterproof notebook, and a pen, maps, a compass, and a GPS.

His pipe would ride in the right leg pocket of his cargo pants, along with a small pouch of tobacco. Why he was smoking again was beyond him. Maybe it was a comfort.

When Scott gave him Jess's dad's black book, he'd teared up. He knew what that book meant to Jess. So he'd put it in two Ziploc bags for protection and planned to carry it in his shirt pocket. It added a couple of extra ounces to his load, but in honor of their friendship, he'd take it.

Ember would carry some of her food and water in her own pack. He had wondered at first how they would be as partners on the trail. She was smart and obedient, but he hadn't bonded with her as closely as with Sprite or his military working dog, Rock. He didn't know why. Maybe it was because she was the second dog in the house, or maybe because he'd had Laura to talk to.

Once he decided to hike the AT, Nate thought it would be good to have a dog along. He'd been having more trouble with PTSD since Laura died, waking up suddenly at night, struggling with depression and panic attacks. His doctors, listening to him, agreed, and so Ember joined the trip.

As near as Nate could tell, with Jeff's help, he had it all planned out. But that night, he didn't sleep well. He was restless, either from excitement or anxiety. So he was glad when the sky began to get light, and he could get up and get gone.

April 1. Nate fed Ember at the hostel, then left her so he could get a good breakfast of eggs, bacon, waffles, and coffee. Then, he returned for his dog, put on her pack, gave her a good pat, and they set out.

The AT runs right through Damascus, so the first little bit of their hike was through town, through an arch erected by Boy Scouts, past the outfitter and another hostel, and down the road. The sky was clear, and the sun was shining. The tiny thermometer hanging on the zipper of his jacket read thirty-two degrees. It was a right fine day for a walk in the woods, he thought. A right fine day.

They crossed a road and headed up a set of steps. With the trail stretching before him, he took a deep breath and he prayed, a habit he couldn't break even though God seemed silent. He was stepping into the woods, without Laura, without anyone, just following the white blazes that marked the AT.

He reached down and unclipped Ember. The artificial leg made trekking poles mandatory. Balance, especially on the uneven, rocky surfaces he anticipated, was difficult. But managing the poles while also dealing with a dog on leash was a pain.

Nate patted his dog and adjusted her pack. "Let's go, girl," he said to Ember. "We've got a ways to walk today. Stay close now, hear?"

24

I woke up early and looked at my watch. 6:04 a.m. April 1. My heart sagged. April 1, the day Nate would start his hike.

I felt fear grip me, a physical ache like a fist squeezing my gut. I was afraid for him. I'd hiked with that man in the woods on searches. I'd seen him struggle with balance. I'd seen him fall. I'd seen his stump get so chafed it would bleed. I couldn't imagine him living on his own, *hiking* on his own, in the mountains for weeks.

But even more than my concern for his physical safety was my confusion and fear over his inability to access his faith. He was the most spiritual man I knew. He thought deeply and loved Jesus fiercely. He'd been my spiritual mentor since I met him. If Nate could fall away, what hope was there for me?

Immediately, phrases from verses jumped into my head, verses like, "He who began a good work in you will bring it to completion," and "no one will ever snatch them out of my hand." But the fear gripping my gut was strong.

I didn't know what to do. Didn't know what I *could* do. So I prayed for Nate. I prayed for his protection, and I prayed, most of all, that he'd grab hold of his faith again, and until he did, that God would hold onto him.

Whatever happens, Nate had always told me, *let it drive you to God.*

And so I let this "whatever" drive me to God.

I got up, showered, got dressed, fed Luke, grabbed a quick hotel breakfast, and left. I wondered if I'd beat the FBI to the office.

The sun was just coming up as I drove into town. Spotting a doughnut place, I stopped and bought four dozen plus a container of hot, fresh coffee. Despite all the jokes, cops really do appreciate a little friendly, sugary treat when they're on a long job.

The tired and discouraged crew in the bullpen perked up when I walked in with that food. "Don't give any to my dog," I said loudly, "even if he swears he paid for them." Luke sat nearby trying to look particularly handsome.

Robert came out of his office to see what the fuss was all about. "So update me," I said after he grabbed a doughnut and thanked me.

He shook his head. "Not much new. We got a few tips last night, and we followed through, but they didn't pan out. Her parents got here late. Dad was ready to go out on his own last night. I booked 'em in your hotel. I expect them back down here this morning. The folks from Charlottesville will be here in an hour."

"Did you go home at all?"

He shook his head. "Slept in my office on the floor."

"May I look over the leads?"

"Help yourself."

I was just beginning to do that when someone in the bullpen shouted, "Boss! Boss! We got her!"

"What?"

Everyone stopped talking. I stood up. An officer handed Robert a piece of paper. "She's at that address. She's alive!"

Big cheers. Joyful chaos. Robert turned to me. "Let's go. C'mon, Jason! Cherie!"

I gathered up my stuff, including Luke, and went out to my Jeep, my heart light for the first time in days. Jason jumped in with me and Cherie rode with Robert. I followed him east toward the mountains. We turned off the two-lane road onto a long, winding driveway and parked in the yard of a small, one-story house with blue shutters. A metal garden chair sat out front, near a garden whose blooms had faded and gone to seed. A cylindrical bird feeder hung from a shepherd's crook-shaped metal pole in the middle of the garden.

An older woman with white, curly hair opened the door as we walked up. Robert showed his badge. "Come in, come in! I'm so glad you're here."

I'd left Luke in the Jeep, which was a good thing, because the house was small. I half-expected a yappy little dog to come out barking at us, but no. As we stepped into the house, directly into the living room, I saw a young woman sitting in a chair next to the fireplace, stroking the head of a beautiful golden retriever.

Good therapy, I thought. *The best.* I decided I liked Mrs. Chambers, a lot.

Robert Porter showed Julia Whitaker his badge, then introduced everyone else. He gave her the choice of talking in private to Cherie Towson, an officer specially trained in sexual assault, or speaking to all of us. Barefoot and wrapped in a blue blanket, Julia responded, "I can talk to all of you."

Her face was attractive, I thought. Her cheekbones would be the envy of models. She had leaf bits in her blonde hair and a scratch down one cheek, testimonies of the trauma she'd just undergone.

Robert stepped back to give Cherie room. She pulled a chair up in front of Julia, giving her a focus point. She told her that her job was to talk to sexual assault victims.

Julia interrupted her. "He didn't."

Cherie stopped.

"He didn't assault me. He was going to. But I got away."

"I'm so glad," Cherie said. "You were so resourceful! And brave." She reached out and touched Julia's hand. "I'm really proud of you.

Let's hear the whole story. Take it from the top."

As Julia shared her story, I could barely breathe. Smart and articulate, her emotions veered between fear and anger and grateful relief.

"After my car broke down," she began, "I started walking toward a gas station. It was within sight. This guy in an old Chevy Impala pulled up and offered to give me a lift. I refused. He pretended to drive away but then he pulled over, got out, chased me down, and wrestled me to the ground."

Is that what Luke smelled? Down the hill and in the weeds? I wondered.

Julia went on. "He had handcuffs, you know? Those plastic things? And a gun. He tied my hands behind my back and forced me into the back of this car on the floor. Then he got in and started driving. He told me he'd shoot me if I moved.

"I prayed, hard. I was terrified. After a little while, I told him I had to go to the bathroom. I told him if he didn't stop I was going to pee right there in his car. I felt him turn off the main road onto some rutted lane. He stopped the car and pulled me out of the back. We were at a park or something with a detached restroom building. Deserted. I prayed and prayed.

"I told him if he didn't take those wraps off I'd just pee all over myself. He argued with me, but I pretended to start crying. I acted weak. So he cut them, and he told me if I tried anything, he'd shoot me. I promised him I wouldn't try anything. I said, 'We're in the middle of the woods! Where would I go?'

"He made me take my shoes off, then my pants. I guess he figured I wouldn't run away from him barefoot and half-dressed.

"I went into the restroom. Praise God, the door had a lock on it! So I locked it, then went into a stall and locked that door. My cell phone was outside in my pants. I couldn't call for help. I was panicking, worried he would do something crazy, like try to break down the door with his car once he realized I'd locked it. I had to try to get away.

"There was a small window up high, near the ceiling, on the back side of the building. It didn't look like I'd fit through it, but I had to try. I climbed up on the toilet and forced the window open. I wiggled and squirmed my way out, and then I dropped down as quietly as I could.

"The woods were full of dry leaves. I was so afraid of making noise! But I slipped away from that place, disappearing into the woods. I heard him yelling. Pounding on the bathroom door. So I started running and I ran and ran and ran until I was out of breath.

"The rocks and brambles cut my feet. I fell twice, maybe three times. I got to a place where there were some huge trees that had fallen down. I couldn't run anymore. I crawled under that pile like a rabbit. I covered myself with leaves, trying to stay warm, and I prayed."

Julia took a deep shaky breath. "Thank God he didn't come after me. Eventually, I heard his car start. I didn't think I was near the road. I heard his car move away. But I was afraid to move so I just stayed there, hunkered down, all night, waiting for dawn.

"When the sky grew light, I started walking. I was freezing cold. I found a stream and decided to follow it. Then I saw the light in this house. I was afraid of who might live there, but by that time, I was so cold and exhausted, I had to take a chance." She looked at Mrs. Chambers. "I'm so grateful it was you."

Mrs. Chambers patted her arm. "Me, too, honey."

"You were very smart, and very brave," Cherie said gently. "So, once again, just to clarify, did he assault you?"

"Sexually? No. But he was going to. I'm sure of it."

"Are you hurt?"

"Cuts and bruises. Nothing big."

"Did you clean yourself off or shower or anything once you got here?"

Julia shook her head. "I watch cop shows. I know not to do that."

Cherie smiled. "Good. Julia, you saved yourself. Good job. Now what's going to happen is this: Detective Porter probably has some questions for you if you're okay to talk. Then, we're going to take you to a hospital where they'll examine you and collect any evidence that's on you. You'll be able to see your parents then."

"My parents are here?"

"Yes, we called them. We'll get a formal statement from you. Then you'll be free to go. If you'd like a police escort we'll arrange that. Or you can go home with your parents if you swant."

Julia shook her head. "I'm not letting that man make me miss the rest of the lacrosse season. No way."

"Good for you, Julia." Cherie turned to Porter. "You have some preliminary questions?"

"Yes, thank you. Julia, we'd like to find this guy ASAP. Before he can try this again. Can you give us a description of him and/or his car?" Porter asked.

"It was dark. When he stopped to offer me a ride, the dome light wasn't on. As he pretended to drive away, he must have put on a ski mask because when he chased me, he had one on.

"By the way he moved, I thought he was an older guy. Definitely not college age. But I'd say he was white. He had on dark clothes. Not jeans, more like clothes a workman or a mechanic would wear. In fact, his jacket looked like it should have a patch up here." She touched her upper chest on the left side. "One thing, though, he smelled bad. So did his car."

"What do you mean by 'bad.'"

"Like he hadn't showered in a while. A long while. And he talked like a hick."

"A hick?"

"Right. Not just southern, a hick. Used bad grammar and all that."

"And the car was a Chevy Impala?"

Julia nodded. "Dark blue or black. My dad used to have one. I recognized it." She hesitated. "Oh, I think the last two digits of the license plate were 64. I can't remember the rest of it."

"Good job," Robert said. "You're amazing."

Julia blushed.

When Robert finished, I spoke up. "Julia, do you think you could tell us where that bathroom was?"

She looked down and bit her lower lip. Then she slowly shook her head. "I was on the floor of his car and couldn't see where he was going. I kept trying to memorize the turns, but I quickly lost track.

"I can tell you it was probably within four miles of here. I'm guessing I ran about thirty minutes, maybe a little more, then I walked for at least twenty minutes before I got here. I was running slower through the woods than what I can run in the open, so maybe I was clocking a nine-minute mile. So figure I ran about two and a half or three miles, then walked another mile . . . so within four miles." She looked up.

"Thank you," I said. "That's very helpful. What did you see first when you saw the house?"

"The lights in the windows."

"I'm trying to figure out what direction you were coming from."

"Oh." Julia frowned again. "I saw a clothesline and a big silver tank. I walked around it to get to the front door."

I smiled. "Thank you." Then I looked at Mrs. Chambers. "Is that an oil tank? Propane?"

"Propane. And it's out there." She pointed to the east end of her house.

"Can you think of a restroom like what she's describing out in that direction?"

Mrs. Chambers shook her head. "No, I can't."

"That's all right. We'll check the maps."

We thanked them both and Julia went with Cherie to the hospital. Robert, Jason, and I huddled in Mrs. Chambers' yard. "I'd like to try to find that restroom," I said.

"What are you thinking? Just ride around and see what you can find?"

"Essentially, yes."

"Jason, why don't you go with her. I need to get back to the office."

"Okay, boss."

Robert looked up at the blue sky and took a deep breath. "It's a good day. A really good day."

. . .

Jason Black had his phone out and a map app pulled up by the time we got in my Jeep. He was searching for any place—a campground, a club, a park—any place within a four-mile radius of Mrs. Chambers' house that might have a free-standing bathroom like the one Julia described.

I did the same, and together we made a list of possibilities. Then we drove around and checked them off one by one. Nothing.

"I got an idea," Jason said. "Let me make some phone calls."

While he stood outside my Jeep making calls, I texted Scott. *Found her. Alive! She escaped. Gutsy girl.*

Congrats! Coming home? he texted back.

Not quite yet. I'll let you know.

Jason got back in the car. "Let's go back to Mrs. Chambers'."

We were close, so I drove there and parked in her driveway.

"I'm going to ask her if we can hang out here for a bit," Jason said.

"Ask if I can let Luke out!" I called after him.

Mrs. Chambers was happy to have us there. She said she'd keep her dog inside. I let Luke out, and he began sniffing around her yard. Fifteen minutes later, another officer showed up. With a drone.

I'd been around drones before on searches.

I was always secretly a little proud when a dog found the person, not a drone. But in this case, as far as I know, no dog had been trained to locate restrooms, so I was like, have at it.

Jason and I watched over Officer Campbell's shoulder while he flew his device over the woods around Mrs. Chambers' house. "What's the range on these things?" I asked.

"Depends on conditions, especially the wind. This is a commercial product, and I expect I'd get at least ten miles on a day like today," he said. "The wind's coming from the south at about four or five miles an hour, and you are particularly interested in east, so we'll see how far we can push it."

After about fifteen minutes I grew bored standing there watching a small screen. So I looked around, found a good stick, and started playing fetch with Luke. He'd been quiet for hours and I knew he could use the exercise. Plus, it was fun for me and for him.

Fetch was a "no rules" game for us. I let him do anything. So every once in a while, he'd play keep-away, appearing to bring the stick back to me but then swerving at the last minute, keeping just out of my reach. I'd pretend to be mad and chase him. And then he'd repent and bring the stick back.

Sometimes, I'd delay throwing the stick. I'd hold it high over my head and make him jump for it, or behind my back and make him find it. Or I'd throw it, then pretend to run after it myself.

As I said, it was fun. And both of us were ready for a little fun.

After a while, I held up my hands and said, "That's all," the signal for the end of our playing time. He went off and began chewing up the stick, and I turned back to the men and the drone screen.

"Hey, what's that?" I said, pointing to a bright triangle on the screen.

25

My exclamation caught Officer Campbell's attention. He manipulated the drone into a different angle. The triangle disappeared. "Sun's reflecting off something," he said.

"Let's mark that spot."

We noted the coordinates. "I don't know," Campbell said. "It could be a piece of metal, or a small pond. Let me go lower."

He brought the drone around again at a lower altitude, and there was a momentary flash, but it was impossible to see what it was. By the time he brought the drone around again, we didn't see it. "Sun's moved," Campbell said.

I thought about it. The area the drone was surveying was forested, with few openings and no visible buildings. According to the map on my phone, there were no houses or other structures there.

But it was 5.3 miles by the way the crow flies from the place we were standing.

Maybe I was restless. Anxious. But I looked at the two men and said, "I want to go check that out."

"I don't think it's anything."

"She said the restroom was dark brown, right?" Jason said. "That wouldn't reflect."

"Still, it's in about the right place. I want to see what it is."

Campbell nodded. "Okay. I'm ready for a break. You have the coordinates?"

"Yes," I said. "Jason?"

He hesitated, but then he said, "Yeah, sure, I'll come along."

"I'm going to go get some lunch," Campbell said. "Text me if you want to resume here."

I loaded Luke in the back of my Jeep, and we set off. I could feel Jason's skepticism. "Thanks for coming," I said.

He shook his head. "Can't see sending you off in the woods by yourself. I'll see this out."

Jason navigated while I drove. Following the GPS coordinates took us down a tiny back country road with no markings at all and nothing in the vicinity that we could see.

"Wait, we've missed it," Jason said, staring at the handheld GPS I'd given him. "Go back."

I turned around on the road and crept back the way we'd come.

"There, there!" he said, gesturing.

What I saw was barely a driveway, a lane, overgrown and rutted. "Okay," I said, turning into it.

A little way down the driveway, we came to a small creek. "Hold on!" I said. "Let's get out here."

Jason looked at me like I was crazy.

"If we drive through that we'll be obliterating any tire tracks on the other side. We may need those, so let's go on foot. Just so you know, I'm taking my dog and my gun."

He went along with it.

We parked. I got Luke out of the back and leashed him up. Then we walked further down this rutted, rough road, being careful to stay to the side, Jason carrying the GPS. We saw nothing around us to the left or the right, just trees and underbrush and an occasional bird.

"Hey, look at this," I said, drawing Jason's attention away from the GPS. Off in the bushes to the left I saw an old wooden sign, lying on the ground, half obscured. I pushed the undergrowth away. "Camp Friendship," I said.

"Weird," he said. "I've never heard of that."

We walked on about another hundred yards, him on one side, me on the other. The driveway widened out a little. And then we saw it. Ramshackle cabins in a semi-circle, and to the left, back aways from them, an old bathroom building. It had a silver vent pipe on the roof.

We stayed back, sheltered in part by the bushes. If this is where the unknown subject had brought Julia, could he be here? Living here?

Jason gestured he was going to move to the right to check out the cabins.

I stayed put, well aware of the baby in my belly.

With my gun in my hand, I watched as he moved stealthily through the woods, methodically moving from cabin to cabin. When he got to the fourth one, he waved. All clear. Then he gestured he'd check out the bathroom building. I watched him walk over to it, disappear behind it, emerge, and try the door, which was locked. He motioned me forward.

I holstered my gun, and Luke and I walked over to Jason, staying close to the bushes so we wouldn't mess up any footprints or tire prints that happened to be there. "Nothing, huh? Do you think this is the place?"

"Yes. Come look at this."

I followed him to the back of the building. There, about eight feet off the ground, was an open window. "Wow. Let's send that to Porter. See if we can get Julia to ID it."

We both took pictures, and he texted his to Robert and also Officer Campbell, the drone operator. "We should look around for her stuff," he said.

I took Luke off leash and let him sniff the area on his own. He'd be smelling wild animals, I knew, and the occasional stray dog. But maybe, just maybe, he'd find her pants and cell phone if the perpetrator had pitched them into the woods.

"We need to mark this off as a crime scene," Jason said. "But I don't have tape with me."

"I've got some in the Jeep."

He stared at me.

I grinned. "You never know when you're going to need it."

Within half an hour, Detective Porter, an evidence response team, and several other officers were on the scene. Then Julia and her parents arrived, escorted by Cherie.

Julia, now cleaned up and dressed in sweats and a jacket, looked lean and athletic. Her blonde hair lay captured in a scrunchy at the base of her neck. She looked carefully at the restroom, then asked to see the back of the building. When she saw that small window, she said, "This is it. This is the place."

Yes! My heart jumped. The chances of getting this guy now increased exponentially. Already evidence techs were making casts of the tire treads in the driveway and the footprints. Others were inspecting the whole property for any indication he might have been staying there or anything he might have dropped. A couple of guys with a battering ram busted open the door to look for evidence in the bathroom. The men's side was open, so they went in there, too.

Detective Porter came up to me. "Good work, Jess. I really appreciate it." He shook my hand. "We never really talked about a consulting fee."

I smiled. I was pretty sure the search for the two

missing women had blown his budget. "This? This is pro bono. I needed a win."

"And so did we all. Thanks so much for all you've done." He answered a question from one of the investigators, then turned back to me. "You want to head on home now? I think we got this from here."

"Yes, I'll take off. I'll type up a statement and send it to you."

While waiting for Porter and the others I had moved my Jeep, which was a good thing because I would have been completely blocked in if I'd left it where I originally parked it. I said goodbye to Jason, loaded Luke up in his crate, and headed back to the hotel, where I checked out and started home. I texted Scott that I was on my way. I didn't hear back from him, but I figured he was busy with the horses or something.

The shadows lengthened as I drove east, the sun dropping behind the mountains. I looked hard for the first signs of spring, for leaf budding or daffodils or even crocuses. Nada. Nothing. So I switched gears and thought forward to what I'd fix for dinner and what Scott and I might do this evening.

Now that the intense excitement was over, fatigue seeped through me. I straightened up in my driver's seat. I'd been warned about "pregnancy brain" and staying alert while driving. I turned on the radio and heard a weather forecast.

Clear tonight. Lows in the lower thirties in the valleys and mid- to upper twenties in the mountains. Sunny tomorrow, highs in the forties.

Which made me think of Nate. Did he have the gear for the cold overnights? Would he be alone out there on the mountain? How would he cope with his leg, with falling and getting up? He'd be sleeping on the ground. How was he supposed to get up with one leg?

A familiar feeling gnawed at my gut. Fear. *I can't control him,* I said to myself, trying to get a grip. Truth is, I can't. I can't even control me.

26

Nate found a place to camp and paced off a couple of trees. Just right, he thought. He pulled out his gear—a hammock, tarp, quilts, and the rigging to hold them up.

He and Jeff had debated what he'd use for shelter on the trail. Jeff had a sweet little ultralight tent that he'd carried on his thru-hike. Most people had something like that. But Jeff had a friend who'd used a hammock, and the more he and Nate talked about it, the more they thought it would work well for him.

In a hammock, he wouldn't be sleeping on the ground, so getting up, always clumsy with one leg, wouldn't be a problem. He could rig the hammock low enough that he could sit on it to get his leg on and off, put his shoes on, or check his stump. And over it, Nate could erect a rainfly that would be big enough for Ember to sleep under.

Backpackers had strong opinions about tents vs. hammocks. Nate had read a lot and tried both. In the end, he'd chosen the hammock. He'd practiced with it at home, setting it up in the daytime and in the dark, and once even in the rain. Slung between two trees under a rain-shedding tarp, its thin fabric augmented by quilts for warmth, the hammock was, in his mind, "right comfortable."

Then again, after hiking for hours he felt like he could sleep on rocks.

Nate set up camp near Saunders Shelter, a three-sided building big enough for eight campers. Near it lay a water source and a privy. He'd wondered if he'd see other hikers there but so far the place was empty.

Of course, he could have just slept in the shelter, but he'd decided to avoid shelters if he could. One reason, mice. Another one, snorers.

The temperature dropped quickly after sunset. Nate skipped making dinner. He'd eaten a protein bar and some cheese and jerky on the way to camp to save time. He fed Ember a high-quality freeze-dried raw food, rinsed her bowl, and put it in the food bag. Then he placed the food bag in the bear box, a metal box secured with a clasp and carabiner. He secured his pack on a nearby tree.

Finally, he was ready for bed. Almost. He got into the clothes he'd brought for sleeping. He sat on the hammock and removed his prosthetic leg and cleaned his stump. In the light of his headlamp, he thought it looked good, a little pink in just one spot, but basically good. It would be good for it to air out overnight. Then he changed his mind and put his leg back on. This first night out in the wild, he wanted to be prepared for anything.

He whistled for Ember, who came bounding out of the woods. He petted her head and said, "Okay, now, bed." *Bed* was her command to lie down on her mat until he told her to get up. She'd gotten good at that at home, but Nate wondered what she'd do if a wild animal came snooping around. "I guess I'll find out," he muttered to himself. He lifted his legs into the hammock and covered himself with the quilt.

Settled and warm in his bed, loneliness hit him hard. It sucked the life out of him, hollowing his gut, leaving a dark void inside. Laura was gone. He was alone. Again.

An owl hooted in the night, a Great Horned Owl, if he remembered the call right. Nate lay still, listening. A second owl responded from far off. The two went back and forth for ten, maybe fifteen minutes. And while Nate listened, exhaustion overtook him, and he drifted off to sleep.

27

A couple of times on the drive home from Harrisonburg I rolled down the windows partway, letting cold air pour in to wake myself up. Glancing in my rearview mirror, I saw Luke lift his head and open his mouth, smelling all the smells in the fresh air.

By the time I got home it was dark. I pulled into our driveway and was surprised to find Scott's car was missing. Where was he? The barn was buttoned down, and just the one light in the window that we always left on was burning.

I started to call him, but Luke whined in the back, and I decided to wait. I turned off my Jeep and let Luke out of the back. He immediately went running around, nose to the ground, but instead of doing a perimeter search, he ran right up to our front door.

Sprite. I'd forgotten she'd be inside. I grabbed my SAR pack and overnight bag, as well as Luke's food and followed him.

"Well, hello!" I said as I opened the door. The little springer spaniel acknowledged me with a wag of her stubby little tail but then went straight for Luke. "Y'all go on outside," I said. "Go on!"

I set my things down and flipped on the light in the foyer. Immediately, I noticed a package from

Amazon on the small table. I wondered what it was. I didn't remember ordering anything. Probably another book for Scott, I concluded.

But it was addressed to me. Quickly, I ripped open the bag and pulled out a beautiful leather copy of *The Heidelberg Catechism*. My heart thumped. I found the gift note. It read, *Sorry I destroyed your favorite. Grace and peace. Your brother, Nate.*

My vision blurred.

I had barely recovered from that when my phone rang. Scott. I answered, hoping to hear that, wherever he was, he was almost home. But no.

"Where are you?" he said.

I could tell right away something was wrong. "Home. What's up? Where are you?"

"UVA Medical Center."

Was Scott hurt? Nate? Dramatic scenarios, like thunderclouds, formed instantly in my head. "What's wrong?"

"It's Amanda. She . . . she may be losing the baby." His voice broke.

"Oh, no, Scott!" Dizzy, I sat down on the stairs. "I'm so sorry. Let me feed the dogs and I'll be right there."

"No. I don't want you to come. We may be here all night."

"Is Ethan there with you?"

"Yes."

"What happened?"

"She began bleeding. Ethan called her doctor. She said to take Amanda to the ER, and she'd meet them there."

"Are they still hearing a heartbeat?"

There was a pause. "I don't think so."

I suddenly felt sick. Amanda was about thirty-four weeks into her pregnancy. Was a baby viable at thirty-four weeks? My mind raced. "Scott, I want to come down there. Just give me—"

"No!"

I heard him choke back emotion. It took Scott a minute to get himself together. "No, please, Jess. I need you to do something at home, and most of all, I need you to take care of yourself. Stay home."

I backed off, a cold chill coming over me. I'd never heard my husband so emotional. "Okay, Scott. What do you need me to do?"

I listened as he told me to call a neighbor and ask him to take care of the horses, let Kathryn know that Saturday might not be a good time to come down, and he asked me to pay two bills that were sitting on his desk. "Oh, and take care of Sprite," he said.

"Sure, I can do all that. But call me, okay? Let me know what's going on. And tell Amanda I love her and I'm praying for her."

"Right. I've got to go. Love you."

"Love you, too." I responded and clicked off my phone.

In this world you will have tribulation, Jesus said.

Truth.

I had no time to look at the book Nate had sent me. Our neighbor wasn't home, so I ended up feeding the horses myself. That wouldn't have been a problem except that I had to go up into the loft to get hay, which was a little awkward, but I did it. Four horses eat a lot, especially when it's cold.

While I worked I thought and prayed and thought some more. The idea that had struck me driving home from Harrisonburg hit me again. I played around with it, then shoved it to the back of my mind. I couldn't act on it until we got through this situation with Amanda.

I said goodnight to the horses, turned off the barn lights, and Luke and I headed to the house. The air was cold and clear, a beautiful night really, with a half moon and plenty of stars visible. I wondered if Nate was seeing it, if it was clear where he was, if he was sleeping out or still inside somewhere.

Back inside, I fed the dogs, put fresh water in their bowls, and stared at the open refrigerator hoping something would appear on the shelves that I felt like eating.

Nada. Nothing. But Baby Cooper was kicking up a storm, demanding *food.* So I pulled out eggs and cheese and made scrambled eggs.

I sat down to eat, but I couldn't stop thinking about Amanda. I pulled out my pregnancy book and looked up if a baby could survive at thirty-four weeks. The good news is they can, and usually do. My book said the survival rate was 80 to 90 percent. *Yay for that!* I thought.

Then I looked up "bleeding in the third trimester." I started reading about placenta previa and placenta abruption. The more I read, the more concerned I was. Then I started feeling sick.

I shut the book. *How does anyone ever get born?* There were so many things that could go wrong and so many that *had* to go right. No wonder so many women died in childbirth.

But Amanda couldn't die, could she? That wasn't a thing now, was it?

I got up from the table. Took my plate to the sink. And nearly threw up.

I turned out the lights and left the kitchen. On my way upstairs, I grabbed my overnight bag and the book Nate had sent me and carried them both up with me. Luke and Sprite followed me. I dropped my stuff in our bedroom, then walked into the nursery we'd prepared. "It would be too much, God," I whispered, "if something happened to Amanda, too. I mean, first Laura, now this? If she loses the baby, that would be horrible. Tragic. But her, too? No, Lord, that would be too much, way too much, for us to bear."

A cold fear swept over me. I had no control over anything, not over what could happen to Amanda or Nate. What happened to Laura. All the people important to me. No control even over my husband. I was as helpless as a child who kisses her father goodbye in the morning and never sees him again.

I turned and walked into our bedroom and unpacked my overnight bag, jerking the clothes out one by one. I threw them into the hamper and tossed the bag in our closet, kicking it to the back. Then I walked into the bathroom and turned on the shower, hoping the hot water would drive away my fear.

It didn't. I dried off, slipped into pajamas, and crawled into bed with Nate's book. I felt the texture of the cover. I traced my finger over the engraving and the gold letters. I smelled the leather. Then I flipped it open to a random page. I read, "What do you understand about the providence of God?"

I slipped deeper into the covers. Luke was already snoring, lying on the floor. Sprite had curled up next to him.

I kept reading. "Providence is the almighty and ever present power of God, by which he upholds, as with his hand, heaven and earth and all creatures, and so rules them that leaf and blade, rain and drought, fruitful and lean years, health and sickness, prosperity and poverty—all things, in fact, come to us, not by chance, but from his fatherly hand."

I closed the book. "Lord God," I said, "if this is your hand, it's pretty heavy on us right now. Have mercy, Lord. Help us. Especially Amanda and Scott." Then I added, "And please don't forget about Nate. You promised you'd never leave us. That you'd finish what you began in us. You cannot lie, so I'm trusting you, Lord, to bring Nate back to his faith. Heal his heart. Comfort him. Give him grace to get through this loss."

I wanted to stay awake until Scott got home, but my body was too tired. I fell asleep with the light on and the book still open. I slept like a rock until, sometime in the middle of the night, I heard Luke give a low woof. He rose and padded downstairs but sounded no further alarm, so I drifted back to sleep. At some point I was vaguely aware of the shower running. Then I felt Scott slide into bed. I turned to look at him.

"She's okay," he whispered.

"The baby?"

He shook his head and pressed his lips together. My heart grew heavy. He kissed me softly. "I'll tell you more in the morning."

I didn't want to let him go. "Scott, honey, what about you? Are you okay?"

He snuggled closer. "I will be."

We held each other close, lying perfectly still, each hoping the other would fall asleep, both of us wide awake. I tried to wrap my mind around the loss of Amanda's baby, Scott's first grandchild, the one we'd pictured being so close in age to Baby Cooper. I tried to put it all together—the rape, Amanda's pregnancy, her decision not to abort, and now this. Where was God in it? Why had he allowed all this to happen? It was one horrible circumstance after another, a nightmarish parade of events.

These thoughts swarmed in my head like bees harassing me. My husband's breathing had still not deepened. He must have been thinking, too. Finally, I whispered, "Scott?"

"Yeah?"

"I can't sleep."

"Me either."

We pulled apart. "Let's go downstairs," I said. "I'll make you something to eat."

By the time I had eggs, toast, and tea ready for him, Scott had a fire going in the fireplace. We sat in the living room, the golden light playing around us. The dogs, confused by our middle-of-the-night wandering, had followed us downstairs, collapsing on the floor in a heap.

I sipped my ginger and lemon tea. "Talk to me, Scott. What happened?"

He stared at the fireplace, the golden light reflecting off his skin, his eyes sad. "She noticed she hadn't felt the baby move for a while, but she didn't think much of it at first." He went on, talking about the bleeding, the pain, Ethan taking her to the hospital. "Right after I got there, Amanda started hemorrhaging." He gave his head a shake, like he was trying to dislodge those images. "Blood everywhere. We rang for the nurse, and," he ran his hand over his face, "they whisked her out of there. She was terrified. Ethan and I, we stood there stunned, not knowing what to do. A nurse came in and asked us to leave so they could clean the room. We almost lost her, Jess. She almost bled to death."

"That must have been scary."

"We sat in the waiting room and drank terrible coffee. I told Ethan how much I appreciated him standing by her, that I knew she wasn't easy, and that I regretted so much about her childhood." Scott took a deep breath. "Ethan really loves her. He's a great guy. I really, really hope she's smart enough to marry him."

"So what happened with the baby?" I asked.

"Apparently, the placenta pulled away from the wall of the uterus."

Placental abruption. I'd read about that.

"That's what caused all the bleeding. They had to do an emergency C-section. They delivered a perfectly formed, tiny baby girl. She just . . . just wasn't breathing."

"Oh, Scott, I'm so sorry!" I grabbed a couple

of tissues and handed them to Scott so he could wipe away the tears filling his eyes.

He looked at me. "I shouldn't be telling you all this. It won't happen to you. It's very rare."

"I want to know. I need to know. Everything."

So he went on. "They wrapped the baby up in a little blanket so we could see her. She was just . . . perfect. Tiny hands, tiny nose. Beautiful. Ethan and I both held her as Amanda was coming out of the anesthesia. The nurse offered her to Amanda and at first Amanda said no. But then, she took her, took the baby, and she just sobbed. It broke my heart."

"I'll bet."

"The hospital staff was very kind. They didn't rush us. They gave us time to be with her—her name is Mia, by the way, Mia Cooper. Someone came in with a form to fill out, asking about releasing the body to a funeral home. I hadn't thought about any of this, and obviously, neither had Amanda. So I gave them the name of the funeral home that Nate had used with Laura." He checked his watch. "I need to go down there today and pay them and make the rest of the arrangements."

"I'll go with you."

I could tell that from his expression Scott was going to tell me no. But he obviously thought better of it. "Thank you." He stared at the fire. "There's a family burial plot up on the rise beyond the paddock. I'm going to call the county and see if we can bury her there, if it's all right with you."

"Of course."

"I'd always envisioned Amanda's baby growing up here or visiting us here. That would be a way of keeping her close."

"Would Amanda want that? Or do you think she'd just want to put all this behind her?"

"I'll ask her once she's recovered a little. We have time." He closed his eyes and shook his head. "Hey, come here," he said, gesturing as he turned sideways on the couch.

I moved toward him, and he took me in his arms. I laid my head on his chest, heard his heartbeat, felt his breathing. "She's young. She'll recover," I said.

"Physically, yes. But emotionally? She has no ballast, no keel to keep her steady. She is so smart, but man, she is all over the place emotionally."

"Who isn't a little crazy at that age? She's young, Scott. Give her time. When will she be released from the hospital? Is she coming back here?"

"She'll be in the hospital three or four days, they said. I assume she'll come here."

"I'll get things ready for her. But Scott, one thing, let her decide about the grave. That may be hard for her, having Mia here, a constant reminder."

He squeezed me gently.

28

The sun's light woke Nate the next morning just before seven. He sat up, dropped his feet over the side of the hammock, and looked at Ember. She was on her mat, tail sweeping the ground, looking at him with expectation. "Okay, girl!" he said, and she leaped to her feet and came to him, all energy and sass.

She was a pretty girl, with her deep brown eyes. Impossible to see at night, so he had a little red light he put on her collar in the dark. He stroked her head and spoke gently to her. "You were a good girl to stay in your bed. A good, good girl," he said. "Go on, now," and she did, snuffling around the empty camp.

Nate shivered in the cold. Whew! The tiny thermometer he carried read 22 degrees. He'd left his clothes in a stuff sack nearby. He quickly changed into them. The convertible, zip-off pants made it easy to get his leg on and off. Then he slid into his hiking shoes.

That was another hiker debate—boots or shoes. Boots support your ankles, but shoes are lighter. He wore boots for SAR, but because he'd be hiking such a long way and for so long every day, he'd switched to shoes for this trip. But he'd stuck with Merrell. He'd been wearing Merrells for a long time.

Alls I have to do today, he told himself, *is hike. Put one foot in front of the other. Keep goin' 'til I get there.*

He fed Ember, then made his own breakfast. The tiny Solo stove he'd bought ran on wood—twigs and sticks, really—a readily available fuel he didn't have to carry. He'd been told it would burn even when the wood was wet. He'd tried it at home and found it to be true.

So he grabbed some little pieces of wood from around the camp and fired up the stove. He boiled water in a small pot and made a cup of coffee. He boiled more, then divided it between two envelopes of instant oatmeal. Apples and cinnamon. Perfect. Enough to get him started.

He packed up, filtered water from the nearby stream, and signed his trail name, Dog Man, in the logbook at the shelter. Jeff had told him to pick a name before somebody picked one for him. So he did.

Then he whistled for Ember, and they were off. Their hike took them parallel to or actually on the Virginia Creeper Trail. "Virginia Creeper" is the name of a plant that some call a weed. The trail was a former railroad right-of-way. Where the AT and the Virginia Creeper Trail ran together, Nate kept Ember on leash. She wasn't used to dodging bikes.

And bikes did come, including groups of moms and dads with kids, whole families out for a ride.

It must be spring break for some people, Nate thought, nodding to them as they went by.

The next day, he was back on the narrow AT in the woods. He saw his first hikers around ten that morning, a couple of guys coming southbound, students from Virginia Tech out for a couple of days in the woods. They told him they had planned to hike on in to Damascus. "You'll be movin' at a right good clip," Nate said, "but you should make it."

He told them what was ahead on the trail, and they did the same for him. "See any ponies?" he asked them.

"A small herd of them, about six. They'll eat your lunch if you don't watch out," one of them said.

Nate laughed. "I'll be careful. Y'all take care now," he said, waving goodbye. He watched them as they continued down the trail. They reminded him of "his boys," the students at the community college where he worked. He missed them.

Ain't nobody makin' you do this, he told himself. *You can quit right now if you got a mind to.*

But he couldn't quit. Not really. He couldn't walk back into his "new normal" life without Laura until he'd either found God again or quit trying.

So he walked on. One foot in front of the other, day after day.

Near a bridge, Nate experienced his first "trail magic." Someone had left a small cooler full of candy bars next to the trail with a sign on top that said, TAKE ONE—OR TWO! He helped himself to a Snickers bar and stuck it in his pocket.

Jeff had told him about trail magic, the random, unexpected food gifts left for hikers, and trail angels as well—people who supported hikers in person by providing food or rides or extra clothing or even a free place to stay. Then there were the "hiker boxes," containers at hostels or other trail locations in which hikers donated clothing or gear or food they no longer needed, inviting other hikers to help themselves. A unique community had developed around the AT, people helping people enjoying the freedom of the trail.

The portion of the trail Nate was on that day was relatively flat and wide, which meant he could think about more than just navigating the ground beneath his feet. Jeff told him that once he'd found his stride, all kinds of things would bubble up in his mind. "It can set a lot of things right," Jeff had said.

Unable to get along with his father, he'd joined the Marine Corps after high-school graduation. By some miracle he'd been assigned to the military working dog unit in Texas. At first, he was just cleaning kennels and doing general maintenance. Then an aggressive, hard-headed German shepherd named Blitz arrived back from the field. Deemed unmanageable, Blitz was destined for release—or worse. Nate took to him. He didn't like it when people gave up on dogs. On his own time, he began hanging out near Blitz's kennel, then *in* Blitz's kennel.

Back home they used to say that Nate had a way with dogs. Before long, the Marine Corps found out Nate had a way with Blitz. After Nate worked with him for a couple of weeks, the dog began to relax. Wag his tail. Follow commands.

When the sergeant walked by the kennel and the formerly reactive dog didn't charge him, he asked what happened. "Private Tanner, sir," the corporal said. "Private Tanner's what happened."

At the next opportunity, Nate was made corporal and became a dog handler. He got a new dog, a Malinois trained to find explosives, and together they shipped out to Afghanistan. Rock found buried IEDs. Together, they saved many lives.

Nate didn't mind being deployed. He'd heard that Laura got married. There was nothing more at home to miss. So he did his job, walking dusty roads in front of vehicles, following his dog who was following his nose.

His service in Afghanistan ended when an RPG blew up the vehicle he was riding in, killing everyone but him, including his dog. He arrived back in the States wounded and broken.

That's when he met Peter. A double, above the

knee amp, Peter was irrepressibly cheerful and obnoxiously Christian. It was all "Jesus this" and "Jesus that" with Peter. At first, Nate hated him. What right did Peter have to be so happy?

If he could've punched Peter to shut him up he would've. Instead, Peter eventually won him over. Nate's eyes were opened, and he was born again.

Thinking about it now, walking in the woods, Nate had to smile at Peter's method. He'd sneak chocolate milkshakes into the hospital, contraband that Nate couldn't resist. Then he'd talk about Jesus while Nate's mouth was full, and he couldn't argue with him.

"Lord," Nate said out loud, remembering. "That man was one of a kind."

After a medical discharge from the Marine Corps, Nate found a job at a community college near Charlottesville. He cut grass and did general maintenance while struggling with PTSD and depression. When he admitted to his therapist that he missed working with dogs, she did some research and discovered a local volunteer organization, Battlefield Search and Rescue. Before long, Battlefield would be the latest to discover that Nathan Tanner had a way with dogs.

Learning about SAR had pulled him out of his depression. Eventually, he got a dog named Maggie, then Sprite. Sprite was a cheerful pup, small enough that he could take her places, including work. Soon, she was riding with Nate on the big mowers, then accompanying him to inside job sites. The kids at the college started calling him the Dog Man, joking with him while they played with his dog. Dogs build bridges, Nate learned.

"Ah, I miss you, Sprite!" he said out loud. He stopped and took a long drink out of his water bottle. Maybe he'd been wrong to leave her. Maybe he should get Jeff to bring her next time he came. "Nah," he quickly realized. "That'd be selfish. This hike would kill her." Sprite was better off with Scott and Jess.

Jess. Jess, who'd tracked down Laura and brought her back into his life. "She's a nosy rascal," Nate said out loud. She'd seen Laura's picture in his wallet and started asking questions. Then, when he'd lost his leg, she'd found Laura, and Scott had brought her from western Virginia as a surprise.

Jess. Stubbornly agnostic. Hard-headed. Argumentative. And deeply wounded. He'd picked up on that pretty quick.

That girl's come a long way, he mused, and it struck him that only a Great Love could change a person the way Jess had been changed. That made him pause. Think.

Then he moved on.

He knew he'd offended her. He'd hurt her, not responding to her after Laura died, walling himself off. Truth was he just couldn't deal with the emotional torrent that talking to her would release in him. And he especially didn't want to upset her. She'd been wanting a baby since she and Scott got married. Now was not the time for her to be bearing other's burdens, especially not his.

So he'd avoided her. And hoped she'd understand. But he suspected she didn't. She was persistent, that one.

By the fourth day into his hike, Nate had worked out a system. Wake up at dawn, feed Ember, eat, pack up, hike until lunchtime. Stop. Check and clean his stump. Walk again until he'd reached his goal for the day. Set up camp. Check his stump and his one remaining foot for blisters. Feed Ember. Eat dinner. Be in bed by "hiker midnight," about 8:30.

On the fifth day, Nate stood next to a rustic wood fence in Grayson Highlands State Park, staring at the view, one blue mountain ridge after another stretching into the distance. The beauty took his breath away.

They were old, these mountains, the oldest on the planet according to geologists. They'd been home to generation after generation of Tanners, including him. Looking at them he felt grounded.

Unlike the sharp-peaked Rockies, the Appalachian Mountains were rounded at the top, folded, worn down by years and years of rainfall and snow and rock-splitting ice. They looked friendly, like a person could get lost in them and still live. Which was kind of what he was doing now with the help of some freeze-dried food and Jeff.

Nate dug his phone out of his pack and took a picture. He wanted to remember this place. There was something here that touched his heart—something he couldn't quite grasp. Maybe later it would come to him.

After one more long look, he called Ember and walked on. The trail had taken him up past the tree line into the rocky meadows—called "balds"—at the top of the mountain. This is where the ponies lived. Blight had killed all the native chestnut trees, leaving these rocky mountaintops. Farmers used to graze cattle on the balds. After the farms became a park, someone had introduced the ponies to keep the brush down. Small and sturdy, the ponies were only partly wild. In fact, they could be downright pushy when hikers had something tasty to eat.

Nate saw Ember alert, her head raising and her ears pricking up, and he put her on leash. Moments later, they came across a small herd, some solid, some brown and white. A few mommas and their babies, and one small stallion stood apart, watching. Nate ignored them, curious to see what the ponies would do.

Sure enough, a brown-and-white mare fell into step behind them, probably hoping for a handout. "You'd love this, wouldn't you?" Nate said, an image of Laura in his head. "I'd have a hard time makin' sure you didn't try to sneak one in the truck." He grinned, thinking about it.

He realized a few minutes later that was the first time he'd smiled thinking about Laura since she died. "Oh, Lord," he said reflexively, but the rest of that prayer got stuck in his throat.

He met Jeff at the parking lot in the late afternoon and they drove into town. Nate was going to take a zero the next day, so he got a hotel room. While Jeff checked his prosthesis, Nate took a shower. Jeff had brought the clean clothes Nate had packed ahead of time, along with a fresh supply of food. Once Nate had showered, Jeff checked his stump. "It looks great," he said. "How's it feel?"

"Pretty good. Being able to zip those pants legs off and clean it midday helps, and the new stump socks fit good. I think it's doing okay!"

"You want to keep hiking?"

"Yessir, I do. It's been good for me."

"Did you fall yet?"

"Nope."

"You sleeping okay?"

"Man, that hammock is perfect."

"How's the depression?"

Nate shook his head. "When I saw the ponies up there, I couldn't help but think about my wife. But I smiled when I did. There was a joy in it. I ain't felt that since she died."

"Good." Jeff grinned. "I told you, hiking is a good tonic."

"That it is."

"You want to meet again in five days?"

"Let's make it seven. You don't need to be runnin' up and down 81 for me all the time."

"Seven? You sure?"

"Yessir, I am. I'll call if I need you sooner. I appreciate all you done for me, Jeff. Especially telling me to take a hike." He grinned. "That ain't the first time I been told that, but at least you meant well by it."

Jeff laughed. "We'll make it seven days then. But call me if you have any trouble, okay?"

"I will." Nate looked at his watch. "Can I buy you dinner?"

"No, man. I got to drive back tonight. Can I drop you at a restaurant?"

"There's one right here. I'll be fine."

Jeff gave Nate a quick hug and patted Ember. "I'll see you in a week!"

"Right."

29

Following the loss of Baby Mia, Scott and I were all about helping Amanda, or trying to. Understandably, she was an emotional wreck, angry one minute, sad the next. Released from the hospital, she came to our house to recover from the C-section. She was in a lot of pain and had trouble sleeping.

When she first got to our house, she told Scott he could do what he wanted with the body—she didn't care. We knew that wasn't true, but we didn't argue. She didn't want to deal with a funeral or even the funeral home, she said. So Scott did it all.

Scott got permission from the county to bury the baby at our farm. He hired a couple of neighbors to dig the grave. Together we picked out a little white casket. By that time a week had gone by, so he approached Amanda again and she agreed to the burial and said she would attend as long as no one else was there but us. "No ministers!" she said, emphasizing her words.

I told Kathryn all this when she called. "She's so resistant!" I said.

"You and Scott are doing the right thing," she replied. "This isn't the time to try to convince her that God loves her."

"I know," I said, sighing. I often heard some of Nate's wisdom in Kathryn, and I wondered about her story. When did she come to faith? How? Was she one of those people raised in the church, who couldn't remember not knowing Jesus?

I'd told her we were burying the baby at the farm in two days. She thought that was sweet and volunteered to help if she could. "I think we'll be fine," I said.

The April day was sunny and cool. Ethan drove Amanda across the field and up to the little graveyard in his truck. Scott had positioned a chair so Amanda could sit. Daffodils planted long ago by some other mourner nodded their cheerful yellow heads. A tiny white coffin rested beside the red earth grave.

Scott said a few words, exactly what I don't know because I was fighting to keep myself together. That casket was so small! That baby should have grown up to be wearing a little white dress at Easter. Instead, she lay in a white box. Sorrow filled me, sorrow for Amanda and for Ethan and for Scott. I automatically put my hand on my belly as if I could protect Baby Cooper— and myself—from grief.

Scott prayed a short, simple prayer. He was taking a risk that Amanda would protest, but good for him. He needed to recognize God there at that little grave, and I needed it, too, even if it did irritate Amanda. That was Scott. He was who he was.

Amanda, dressed in her robe, her long blonde hair blowing in the breeze, watched as Scott and Ethan lowered the casket into the grave. I wanted to put my arm around her or take her hand, anything to show support for her, but a glance from her fended me off.

Tears blurred my eyes. Two deaths in such a short time. First Laura, now little Mia. Laura's death had blown up Nate's life as effectively as the RPG that ended his service in Afghanistan. Now, what would happen to Amanda? She didn't have the maturity or faith that Nate had. How would she cope? I felt a shiver of concern run through me.

I wanted to talk to Nate. Old Nate. I wanted to ask him why Amanda's baby had to die while mine lived on. Why Scott had to go through this loss. How I could help Amanda. I wanted to know that God was right here right now, entering into this suffering with us, the way Nate promised me that he was, as our omnipresent, immanent God. I wanted to ask what happened to babies who die. Where do they go?

But Old Nate was gone, carried off by grief. And I wasn't sure I'd ever get him back.

When Scott was finished he brushed off his hands and walked over to us. "Ethan's going to take Amanda back to the house."

"I'll go back, too," I said.

So I walked past the nodding daffodils, out of the old iron gate, and down the small rise, following Ethan's truck with Amanda in the passenger seat. Behind me, Scott had stayed and was covering that little casket with dirt. Such finality.

As I neared the house, I was surprised to see Kathryn's blue Forester parked out front. I went inside and found she'd prepared a meal for us. There was a breakfast casserole in the oven, soup on the stove, the fixings for sandwiches on the table. A beautiful brunch spread. "I wanted to do something for you all," she explained.

I gave her a long hug. "Thank you."

"Amanda," she said, "can I get you some tea?"

"Yes, thank you."

"Go in the living room," I said. "Take the recliner. We'll bring it to you."

"How'd she do?" Kathryn asked in a low voice when Amanda had left.

"Stone-silent."

"Why don't we go sit with Amanda?" Kathryn suggested. "Tea?"

"Sure."

Sitting in Scott's recliner, with the two of us on the couch, Amanda suddenly opened up. "I didn't know her," Amanda said. "I mean, it wasn't like she was two or three and we had a relationship." She shrugged. "It's no big deal."

I bit my lip.

"I don't know why Dad's doing all this. The casket, the funeral, burying the body here. It's not like she was a real person."

Oh, but she was.

"I mean, I didn't even know if she was a boy or a girl. I didn't even *want* to know."

I fought to keep my mouth shut. I knew what it was to have a baby growing inside you, to imagine its future from the moment you realized you were pregnant, to anticipate a stream of birthdays, to feel baby kicks and baby hiccups, to have your body taken over by this little one, to give your body willingly so another could have life. You *do* know that child, no matter what Amanda claimed. She knew her baby on some level, and now she had the hard job of grieving her—or she could live in denial.

Ethan came in. He'd gone back to help Scott finish up. He stood, looking awkwardly at us gathered around Amanda. "Your dad will be here in a few minutes." Amanda didn't respond.

I took that as my cue to leave. "Thanks, Ethan." I glanced at Kathryn, who got the message.

"We'll be in the kitchen," she said. "If you need anything, just yell."

"I need a little break," I whispered to Kathryn. "I'll be back down to help you in a few minutes."

She nodded. I walked upstairs, my heart heavy, my hand gripping the dark wood banister. Both dogs followed me. "Wait," I said to them, holding out my hand in a "stop" signal in the hallway. I went into the baby's nursery and closed the door.

I sat down in the oak rocker. I could see the dogs sniffing under the door, trying to figure out what I was doing. Then I heard a heavy thump as Luke laid down.

I pulled out my cell phone. My eyes lifted up to the cowboy art print. I rocked back and forth slowly, thinking.

I didn't care what anyone said, or even if he responded, I needed to text Nate. I would choose my words carefully, but I needed to tell him. To ask him my questions. To touch base with my friend, my spiritual mentor.

And so I did. I wrote a long text about Amanda and the baby and Scott and all of my why questions and then about him and my concerns for him. In the end, I told him I was trusting God to honor his promises, to finish the work he'd begun in him, to never leave him or forsake him. Then I clicked off my phone and let the tears come.

Scott found me, no doubt cued by the dogs lying outside the nursery door. We had a little moment together, both of us emotional. Then I hiked up my big girl pants, took my focus off myself, and I told Scott I thought he'd done a wonderful job with the whole burial, honoring Mia, honoring life. "Loving and strong" is the way I described him. And he was. Is.

"I was looking forward to that baby," he said softly.

"I know you were."

"I was hoping the baby would help Amanda settle down, find some stability . . ." His voice trailed off.

"She's still young, Scott."

"I know."

"She's had a lot of trauma."

"And this is one more big one. I just don't know what else I can do for her," he said.

My eyes searched his face. "None of this was your fault."

"If I had just—"

"Stop," I said. "What happened, happened. Let it go. You've been there for her these last few years. Now let the rest of it go."

He hesitated.

"You have limited agency, Scott," I said, repeating words back to him that he'd spoken to me. "Leave it to God."

He took me in his arms again. "I love you."

As we stood there together, our breathing synchronous, our bodies warm, I realized I never wanted anything to come between us, to break this love. I looked up at Scott. "I texted Nate."

He raised his eyebrows.

"I had to. I just needed to tell him what happened."

"Did he respond?"

"I just sent it, just now. At the funeral, I was standing there wondering why her? Why not me? I'm so used to talking to him about those things."

Scott nodded.

"Even if he doesn't text back, I just . . . just had to tell him what was going on."

"I get that."

There was more. "I figured out about where he is."

"What?"

"I got an Appalachian Trail Guide. I figured out that a lot of hikers can do fifteen or twenty miles a day, but I'm guessing Nate will do eight, maybe ten, if that. So yeah, I know about where he is."

To my relief, Scott grinned. "You are persistent. He said you would be." He kissed me. "Promise me you won't try to find him."

I closed my eyes and pressed my lips together. That was exactly what I was thinking of doing. "I could take him food," I suggested.

"He has people for that."

"We could both hike with him for a day."

"He wants to be alone."

"But . . ."

Scott gently touched my lips with his finger. "All you can do is pray. I'm sure he'd appreciate that."

30

After a couple of weeks on the trail, Nate could feel his body growing stronger. Some days he found himself walking down a narrow path through high, grassy meadows. Other days the trail took him over forested rocky paths. Sometimes it was wide and easy and other times it was a trace. He followed white blazes across creeks and up through boulder fields. Because he couldn't feel his footing with his left leg he had to watch where he was stepping. Once, that made him miss a turn. When he ended up at an impenetrable mass of rhododendron bushes, he realized his mistake.

His trekking poles helped him maintain balance and find his footing, especially as he crossed streams. Despite the poles, he'd fallen once, tripping over a protruding rock. Sprawled out on the path, Ember had rushed over to him and licked his ear, which was about the only first-aid skill she had. He'd managed to get up, suffering only a couple of bruises and a scraped hand. He was thankful for that.

A couple of groups of northbound thru-hikers had overtaken him the second week. He'd hiked with one bunch for a little while, but his pace was too slow for them, and they were soon on their way. He'd had lunch with another group, three men and a woman. A couple of times, he'd camped near a shelter with a bunch of rowdy young men. He ignored them, reminding himself he would have been just like that in his early twenties.

One time, though, a bunch of kids camping near him got really drunk. They were loud. He heard glass breaking. They had a fire in a pit that roared high into the sky.

He couldn't sleep. Anger filled his heart. Why did they think getting crazy drunk was funny? Did they know? Didn't they realize what could happen?

He thought about going over there, lecturing them about alcohol. Telling them how stupid they were being. Getting drunk like that, they could kill somebody. Somebody like Laura. Maybe not here in the woods, but somewhere.

He got up. Looked over to where their fire was. There were a bunch of them. He counted nine. All young men.

He checked his watch. 3:20 a.m. These were clearly not hikers.

He pulled on his clothes. Laced up his hiking shoes. Ember watched him carefully. He told her to stay and started to walk over to them. She whined.

The sound stopped him. He was alone. No backup. No weapon. Nine young men, roaring drunk, versus him with a dog who was trained not to be aggressive.

Common sense prevailed. Forget it.

He turned, packed up his gear, and quietly left.

Nate hiked, his headlamp his only light, for several hours. After a difficult climb, he got to an overlook, ready to rest.

He was just in time to watch the sunrise. He sat down on a rock, Ember next to him, as black turned to gray and gray became blue. The sky was undercast—clouds lay below him like a white comforter, settling in the valleys and covering the lower hills.

The beauty of it settled his heart. It took his breath away. "He is coming with the clouds," Nate said, reciting Revelation 1:7 from memory, "and every eye will see him, even those who pierced him." Reacting to his voice, Ember licked his ear, then she laid down next to him, resting her head on his leg. As a pink light appeared in the eastern sky, he stroked his dog, breathed slowly, and let the beauty of dawn bathe his soul.

Soon the sun's rays pierced the horizon like javelins, turning the clouds golden. Nate felt the warmth on his face. His eyes watered. "Lord, if I could be with you right now, I would. I'd wanted to go with Laura to that appointment, remember? She didn't want me to. Said it was no big deal.

So I stayed. I stayed, and she died, in that little car. Because of a drunk.

"Lord, last night I couldn't sleep. Those boys, they kept me awake. So drunk. Rowdy. Laughin' like they were so clever. And I laid there in my hammock listnin' to them, gettin' madder 'n madder.

"It was a drunk killed my Laura. And I'm 'sposed to forgive him. Forgive him? Are you kidding?"

Nate sat there, Ember's coat smooth under his hand. The sun rose higher, its rays heating his chest. It began melting away the clouds hanging below him. "I think that drunk driver's what's got me tied up, Lord. That's what's got me wrapped around the axle. I'm so angry."

He sat silently watching the birth of the day, the rock cold beneath him, the sun warm on his face. Ember whined, breaking the spell. "Time to get up," he said. "Let's go." He scooted backward until he found a way to boost himself to his feet. Safely back from the cliff, he shouldered his pack, looked up, found the white trail blaze, and moved on.

Blaze to blaze, one day at a time.

31

Five weeks after Amanda lost her baby, I entered into my third trimester. My hips hurt. I was definitely more tired. My belly was for sure bigger. I'd noticed I'd started dropping things as my joints loosened, preparing for childbirth.

I decided I needed to wrap up my PI cases and not take on anything other than easy background checks for a while. Limit my search-and-rescue activities.

Scott and I would start baby classes before long. He had his dissertation to defend. That was coming up fast, next week! And we were still supporting Amanda, who was trying to finish her semester at UVA, and caring for two dogs and four horses. Plus, we'd gotten two kittens to keep the mice population in the barn down. One was black and white, and the other was solid gray. Watching them play brought moments of joy in a bleak time.

There was one loose end in Harrisonburg I had not yet tied up. I'd hesitated bringing it up because of the sorrow in our house over the loss of Baby Mia. I knew Scott wouldn't want me to leave again. But it was now or never in my opinion. I wasn't going to get less pregnant until the baby was born, and then, well, I'd have a baby. God willing.

Scott stood silently while I explained what I

wanted to do. I braced myself for his objections. But he took a deep breath and said, "Two days?"

I nodded.

"And you'll have an officer with you?"

"Yes. I'll ask for one, anyway. I'm pretty sure Detective Porter will give me someone."

"I don't want you doing it without an officer."

"I understand."

"I can't miss next week."

The defense of his doctorate. "I know."

"And I still have a lot of prep to do."

"I'll make some meals ahead of time so all you have to do is microwave what you want to eat. I'll have Luke with me. I can find a place to board Sprite if you want me to."

He shook his head. "No, she's no trouble."

"So it's just the horses."

"And missing you."

I took a deep breath and nodded. "I'd just like to get this done before I get any bigger. And I want to be there when you make your defense and get your degree. You're amazing, Scott, all you've been through and here you are, getting your doctorate on top of it. I'm so proud of you."

He took me in his arms. "Just don't get hurt, okay? We don't need more stress."

"I promise."

I spent the rest of that day making meals for Scott and getting my SAR pack ready. I lightened it as much as possible. I was already carrying nearly twenty extra pounds of baby weight, and I didn't need to stress my joints more or hurt my back or have a fall because my balance was off.

The next day I loaded up Luke and we drove over the mountains to Harrisonburg. Robert Porter was more than happy to loan me an officer. In fact, when he told Jason what I was proposing, he volunteered to be my escort.

This was my thought: Julia Whitaker's abductor knew about that remote camp and its bathroom. I wondered if he could have abducted Heather Burgess as well? And if he'd killed her, could her body be there?

Luke was cross-trained for both live finds and human remains detection. That is rare, but as I've already told you, Luke is exceptional. My mission for today, then, was to have Luke search that old camp and see if we could find human remains.

As I crossed over the mountains on Route 33, the trees still looked bare. Third week of April is when the trees usually leaf out, but I could tell they were running a little late this year. At Swift Run Gap, the road crossed the Appalachian Trail and I thought of Nate. He was well south of there, I knew. At two miles per hour (at best) it would take him weeks and weeks to get to this point.

I got a sick feeling in the pit of my stomach just thinking about what he was doing. I could do nothing about it, as Scott said, but pray. So I did, out loud, for my friend.

I was meeting Jason at the police station in Harrisonburg. I walked in and the desk sergeant waved me back to the bullpen near Porter's office. Jason rose from his desk as I walked in. Porter came out when he heard us talking.

"How are you feeling?" he asked me, glancing at my belly.

"Just a little tired. Otherwise, doing okay." I changed the subject. "Say, did you get any physical evidence in Julia's case?"

"Hairs and fibers. No fingerprints or DNA. Not yet, anyway. They're still going over her clothes."

"Have you made any progress on identifying the car?"

"We think those plates were stolen."

I nodded. "I promised my husband I'd be home tomorrow, so Jason, if you're ready, why don't we get on with this?"

"Fine by me."

"Did you get those topographic maps?"

"Sure did."

"Okay," Porter said. "Good luck you two."

We would start our search at the old campground. I wanted to drive my Jeep over because it had Luke's crate and my SAR stuff in it. Jason thought it would be a good idea to have a marked police car visible. So we caravanned.

The lane leading to the camp was even messier than the first time we saw it. No doubt all the police vehicles going in and out had added new ruts. This time, though, we crossed the creek and drove all the way up to where the restroom was.

Luke was beyond excited when I dressed him in his SAR vest. Finally, he got to work! "Let's start at the restroom, then work our way around the cabins. Then I'll figure out our next move after that. I'm giving him the command, 'F-i-n-d it,' which is the signal he's looking for human remains. So he may be moving slower than you've seen him before, and we'll just follow quietly and let him do his thing." I gave Jason the handheld GPS and told him how to use it. He was looking at me like something was bothering him. "What?" I asked.

"Why are you carrying that pack?"

"It's . . . it's what I do. Part of the outfit."

"Why don't I carry it?"

I stared at him like he'd just suggested searching barefoot.

"You're pregnant. I'm not. We'll be together the whole time. Let me carry the pack," he repeated.

I felt my face grow hot. Then I slipped the backpack off and handed it to him. "Thank you."

Freed from that burden, I walked Luke over to the restroom, made him sit at heel. When he was settled and looking at me, I gave him the signal and said, "Find it!"

He leaped to his feet and slowly sniffed around the restroom area. I trusted him to know what he was looking for, not squirrels, not mice, not raccoons or possums, but that distinctive smell of human remains. This was a game to him, and when and if he found that smell, we would play, play, play.

While he was using his nose, I was using my brain. Heather Burgess weighed about a hundred and thirty pounds. Carrying that much dead weight through the woods would be a difficult task. If the perpetrator killed her and brought her body here, in all likelihood she'd be buried near to where a car could be parked.

On the other hand, the first body Luke ever found was a young woman murdered and placed in the middle of the woods. The perpetrator was a big guy, a wood cutter, unusually strong.

Julia said the man who abducted her seemed older. He walked with a limp and was heavy set. Would a guy like that be able to carry a body any distance at all?

I watched my dog sniff an area in the middle of what would have been the parking area. He sniffed, went on, and returned to sniff again. Then he looked at me as if to say, *I thought I smelled something, but I didn't.*

"Good boy. Find it!"

We went on, across the clearing, and up to the cabins, Luke working methodically, Jason following us. After two hours we took a break. I gave Luke a snack and let him chew on a bone for a little while. Jason wandered off. I could see he was talking on his cell phone, and I could imagine he was bored. When he came back, though, the expression on his face told me he had found something. "There's another set of cabins over there, beyond that mess."

I looked toward where he was pointing. I saw several fallen trees, a tangle of vines, and heavy underbrush.

"I think we can get to them by going around this way," he gestured toward the right.

"All right. We're ready."

Baby Cooper thumped his approval. He was ready for me to stand up. *You're cantaloupe-size,* I thought. *Not all that big. Quit hogging my body.* I smiled and touched my belly as I stood up.

"You okay?" Jason asked.

"Yes. The baby's just thumping me."

"That's the coolest thing," Jason said, grinning. "I remember that from my wife's pregnancies."

It's cool 'til they want to get out, I thought, but I didn't say anything. I didn't want to hear any delivery stories right now.

We made our way back to the hidden cabins, stepping through brambles and scraping past the thick undergrowth. I caught my foot on an anchored wild blackberry runner and started to fall, but Jason grabbed my arm. "Thank you," I said, my heart pounding.

After that, he stayed close. We got to the cabins, which were overgrown with vines and bushes, and I asked Luke to "find it." He worked hard, but after another couple of hours, Jason and I mutually decided it was enough for the day. We walked back to our cars. I played with Luke a little, then we parted company.

I second-guessed myself all that evening. I called Scott, and he reassured me. "Nate says you and Luke are the best SAR team he's ever seen. Trust your instincts, babe."

I love that man. But I still didn't sleep well. Was I crazy to think there was a link between these cases?

32

After a restless night, I rose before dawn, fed Luke and took him out. I'd forgotten to bring his hotel crate with me, so I put him in the Jeep and went to breakfast. I was hungry but couldn't eat much. I had a few bites of scrambled egg, then grabbed a couple of yogurts and granola bars, jammed them in my pockets, and left.

I got to the small road leading to the camp as the sun was coming up. Jason and I had agreed to meet at seven. It was now 6:40. The sun would be up in ten minutes. Did I dare go into the campground on my own?

Scott said I should have an officer with me. Okay, I would, in just a few minutes. If I didn't drive into the camp, I'd just be sitting out here on the road by myself. Was that really any safer? In fact, wouldn't being in the camp out of sight be safer?

I'm very good at rationalizing what I want to do.

I turned into the lane leading to the camp. I drove down slowly, alert for any sign of human activity. I bounced over the creek, water splashing on my Jeep, and kept creeping forward. My headlights caught a glint of metal ahead. I jammed on my brakes. I moved slowly. Then I saw the word POLICE.

Jason had beaten me to the scene.

I took a deep breath, parked, and got out. "You're here early," I said brightly.

"I had a feeling you would be," he said, grinning.

Am I that predictable?

I let Luke out, then pulled the map out and placed it on the hood of my Jeep. Last night in the hotel, I'd highlighted the boundaries of the area I wanted to search today. "Take a look at this, Jason. Tell me what you think."

He bent over the map, then looked up at me. "It's good. Although to be honest, it all looks the same to me. Woods. Bushes. Fallen trees. Brambles. Creek. And a pregnant lady and her dog." He grinned at me.

"And a guy who's doing his best to hide his skepticism," I retorted.

Jason laughed. "I'll follow you, ma'am. Wherever you want to go. You're the boss."

"No, this guy here is the boss." I patted my belly. "C'mon, Luke."

I walked to the back of the Jeep, grabbed my pack, and put Luke's vest on. Jason followed me, shouldering my backpack as he had the day before. I moved to the edge of Cabin #4, made Luke sit, then told him to "Find it!"

We were searching the area behind Cabin 4 today, working our way up the mountain, then down to the creek. I was puffing as we climbed.

Baby Cooper really was making this tough. At some point, I decided it was highly unlikely that someone trying to hide a body would go up this far, not with all the other more easily accessible places available. So we made a turn, angling down toward the creek.

The wind was different today, coming from the northwest. I could feel the chill. Luke ranged a little farther afield than he had yesterday, still nose to the ground, sniffing. We got to the small creek. Jason helped me cross. As I got to the other side, I looked up and saw something, a pattern in the trees that looked different. "Jason, look."

"What's up?" He looked the direction I was pointing upstream.

"Could this be an old path? Do you see how the trees aren't random? They're about eight feet apart, side to side, following the creek."

He frowned. He moved to see it from a different angle. "You could be right. There's a lot of underbrush, though, growing in that space."

"But it's all weeds. Nothing woody, like rhododendron. Let's walk up there." I called Luke back. Made him sit. Then I gestured in the direction of that opening and said, "Find it!"

We followed him, Jason and I, both of us looking intently at the path. Had it been used recently? Were there ruts? Evidence of human activity?

My eyes were so focused on the forest floor in

front of me that I didn't notice that Luke hadn't checked in for a while. I heard a single, loud bark. My head jerked up. A hundred feet ahead of us, near a large tree right next to the creek, Luke lay quietly, looking at me, his tail wagging in anticipation.

His indication. He'd found human remains.

I walked forward, dreading what I was about to see. I pulled the collar of my coat over my nose against the smell.

The body, what was left of it, was slumped up against the base of the tree. I identified a tangle of dark brown hair, a blue North Face jacket, and a pair of L.L.Bean Duck Boots. Exactly what Heather Burgess was wearing when she disappeared. Then, on the forest floor, I saw it—a small silver Tree of Life earring.

I couldn't help it. I began to feel dizzy. Sick to my stomach. I'd seen bodies before, many times, but this one got to me. I turned away.

Jason was on his cell phone calling it in. I walked as far as I could, grabbed hold of a tree, and threw up.

My dog came up behind me and nudged me, looking for his reward. I remembered his toy was in my backpack, with Jason.

I could not go back. I picked up a stick. "Good boy, Luke, good, good boy." He went along with me, accepting this odd reward, retrieving the stick, tail wagging, while I tried hard not to gag.

"Are you okay?" Jason said.

I jumped. He was right behind me. "I think so." Embarrassment made my cheeks hot.

"Were you sick?"

I nodded.

"It's because of the pregnancy," he said. "My wife couldn't stand the smell of garlic when she was pregnant. She'd throw up every time I brought home pizza." He paused. "The boss is on the way, along with the techs and the chief of police. Good job, by the way. Your instincts were right on." He paused. "Why don't you go sit down in your car? Sip a little water. I'll play with the dog."

Why not? Everything else about this was unconventional.

Detective Porter was blown away that we'd found her. I found my little jar of Vicks in my pack. I dabbed some under my nose to mask the smell of human remains and walked over to the body with him. I hoped against hope I wouldn't get nauseated again. Jason had put crime scene tape around the body. Porter moved inside the tape, squatted next to her, and made notes in his little book.

He stepped back when the forensic team arrived and came over to where I was standing. I was mindlessly petting Luke, scratching him behind his ears. Maybe I was hoping he'd anchor me.

"Good job, buddy," Porter said, petting my dog.

He straightened up and looked at me. "You did it. Amazing."

"Now all you need to do is figure out who this guy is," I said, "before another young woman gets hurt."

He shook his head. "I thought Harrisonburg would be a quiet job!"

"All it takes is one."

"Have you worked serial killer cases before?"

I paused, wondering how much I should reveal. "One. My husband knows a lot more about them. You should pick his brain."

He nodded. "I'd like to do that."

I told him about Scott's upcoming dissertation defense. "He's focused on that right now, but why don't you call him? I'll text you his number."

Robert started to turn away then looked at me again. "Do we draw straws for who tells her parents after we have positive ID?"

"You tell them. I'll call them after you break the news."

An hour later, I checked out of the hotel and headed home. I felt oddly emotional. I should have been elated that my hunch had panned out. Instead, I felt sad. Heather Burgess was dead, her bones scattered by animals. Two parents had lost their daughter, a brother had lost his sister. And a human hunter could still be prowling around the community, looking for a young woman in a moment of vulnerability.

It made me sick.

Swift Run Gap. The sign marked the place the road I was on crossed the Appalachian Trail. *Nate.* I took a deep breath.

There are lots of ways to die that we can't control: cancer, heart failure, random car accidents, murder. Why did Nate have to take this unnecessary risk?

People call me a risk-taker. Scott says I drive him crazy. But when I thought about it, most of the risks I'd taken had to do with protecting someone, like the cop being assaulted on the side of the road. Or Scott himself, after he'd been shot.

Except for that incident when I was running alone in the mountains and that man showed up.

Sigh.

Look, I told myself, *none of us like to be bubble-wrapped. Everyone takes risks. Even driving is a risk. So Nate's taking a risk. Big deal.*

But it was a big deal. All I could do was pray.

33

Nate met Jeff, resupplied, rested, and kept going. The trail took him up west a good ways. The mountains stretched on. Day after day he walked, six miles one day, eight miles the next. Ten. One day, after a tough climb he got to Burke's Garden Overlook, a beautiful spot with a view of an unusual valley, a bowl surrounded by ridges.

He'd read about it before he left for this trip. Geologists say the valley was formed when the dome of the original mountain eroded more quickly than the lower parts. The mountain essentially collapsed in on itself. The ridges, the one he was standing on and the others that formed the ring around the bowl, remained. People called Burke's Garden, "God's Thumbprint."

He stood looking, his heart swelling as he took in the view. Field after field stretched into the distance, some plowed and brown, some green. At the lower elevations, the trees were budding. He found himself talking to God. "Well, that ain't no Valley of the Shadow of Death, Lord. It's broad and beautiful, a valley of life. A place of peace. I can see your hand in it, see why they call it God's Thumbprint. It's like you were signing a painting, a beautiful piece of art, with your thumb. All this," he gestured toward the mountains rimming the valley and the hills beyond, "all this is awesome." He stopped talking and took a deep breath as if he could draw the beauty in.

Ember nudged his leg. He looked down and saw she was staring at something. He followed her gaze. A regal stag stood motionless at the edge of the woods, not more than twenty yards away. His antlers, which Nate knew were shed every winter, were just beginning to regrow. His coat, a beautiful shade of tan, glistened in the sun. His ears flicked and he looked toward Nate. Their eyes met. "He makes my feet like hinds' feet, and he makes me walk upon high places," Nate whispered, his eyes fixed on the deer.

Ember nudged him again. "No," Nate said, rubbing behind her ear. "Leave it. No need to chase that boy. Leave it." She huffed and laid down at his feet, resigned. "Good girl." He looked up again, and the deer dashed off with a flash of his white tail.

"God, thank you," Nate whispered. It was a prayer born of habit, but it ticked a little box in his soul.

He stayed that night next to Chestnut Knob shelter, a former fire warden's cabin with plexiglass windows. He slept outside, in his hammock, rather than use the shelter. He'd gotten used to it by now, and Ember was well-settled.

The sky put on a show. Clear and black, it

made a perfect backdrop for the Milky Way. "The heavens are telling the Glory of God," Nate said. He had to laugh at himself. There was so much of the Word written on the walls of his mind, he might not be able to feel God, but he couldn't get away from his Word if he tried.

Later, lying in his hammock, he realized he'd reached two milestones. He'd hiked a hundred miles on the AT, and for the first time in months he'd laughed.

The next day, the trail took Nate on the ridges around God's Thumbprint. He left the trail at VA 623 short of his eight-mile daily goal and hiked down into the valley. He'd read about an Amish general store where he could resupply and camp the night, and about Mattie's Place where he could get some food. Real food. Real food sounded real good.

Sitting on the porch at Mattie's Place eating a homemade ham sandwich on sourdough bread, he realized he'd missed seeing people. He'd bought a hamburger for Ember and two cinnamon rolls for dessert for himself. Together they feasted and were satisfied.

Nate was sitting there enjoying a fresh cup of coffee when three hikers came out of the store, two men and a woman. "Aww, what a pretty dog!" the woman said, and she bent down to pet her. "What's her name?"

"Ember."

"Hello, Ember. I'm Butterfly," she crooned.

That fits, Nate thought. A wispy blonde, she had high cheekbones and bright blue eyes. She didn't look strong enough to carry a pack, but she had one on.

She looked up at Nate. "What's your name?"

"I'm the Dog Man," Nate said.

She laughed, a fluttery kind of giggle. "These guys are Rocky and Bot Fly. We've been hiking together for three weeks."

"Is that right?" Nate tried to imagine what all that entailed. Were they just friends? Sleeping together? Taking care of each other? The trail was kind of a free-for-all and some folks, well, they took it more freely than others.

She plopped down in the chair next to Nate. "So what's your story?"

That took him aback. He wasn't exactly sure how to answer. So he opted for honesty. "My wife, Laura, died. I didn't want to stay in our house by myself no more. Had to get out."

Butterfly put her hand on his arm. "Oh, I'm sorry." She gave him a gentle squeeze. "Who are you hiking with?"

Nate gestured. "Ember."

"Well you can hike with us, right guys?"

The two men looked up, but they hadn't been paying attention and they had no idea what she'd just said. Before they could answer, Nate responded, "I'm sure that'd be a fine time but I cain't do that. I go too slow for you."

Butterfly frowned. "Really? We're only doing fifteen or so miles a day. What's your goal?"

"Eight. If I do eight I'm makin' good time."

"Eight? Oh." Butterfly looked crestfallen. Then she thought of something and brightened up. "Well, look for Calculator coming up behind you. He's tall, thin, wears glasses. He's an accountant. His wife died eight months ago. That's why he's on the trail. You guys can hike together!"

Nate smiled. "Thank you. I'll look for him."

"You shouldn't be alone, Pops."

Pops. That was a new one.

"You coming?" The taller of the two men stood over Butterfly.

"I'm ready!" She jumped up out of her seat. "Bye!" she said to Nate, and with that she was off.

Nate watched the three of them walk up the hill. He wondered about the girl, if she was okay, if the guys were taking advantage of her, or if they were acting honorably. Did she know how to protect herself emotionally and physically?

The attitudes of young people these days were all over the place. Some thought casual sex was as normal as eating. Others, well, they took a higher view. A lot of guys would take whatever they could get from a young woman. A lot of women would give it, not realizing the consequences.

Each man did what was right in his own eyes.

Ember whined, interrupting his thinking. Nate scratched her ears. "You ain't used to just sitting. You want to play?" Of course she did.

34

I arrived home, tired and a little down. But when I approached the house, I saw something that lifted my spirits. Scott's Suburban was not parked where it usually was. In its place, I saw a black Honda Odyssey. A mom van. With a new-car sticker in the side window.

Seriously? I parked my Jeep and let Luke out. Scott came striding out of the house. "What's this?" I asked.

He kissed me hello. "For you, if you like it."

"Are you kidding?"

"Here, check it out." He handed me a key fob.

I opened the car and sat in the driver's seat. Checked out the rear cargo area. Looked in the back, where the baby seat would go.

Scott narrated the inspection. "It's got all kinds of safety features. Blind spot detection, backup camera, lane departure warning, a large display screen. Plus leather seats and a DVD player."

"Room for a crate?"

"For sure. And more. And it drives really well."

"I like it."

"Want to take it for a spin after dinner?"

"Yes, but how'd you get this?"

"It's ours for twenty-four hours. If we like it, we keep it."

"In exchange for . . ."

"I traded in my Suburban."

"What? You liked that car."

Scott shrugged. "We needed the van. Besides, I think for what we got for it, I can make a pretty good down payment on a pickup. And I think I'll like that even better. Let's go eat, and we'll talk more."

He'd made one of my favorites, Mediterranean Chicken, a skillet meal with olives and sun-dried tomatoes. "I figured you'd be hungry," he said, putting a plate of food in front of me. He served himself and sat down. Then he held my hand and said grace, thanking God especially that I'd come home safely.

I didn't want to talk about dead bodies over such a delicious meal, so I asked him about his dissertation defense, and about Amanda, and the horses, and the dogs, and even the kittens. All that covered the twenty minutes it took us to eat. "I'll put the food away. You go on in the living room, and I'll join you in a minute," Scott said.

I could get used to this.

"Take the recliner," he called out, as I left the room. "Whatever's most comfortable."

So I did. I settled into his recliner. After a little while, he came in and sat down on the couch, and I started talking about my trip. I told him about my theory involving the two possible abductions in Harrisonburg. "I knew my time for strenuous searches was about up," I said, "and I just needed to follow that hunch."

He nodded. "Very smart."

I told him how we searched, and how Jason, whose wife had been through two pregnancies, was so understanding and helpful. "On the second day, I was about to give up. If we had to call it quits, I'd already decided to recommend Porter call out SAR and get more teams out there looking. I felt that strongly about my hunch. At the last minute, I noticed a break in the forest pattern. It looked like there'd been an old lane cut through, running next to the creek, maybe a fire road or a way to haul wood in, or who knows what.

"So I asked Luke to search that path. Jason and I followed him, but I was watching my footing, looking down so I wouldn't fall. I heard Luke bark, looked up, and there he was, lying on the ground, giving me his HR indication."

"So he found her?"

"Yes. He found her remains. The body was very decayed." I closed my eyes and shook my head. "Very sad. Some of the bones were scattered, but I recognized the clothing she had been wearing. And her earring. The Tree of Life. It was definitely Heather Burgess. It kind of looked like she was leaning up against a tree." I saw Scott's eyes flicker.

"I'm glad you found her," Scott said softly, "but

I'm sorry you had to see that. It's never easy."

"That's how I met you, do you remember? You were all Mr. FBI, coming into the woods in your fancy Italian leather shoes, and I was wearing muddy boots, sitting on a log with my dog, trying not to throw up."

"Nate was with you," he recalled.

"Yes, it was my first SAR test. I didn't realize Luke had been partially cross-trained in HRD. We'd found our live target. Then he disappeared. I could hear him barking, but he wouldn't come to me. I went looking for him, and there he was, lying on the ground. He'd found a body."

Scott shook his head. "Seems like a long time ago."

"So much has happened. Finding that body was a shock, but it was also the beginning of something wonderful." I left the recliner and moved over to the couch next to my husband. He put his arm around me and kissed me. "I love you, Scott Cooper. Now, let's go try out that van."

Scott had scheduled the defense of his dissertation, on the effectiveness of three different threat assessment tools in violence prevention in public schools, for the second week of May, before professors left for their summer studies and vacations. He'd submitted his paper a month ago, just before Amanda lost her baby. He told me he hoped he could remember what he'd written.

To say that I am proud of my husband is a gross understatement. He works hard, he's smart, and he truly cares about kids and schools and this country. He believes gun violence in particular can be reduced, especially in schools. In the standoff between the NRA and gun control advocates, according to him both sides were acting irrationally. They were damaging the country.

I was looking forward to sitting in on his defense. Then afterward, I was taking him to a nice restaurant in Charlottesville to celebrate. What he didn't know was that I'd invited Amanda and Ethan, my mother and stepfather, my sister, and Kathryn. Much to my shock, they all said they'd love to come.

It's not a good idea to surprise someone like Scott. He's good with people, don't get me wrong, but law-enforcement types, especially FBI agents, like to know what's coming at them. So, four days before the event, I confessed. "I didn't expect them to come!" I explained.

He gave me grace. "It's all right. I appreciate you inviting them."

He didn't really. Scott doesn't need or like too much attention being on him. He's quick to celebrate others' milestones but would just as soon his go quietly unnoticed.

Don't think he's a humble saint. I think his reticence has more to do with his law-enforcement instincts. He thinks he's better off staying low-key, like an undercover operator. Why? I wondered. So he can get the drop on, say, my mother?

Still, what possessed me to organize a party? After all that had gone wrong, Laura's death, Nate's disappearance, the cases I'd been on, and now the loss of Amanda's baby, I thought we needed a positive evening. And like I said, I was proud of my husband.

"Why don't you invite Dr. Garland?" he suggested.

Dr. Garland? His advisor?

"Here, I'll give you his contact information." He pulled out his phone and shared a contact.

"Sure," I said. "I'll be glad to," but I wondered how he was going to fit in.

Good grief, I didn't even know how *I* was going to fit in. I hadn't seen my family since Christmas. Although she hated the idea I was married to someone in law enforcement, somewhere along the way, my mother had decided that Scott was okay. At Thanksgiving, when his arm was in a sling after being shot, she cut his meat for him for crying out loud. She engaged him in conversation about, of all things, his job. She expressed endless fascination with his research.

I, on the other hand, was accepted, but still only under advisement. At least, that's the way I felt.

I sometimes wondered if my failure to establish female friendships had anything to do with the arm's length at which my mother kept me all through childhood. I'm sure it had nothing to do with the fact that I was drawn, like a moth to a porchlight, to risky activities and high-stakes jobs. While other girls played with Barbies, I was out fighting wars alongside the boys, climbing trees, and playing sports. What can I say? I found boys' activities far more interesting.

Yet now, here I was, locked in a female-only track. Pregnant, round-bellied, and big breasted. Could I make it as a mother? When I wasn't thinking about Nate, missing girls, or bodies, that's what was on my mind.

"There are all kinds of mothers," Scott told me. "Don't worry about it. You're going to be great."

But I did worry. I wanted to be a *good* mother. Connected. I just wasn't sure I knew how.

I bought a new dress for Scott's dissertation defense, a flowy, navy, dotted Swiss A-line. I even bought nice shoes. I hardly recognized myself.

I asked him if he was nervous as we walked into the small lecture hall at UVA. He shrugged, his new black suit flexing with his movement. He'd chosen a pale blue shirt that accented his eyes, and a blue, black, and white striped tie to complement it. He looked terrific, freshly shaven, sharp haircut, new suit, shined shoes, and cufflinks. Mr. FBI.

I laid the fancy cookies we'd bought from a

local bakery on the refreshment table on the side by the pitcher of water and glasses that were already there. He'd explained to me how this usually worked. He'd present, then they'd ask questions. After about two hours, the committee would vote on whether to grant the degree or not. Then, refreshments.

I sat midway back in the room so I could watch everybody. And so I could quietly leave if I had to use the bathroom. A bunch of people, professors I assumed, and students, began filling the rows between me and the third row. The five "judges" came in and sat in the front row.

At exactly two o'clock, Scott began speaking. I absorbed everything, his confidence, the way the professors and students focused on him, how and when the judges took notes. I felt the power of his presentation, the logic of his organization, the clarity of his argument. He held my rapt attention for the entire hour and fifteen minutes, and when the judges began asking questions, I could tell they were impressed too.

In the end, I had one thought—I'm just a girl who likes dogs and muddy boots. Who am I that I should be married to this guy?

But God . . .

We walked out of there at 4:55 p.m., me and Dr. Scott Cooper. "Now comes the hard part," he said as he slid into the car.

I looked at him, surprised.

"This dinner," he said, grinning.

"Hey, that's my family you're talking about!"

"I know!"

"Don't worry, you're the golden boy now." I touched his arm. "Scott, I'm so proud of you. You did so well."

He gave a small nod. "I'm glad it's over. Now I can concentrate on the baby."

The classic Charlottesville restaurant gave us a private room. Ethan was already there. Dr. Garland and his wife joined us. Then my mother and stepfather walked in. My mother took one look at me, commented on the size of my belly, and said, "You're carrying low! Must be a girl."

A flash of near-horror went through me. A girl! How could I mother a girl? What a horrible role model I'd be.

A few seconds later, my sister, having detoured to the ladies room, arrived, took one look, and said, "Wow, you're huge!" Then she added. "You're carrying low. Must be a boy."

I felt dizzy. "Let's sit down," I said.

There was one noticeably empty chair. Amanda would be coming late, Ethan said. "She wanted to drive herself. I'm not sure why." He texted her . . . again.

We waited a few more minutes, then Scott said we should go ahead and order.

So we did, ordering steaks for Scott and Ethan and a variety of dishes for everyone else. I chose a roasted chicken breast with maple glaze, sweet potato mash, and grilled asparagus. All the offerings looked good at this place.

And it was good, all of it, except for the elephant in the room—that empty chair. Ethan excused himself after he ordered and stepped out, I suspected to call Amanda. He apparently got no answer. Once back, he kept checking his phone under the table, while trying to converse with my stepfather. Meanwhile, Scott and I kept the conversation going with Dr. Garland and his wife, psychological terms flying like migrating geese right over me. My mother kept shooting looks at me and the empty chair, while at that end of the table, my sister told stories (despite HIPAA laws) of the patients she'd had lately. Thankfully, she didn't name names.

I never thought that dinner would end, but it did, with another round of congratulations for Scott, and a hearty slap on his bad shoulder from his advisor. My family drove off into the night, while Scott, Ethan, and I tried to pick up the pieces.

"Do you think she's at her apartment?" I asked, while intercepting the server who was about to give the check to Scott.

"I have no idea," Ethan said.

"How has she been lately. Emotionally. Any

chance she'd try to hurt herself?" Scott asked.

Ethan shook his head. "I don't think so. She finished her classes and seemed happy with the way they went. Talked to me about what she wanted to do next year. So I don't think she was deeply depressed."

"Car break down?" Scott suggested.

I paid the bill with my credit card, added a hefty tip, and set the folder back on the table. "Let's drive to her apartment and check to see if she's there," I said.

So we did, Scott silently steering his car through the dark streets, following Ethan.

We got to the apartment building, a nice, brick building near the university and rode the elevator up to the third floor. Ethan had a key, so he unlocked it, and we went in. There, on the coffee table next to a set of car keys, was a note addressed to "Ethan, Dad, and Jess."

Scott's hands shook as he opened it.

I'm sorry, it read. *I hate who I've become. I don't think I'm cut out for the East Coast. I'm going back to California. Ethan, I love you. I'm sorry. I know you'll find someone better. Dad, thank you for all your support. Jess, good luck with . . . the baby. –Mandy*

Scott's hand dropped after he read it, and an expression of sheer frustration came over his face. Ethan dropped to the couch, his face in his hands.

I was furious. On her father's big night, she had to be missing in action? Upstage him with a dramatic exit? To selfishly divert attention to herself? Amanda was as narcissistic as her mother, I declared silently.

My face hot, I choked back my anger. I'd have time to deal with that later. To express it.

Not to Nate, of course, because he was MIA as well, I told myself sarcastically. Maybe, I don't know, to Luke.

I took a deep breath to get a grip. These men needed me. I did a quick triage.

I touched Scott's arm as I walked by and continued over to Ethan. I sat down next to him and put my arm around him. "I'm so sorry, Ethan."

A muffled, half-suppressed sob was his only response.

"You don't deserve this, Ethan," Scott said, his voice trembling with anger. "You've done everything to love her that a man could do." He paraded his evidence in bullet points. Her drinking. Rape. Pregnancy. Through rehab. Depression. Volatile moods. "And now this," Scott said, ending the parade. "She's just like her mother. She'll make you miserable your whole life, and you don't deserve that. You don't!"

He paused, loosened his tie, then pulled it off with a jerk. It cracked like a whip. "She's my daughter, so I can't divorce her. But I'm telling you, son, run. Run as fast as you can away from her," he said, ignoring the fact that Amanda was the one who'd already run, all the way to the West Coast.

Ethan sat silently, head in his hands, with me rubbing his back the whole time. Scott continued his rant until it started to upset me. In his anger, old Scott had begun to emerge. I wondered if Dr. Psychology realized he was talking as much about himself and his first marriage as he was Ethan and Amanda. "Scott," I said, a soft rebuke in my voice. Our eyes met.

Ethan raised his head. Then he stood and faced Scott head on. "Sir, I understand where you're coming from. But I love her."

"Well, you shouldn't . . ."

Ethan raised his hand. "Respectfully, sir, this isn't helping." He paced away, his head down. "Where would she go in California?" he asked, turning around.

"I assume her mother's house. I mean, where else would she go?" I said.

Scott took a more investigative approach. He pulled out his phone and checked the credit card he'd given her, linked to a bank account they shared. "She bought a ticket from Richmond to LAX, via New York. So I'd say she's going to her mother's. Figures."

"When does the flight leave Richmond?" Ethan asked.

"Looks like 7:25 p.m." Scott looked up.

I checked my watch. It was 7:40. She was long gone.

"When's the last time you saw her?" Scott asked.

"I talked to her at three. But I haven't seen her since we had coffee at nine this morning." Ethan gestured toward the coffee table. "Those are the keys to her car. How'd she get to Richmond?" He strode toward the door. "I'll be right back." And he left.

I rose, touching my belly. Baby Cooper had been kicking up a storm. I wondered if he heard his dad thundering. "Scott, I'm so sorry," I said, wrapping my arms around my husband. His body, stiff with anger, began to relax.

"Are you okay?" he asked me.

"The baby's kicking, that's all. I think you scared him. You scared me a little, too."

He sighed. "I'm sorry. She makes me crazy."

"Scott," I said gently, "what if it's all too much for her? Your success, her failures, our baby, her baby . . . the whole picture. What if she just couldn't take it?"

He blew out a breath. "Why not just distance herself from us then. Why Ethan, too?"

"You and Ethan are pretty close."

Ethan came through the door, a frown on his face. "Her car is where she always parks it. So how'd she get to Richmond?" His phone rang. He looked down at it, then answered it. "Where are you?" he said.

Scott and I exchanged looks. Ethan walked back to the bedroom, the phone to his ear. Ten minutes later he came back out and silently handed the phone to Scott.

"She said she couldn't get on the plane," Ethan whispered to me. "I'm going to go get her. But she wanted to apologize to her dad first."

I grinned at him. "Forget all that stuff Scott said," I whispered.

"I already have!"

35

Nate's side trip to Burke's Garden made his next two days' hikes longer, but it was worth it. He was supposed to meet Jeff at the intersection with US 52, near Bland, Virginia, where he planned to take a couple of zero days to rest up. To make their rendezvous, though, he had to hustle.

Halfway there it started to rain. Despite his raingear, Nate was soon soaked to the skin and fighting to keep from slipping in the mud. Loneliness began creeping back in along with the misery. What was he doing, walking through the mountains in the rain with only a dog for company? Even Ember looked depressed.

So it was good when they got to their rendezvous and saw Jeff's car coming down the road. "Hey, man! How's it going?" he said when Nate opened the door.

"Wet."

Jeff glanced toward the back seat. "I covered the back with a tarp."

"Me and the dog'll sit back there," Nate responded.

Jeff drove them to Bland where they found a motel. He knew the drill. Nate checked in and dried off Ember, then headed for a hot shower. Meanwhile, Jeff spread his wet gear out in the room. Fortunately, the trick he'd shown Nate, using a plastic trash bag to line his backpack, had kept much of Nate's stuff dry. But the hammock and tarp were soaked.

The two days Nate had planned to take off in Bland turned into four days of sitting in a motel, waiting for the rain to stop. Jeff went home. Nate did his laundry, repacked his backpack, tried to watch TV, and charged his phone. Except for taking Ember out and short walks to get food, he was stuck in his room, with nothing much to do but think.

Lying there on the bed, staring up at the off-white ceiling, he thought about things he'd seen on the trail. Intricately woven spiderwebs. Mountain ranges standing shoulder to shoulder, like ranks of soldiers. Undercast clouds at sunrise. The starry sky. Burke's Garden. He'd heard birdsong in the morning. Smelled the scent of grass. Fell asleep to the hooting of owls.

Something Peter had told him so many years ago came to mind. "God has two books," Peter had said, "nature and this one." And with that, he'd handed Nate his first Bible.

The natural things Nate had seen on the trail were part of a book testifying about the Creator God. Design. Complexity. Beauty.

And here, stuck in this dull motel, Nate felt a tug in his soul. He wanted to pick up the other book.

He hadn't opened a Bible since Laura died. Hadn't even brought one with him.

So he pulled out the only thing he had—Jessica's dad's Gospel of John.

Ember jumped up on the bed and nestled down next to his leg. He reached out and stroked her with one hand, holding the small book with his other. And he began to read.

> "In the beginning was the Word and the Word was with God and the Word was God. He was in the beginning with God. All things were made through him and without him was not anything made that was made. In him was life, and the life was the light of men. The light shines in the darkness and the darkness has not overcome it."

Those familiar words washed over Nate, soothing him like cool water. Memories surfaced in his mind, questions he'd had, questions Jess had asked. Conversations they'd had over his kitchen table, their hot cups of tea steaming on the side.

He made a noise, a small groan.

Ember raised her head. "It's okay," he said, patting her. "I was thinking about Jess." She cocked her head. "Yeah, that's right. Jess. Jess and your buddy, Luke."

Ember jumped to her feet and, tail wagging, stood on the bed and looked toward the door. Nothing happened. She turned back to Nate, towering over him, a question in her eyes. "No, they're not coming." She licked his face. "Okay, okay," he said, laughing. "I shouldn't have said his name. Come on, lie down." He patted the bed.

Obediently, Ember snuggled down next to him, resting her head on his leg, her brown eyes fixed on his face. Nate stroked her. "Good girl, that's a good girl."

He rested his head back. Then he continued to read.

36

Shortly after Amanda scrapped her trip to California, she moved in with Ethan. "I don't see the point of both of us paying for an apartment," she said.

"I was the one paying for it!" Scott said when I asked him how he felt about it. "If either of them had asked me, I would have said it was a bad idea. But they didn't ask."

"What would you have said? Why is it a bad idea?"

His mouth straightened into a line. "It's like playing house. I know, everybody does it. But to me, if you love somebody enough to wake up to their face every day, man up and get married. Fish or cut bait. That way you have a lot more incentive to work things out when the problems come."

"Might sound funny coming from a guy who's been through divorce." I rubbed his upper arm affectionately. We were standing in the kitchen, waiting for the coffee to finish brewing.

He put his arm around me and gave me a little squeeze, showing me he wasn't offended. "I know better now."

I as much as lived with my boyfriend Mitch years ago. Scott knew about that. We'd been open about our pasts. "You can't stop love," I said, and I stood on my tiptoes to kiss him.

"Look where that got you," he said.

Indeed. Love got me twenty-five extra pounds, aching hips, muscle cramps, sleeplessness, heartburn, and a popped-out belly button. In other words, I was in my eighth month.

A week later at 3 a.m. my phone buzzed. Nate? I grabbed it off the nightstand in a panic.

Nope. Not Nate. A callout, a despondent teenager, twelves miles east of our home. She was involved with an older boy, her parents took her phone away, and boom, she disappeared.

Pregnancy or no pregnancy, I wanted to help. It was close by our home, not in the mountains, and what's more, I thought I recognized her last name from one of the churches we'd tried out.

I slipped out of bed, being careful not to trip over the dogs. I opened the closet and eased my SAR pack out, then tiptoed into the bathroom.

I couldn't get my SAR pants on over, or even under, my belly, not even the dark blue maternity pants. So I slid into sweats. I put on a bra, a T-shirt, and planned to steal one of my husband's long-sleeved shirts on my way out. It was warm enough outside I wouldn't need a jacket. I put on my boots, noting even they were feeling small, turned off the light, and opened the door back into the bedroom.

Scott was sitting on the edge of the bed, dressed. "You're not going alone," he said, matter-of-factly.

"What?"

"Whatever it is and where ever it is, you're not going without me."

"You have work tomorrow. Today." I corrected myself.

"Not. Without. Me."

I gave up. "Okay, then. Let's go."

I started to pick up my SAR pack. Scott took it from me.

"We'll leave Sprite here but take Luke. Get water, protein bars, cheese, and I'll get food for Luke," I said on the way downstairs.

I called Bill and told him we were coming. "My husband Scott will be my walker," I said. "No, he doesn't know anything about it. He'll be fine."

We loaded everything in the Jeep, and off we went, with Scott driving. Scott and I had done a lot of things together, but he'd never come on a search with me. Never.

Nora Billingsley lived in a small neighborhood of large suburban-style homes plopped out in the middle of the country. Her parents, I presumed, worked either in Charlottesville or Culpeper. No jobs in our county would support that kind of a house.

Three of us from Battlefield, and our dogs,

clustered around Bill, the incident commander. He had pictures of Nora, who was about five foot four, a hundred and ten pounds, brown hair, brown eyes. A type 1 diabetic, she ran out of the house after an argument with her mother before dinner. She did not take her insulin or other supplies with her. We all knew that was a problem, but we hadn't thought of all the implications.

We were about to continue when Scott said, "She may be suicidal."

Everyone looked at him. "Over a phone?" Bill asked.

"Absolutely. She didn't eat or take her insulin with her. Depending on how fragile her condition is, she could experience high blood sugar if she ate without the insulin or low blood sugar if she didn't eat. Either way, she's not taking care of herself. She may not care if she dies, or she may be planning to kill herself."

"Over a phone?" Bill repeated.

"Absolutely. She's a teenager!"

"Maybe she just forgot it."

"Not an insulin-dependent diabetic."

"All right," Bill said. Consulting with the sheriff, he had marked off an area for an initial search. Then he'd divided it into three segments, and he assigned one to each of the searchers. I thought I got a pretty easy draw. "You really doing this?" Bill asked me, implying I couldn't.

"Of course!" I responded.

He shrugged, then looked at all of us. "Check your radios and plan to meet back here when you're done."

"Come on," I said to Scott. "We're starting out front."

The Billingsleys' house was a new two-story colonial, typical for this part of Virginia, set on about four acres, mostly cleared. The houses on the other side of the road were set well-back, some on wooded lots, others on cleared land. Most of the lots were fenced, and I imagined some of the neighbors had horses or goats.

On the hood of someone else's car, I showed Scott the map and indicated what direction I wanted to take. I could tell he had no clue how to read a topographic map, but now was not the time to teach him. I handed him the GPS, gave him the basics, and then walked Luke over to where I wanted to start.

Suddenly remembering something, I told Luke to stay, and said, "I'll be right back" to Scott. I walked to my Jeep, opened the back door, and pulled out a trekking pole, part of a pair I'd bought just in case I decided to go find Nate on the Appalachian Trail.

I went back to Scott, braced for questions. "What's that for?" he asked.

"Balance," I replied. I tested the wind direction with a puff of baby powder, then sent Luke off before Scott could ask more. "Seek, Luke, seek!"

Luke took off, his lighted vest bobbing like a galloping Christmas tree in the night. I walked straight toward my initial target, while Luke quartered in front of me. Scott carried the pack. "I kind of like having a porter," I said, joking.

"Feels like you've packed this thing with bricks," Scott replied.

We walked toward the fence line I'd picked as my goal. Scott kept asking questions about how I decided which way to go and what the effect the wind would have, especially around creeks and gullies. He really wanted the details about how to search, which was new. "You really do like to study, don't you?" I said, grinning in the dark.

"I guess so," he responded.

We reached my target, I studied the wind again, and then I picked a second goal, and we headed that direction. By that time, we were talking topographic maps. I'd gotten him a topographic map of our property for his birthday last year, quite a romantic gift if you ask me. He'd looked at it, but now, I think, he was beginning to understand how useful it could be.

Our current course took us uphill and into about five acres of woods. I quickly became winded, a fact I tried to hide, but Scott caught on. "Slow down a little," he said, as if he needed the rest.

"Old man," I said.

I was glad I'd brought the trekking pole,

because the woods were full of bramble runners, fallen branches, and other tripping hazards. For the first time ever while searching, I was afraid of getting hurt, or, more correctly, afraid of my baby getting hurt if I fell. The realities of motherhood were already chipping away at my bold, adventurous, free spirit. What Scott would call my "proclivity toward risk-taking."

I was glad Scott was there.

An hour went by, then another half hour. I was reaching the end of my energy. Thankfully, we were almost at the end of my search assignment. The sky began to lighten in the east when I saw Luke suddenly stop and lift his head.

"Look," I said to Scott, poking him. "He has something."

"Another dog? A rabbit? Skunk?"

"The only way he gets to play is to find a human. He knows that. It's called 'training.'"

Luke took off at a forty-five degree angle. "Let's go," I said, following him.

We hadn't gone ten yards before he came barreling back toward us. I suddenly realized I didn't want him jumping on me, not with that energy.

But he didn't. Luke came to a skidding halt, looked at me, and barked. He changed his indication on his own. I swear, he knew I was pregnant.

Good dog, Luke. Good boy.

We followed my dog and just over a little ridge, we found what looked like an old farm outbuilding, a smokehouse or a toolshed. And inside, crouched on the floor, huddled in a pink blanket, was a young teen.

"Nora?" I said.

She nodded.

I could tell immediately she was disoriented. Weak. I looked at Scott. "Use the radio, call it in. Get the location off the GPS." Then I turned back to Nora. "Nora, my name is Jess. I'm an EMT. I'm going to help you, all right?"

She nodded.

I took her pulse. Weak. "When did you eat last?"

"Breakfast."

I decided right then to give her sugar. Her blood sugar had to be low. I dug in my pack, found the juice box I always carried, inserted the little straw, and gave it to her. Her hands were shaking so hard she could barely hold it, so I held it for her.

"Your mom and dad were pretty scared," I told her while she drank. "You forgot your kit." Her kit would have contained insulin as well as emergency sugar.

Nora nodded.

"Was that on purpose?"

She hesitated, but then whispered, "Yes."

"Were you hoping you'd die?"

She shook her head. "I wanted to scare them." Tears came to her eyes. "I'm sorry!"

"It's all right. You're going to be just fine."

We were only about a mile from the Billingsley's house. By the time a sheriff's deputy arrived, I'd given Nora a candy bar to nibble. He helped Nora out to a path where he'd parked his four-wheel-drive truck. As we watched them pull away, I looked at Scott and said, "That's it for me. I can't do this anymore."

He grinned. "Thank God. It's about time!"

Later that day, after a nap and a couple of meals, I was cleaning out my SAR pack, feeling pretty good about finding Nora, when I got a call from Detective Porter. "Hey, I just wanted you to know I'm not responsible for outing you."

"What?" I almost laughed. What in the world could he mean?

"I didn't see the paper until just now."

"What paper? What's going on?"

He blew out a breath. "The student newspaper you contacted? They've been doing follow-up stories on the two abductions. In today's paper, they had an interview with Kevin Burgess. He gave you, by name, the credit for finding his daughter's body."

"He used my name?" I asked, incredulous. "We had an understanding. It's part of the contract!

He's not supposed to reveal my name without permission."

"He used your name, and then, well, the editor made you the headline."

"What?"

"Yep. 'Cooper Cracks Case.' "

Dumbfounded, I stood stock-still, staring at the Garmin inReach, which happened to be in my hand. *How could this have happened? We had an agreement!*

"Jess?"

Robert's voice brought me back. "Send me that article, please."

"Sure. Glad to. I'll send you the link and put a copy of the print edition in the mail. I'm sorry, Jess. I had nothing to do with this."

"Thanks for the heads up," I said. I clicked off my phone, said a few choice words, and called Scott. "Can you believe it?" I said after spewing out the story.

"He probably thought he was doing you a favor. Most businesses love a positive mention in the press."

"Well, I don't! It's in the contract! He can't do that."

"Didn't you tell me he's a lawyer?"

"Yes."

"Lawyers write contracts. They don't read them. Not unless they're on the clock." Scott paused. "What are you going to do?"

"Sue him."

"Really, Jess? Is it really worth that?"

"Absolutely. He violated our agreement!"

"In a paper that is mostly distributed to students."

I could feel myself starting to get angry with Scott. I didn't want that. I closed my eyes and relaxed my jaw. I took a deep breath and said, "What do you think I should do?"

"Let it ride for now. Let's talk about it at dinner."

I didn't respond.

"I just think with the baby coming and everything, well, the stress may not be worth it. Let's think about the consequences. If you decide you want to go ahead, I'll support you. You are in the right on this, but like they say, 'You can be right, or you can be happy.' Some battles just aren't worth fighting." He paused again. "They didn't publish your address, did they? Or your phone number?"

"No."

"Okay. So it can wait. Let's talk about it tonight."

I agreed to that, but I wasn't very happy.

37

Weeks turned into months as Nate moved steadily northward. By June, the days had turned hot. Humid. Long hours hiking the "green tunnel" of the woods led to overlooks with stunning views. Patches of mountain laurel and stands of rhododendron in bloom gave way to towering pines and hardwoods, broken up by grassy meadows.

Deer, possums, raccoons, squirrels, mice, and birds were Nate's main companions. Every day he saw something that gave him pause. Bright orange salamanders in the streams, a new fawn, an eagle overhead, the bright green eyes of spiders at night.

He saw other hikers, but they tended to move on by, his slow pace a deterrent to companionship. That was okay. He often had company at lunch or dinner. He signed the trail logs at the shelters although why he didn't know. He didn't think he'd be back. But it was interesting to read the notes left by other hikers. Once, he'd seen a message to "Pops" from Butterfly, and he had to believe that was meant for him.

He kept Ember close for he'd seen bear scat on the trail. Momma bears kept to their dens until they'd had their cubs, but they were out now, and the little ones were moving around. Black bears were usually eager to stay away from people and dogs, but the mommas could get aggressive if they had babies to defend.

Together he and Ember had handled heat, rain, bugs, and snakes. Trail hardened, Nate felt like they could take just about anything. That thought was challenged one afternoon when they were caught in an open field, a powerline easement, in a violent thunderstorm. Thunder boomed and lightning crackled all around them. He saw it hit the top of a tower and braced himself for the high voltage lines to come down. They didn't. It was still scary.

The air around him was charged with ions. His hair, now trail-shaggy, stood on end. So did the hair on his arms.

Thunder rolled. Rain fell in sheets. Would they be safer under the trees? Lying flat on the ground? He had no idea. Ember clung to him, pressing against his leg, her ears twitching, her eyes glancing around. A loud crack drove him to the ground as a bolt of lightning split a tree near them on the edge of the field. As Nate watched, the twenty-inch diameter oak creaked, then groaned, then leaned, then fell into the easement, barely missing the powerline tower, shaking the ground as it hit.

Soaked to the skin, muddy, and scared, Nate made a decision. "C'mon Ember," he said, struggling to his feet. "Let's get out of here." He hefted his pack back in place and moved as quickly as he could, deeper into the woods, further away from all that electricity. They'd find the trail again later, when the storm was over. Ten minutes in, he came upon a grove of smaller trees with a huge boulder in the middle. He huddled down next to the rock, his shoulders hunched against the rain, Ember draped across his lap. Together they waited. He prayed.

They ended up staying next to that rock all night. Nate wasn't sure he'd find the trail again in the dark. As the sun came up the next morning, steam rose from the land and Nate rose from the ground, stiff and sore.

He could use a shower. And a dry place to rest. But he'd just had a break before the storm, in Pearisburg, so he wouldn't have another one for a week. Wet and miserable as he was, he had to keep going.

This part of the hike was reminding him more and more of war. Misery, followed by terror, followed by day after boring day of the same thing, only now it was walking. The good thing was, he had a dog with him like he did in Afghanistan. Also, the scenery was better. And nobody was shooting at him.

Worn down, Nate found trail magic at just the right time.

Two days after the storm, the trail crossed

a road. As he approached that area, Nate could smell something. Meat. On a grill. Fresh food? Really?

He emerged from the woods and saw a sight that made him grin. At the trail's junction with the road, in a small parking lot, a group of trail angels had set up grills, a table, and coolers full of drinks. Their banner read "Split Oak Community Church" and they were giving away food to hikers.

He was all in.

"Welcome!" a middle-aged man said. "What's your name?"

"I'm the Dog Man," Nate said. "What you're cookin' smells mighty good."

"It's just hamburgers and hot dogs but help yourself."

"Looks like steak to me," Nate said, grinning.

"Get your dog some. She must be tired of kibble."

"Yes, sir, she mentioned that last night."

The guy laughed. Nate found out the group did this twice a month during hiking season. A simple ministry, but such a blessing. He filled his plate with two hamburgers and two hot dogs, potato chips, and a Coke. "Thank you. You got no idea how much this means to me."

A woman tugged his sleeve and invited him to sit in a lawn chair while he ate. He had to look at her twice, she reminded him so much of Laura.

Same slim figure, same height, dark hair. "Yes, ma'am," he said. "Thank you."

He had no sooner sat down than a guy came and sat next to him. He was clean and clean-shaven, obviously part of the group, not a hiker. He had on khaki cargo pants, a blue T-shirt, and Nike running shoes, and he had a Coke in his hand. "Go ahead and eat!" the man said. "I just wanted to find out who you are and where you're headed."

Nate nodded. He'd just taken a large bite of food. "This tastes so good!" he said, once he'd swallowed. Ember lay at his feet, looking up expectantly. He finished chewing and wiped his mouth. "Through Virginia is all."

"Oh, so not a thru-hiker?"

"No, sir. Couldn't make it that far. Be lucky to make it through Virginia."

"Why's that?"

"Hiking on one leg."

"What?"

It was the first time Nate had told anyone on the trail that he had a prosthesis. He'd kept that information private. All someone had to do to overwhelm him was come at him when his leg was off. But something told him this guy was safe.

"Lost my leg a while back. Just got a new one with a microprocessor that helps with my gait. My prosthetics man suggested I try walkin' the trail with it. So I am."

"That's amazing. Where'd you start?"

"Damascus."

"So, what's that, two hundred miles?"

" 'Bout that."

"On one leg." The man blew out a breath. "Whew, man. What'd you say your name was?"

"Dog Man. Nate, really, Nathan Tanner."

"Nate, I'm Peter Brenner. I'm the pastor of this church."

Peter. The name resonated with him. Nate nodded. "Good to meet you." He bit into his hamburger and glanced back toward the sign. "Split Oak Community Church, right?"

The pastor nodded.

"Pretty gutsy church to put 'split' in its name." Nate grinned.

Peter laughed. "The property the founders bought to build on had a huge oak on it, split right down the middle by lightning." He gestured with his hand. "I guess they figured if they named it 'Split Oak' lightning wouldn't strike twice."

Nate chuckled. He took a long drink of cold, sweet Coke. This guy had an easy way about him, a likeable way. "I had a friend named Peter," Nate said.

"Oh yeah?"

"He's the one told me about Jesus."

"Is that right? Tell me about it."

Nate took a few more bites. "I was in the burn center, just back from Afghanistan." He lowered his hamburger and told the pastor about Peter the double amputee who couldn't stop talking about Jesus. How over time Peter made Jesus so real. How he explained the Gospel. How he gave him a Bible to read. How one day, Nate realized it was true. "Totally changed my life," Nate said.

Peter smiled. "It does do that. Tell me about the tattoo." He pointed to the large anchor on Nate's arm.

Nate's mouth suddenly went dry. He gave the last bite of his food to Ember and took a swallow of Coke. Across the way, the woman who reminded him of Laura was helping another hiker fill his plate.

"We have this hope as an anchor for the soul, firm and secure," Peter prompted. "Is that what the anchor stands for?"

Hebrews 6:19. Nate said the verse reference silently in his head. He blew out a breath. "It ain't feelin' so secure right now."

"Hmm. What happened?" Peter asked.

Nate's chest tightened. "My wife died," he said, fighting to keep his voice steady. "Killed by a drunk driver. I couldn't stay in that house alone no more. Had to get out."

Shock widened Peter's eyes. "That's terrible. How long ago was that?"

"January."

Peter put his hand on Nate's shoulder. "That's a terrible loss, Nate. I'm so sorry." They sat side-by-side silently for a while, then Peter asked how it happened. Nate described it. When he got to the end, tears filled his eyes. Peter left some space before he said, "What a shock."

Nate couldn't respond. He looked down, pressing his fist just under his nose, trying to keep from falling apart right there in the middle of the trail magic crowd.

"How long had you been married?"

He told him.

"Kids?"

Nate shook his head. "Knew her in high school. Got reconnected a few years ago, same time I lost my leg. Cain't understand why God brought us together just to rip us apart again." He handed Ember the last bite of the hamburger, then picked up a hot dog. He told Peter the whole story, his and Laura's story, the hot dog getting cold in his hand.

Peter listened carefully. He asked a couple of good questions and reflected back what he'd heard. And then he said, "A lot of guys come out here trying to find God or run from him."

Nate shook his head. "I ain't runnin' from him, I'm trying to walk toward him. I know God's here. I just cain't feel him. I've lost the sureness of it. But he don't change. I think the block is in me."

"Are you angry with God?"

"Frustrated, maybe. Like I said, cain't figure

out why he took her." He took another bite. "But I been thinkin' about it and really," Nate shook his head, "really, I think I'm mad at the guy who killed her."

Peter nodded. "Understandable." His brow furrowed. "What would you say to him if he was standing right here?"

Nate's eyes narrowed. "Truthfully, I think you'd have a job on your hands keepin' me from killin' him." The moment he said those words, he felt a rush of emotion. He hadn't admitted even to himself the depth of his hatred for Joshua Cranmer. He handed the second hot dog, bun and all, to Ember.

"What do you know about this driver?" Peter asked.

"His name. The fact he had prior DUIs. That he drove his big honkin' truck right through a stop sign and into my wife. That he had no business," Nate hesitated, "no business drivin' with a blood alcohol level as high as it was."

"Family?"

Nate shrugged. "Don't know."

"Maybe it would help to know a little more."

Nate didn't respond.

"Was Laura a believer?" Peter asked. Nate nodded. "And you are, too." Nate nodded again. Peter took a deep breath. "So you are in Christ, and so is she." Nate turned and looked at him. "Only you are here, and she is there."

At first he frowned, then, like a curtain gradually opening, Nate began to see it. *We both loved Jesus. We both had the Holy Spirit in us. We both were, are, connected to Jesus.* He sat perfectly still, the sounds of the crowd around him fading, as he processed those thoughts. *We are connected through Christ and always will be.* He felt a surge of hope.

"So you'll see her again," Peter said, continuing, "and when you do it'll be in the presence of Jesus, both of you covered by his great love. It'll be different but you'll meet again."

"Yes," Nate whispered.

"No more sorrow, no more tears."

"Yes," Nate said, tears in his eyes, "and everything healed."

"Everything." Peter put his arm around Nate's shoulders.

What Nate expected would be a fifteen-minute stop for a hamburger turned into a two-hour marathon discussion with Peter, covering everything from Laura to Afghanistan to dogs to God and grief. He told Peter about Rock, his explosives-detection dog in the military, about search and rescue dogs, about Jess and Luke, about Sprite and Ember. And then back to Laura, and the love he felt for her, about his failure to protect her, and about losing touch with God after losing her.

Peter listened, nodding appropriately, frowning at times. He questioned Nate's perception that he had failed to protect Laura. "Unless you kept her in a bubble, you couldn't perfectly protect her." When Nate looked unconvinced, he tried a different tact. "Her death was not in your control, Nate. Only God is omnipotent."

"I know that in my head."

"Sometimes it takes a while for the heart to catch up." Peter paused, then continued. "I know somebody in my church whose husband died a year or so ago. She says she sometimes has to take life fifteen minutes at a time. If she can just hold on for fifteen minutes, she tells herself, things will be better. She does that over and over all day long. It kind of reminds me of you. You're walking one mile at a time, day after day. It may not feel like you're making progress on an emotional level, but I believe you are."

Nate cocked his head.

Then Peter invited him to come home with him, spend a night or two. "I think my family, especially my teenagers, would love to meet you. My wife's a good cook, and you could rest that leg."

Nate thought about it. It was tempting. But then he declined. He needed to keep going. And he felt too dirty to be a guest in someone's home. "I got to keep walkin'. My friends are about to have a baby. I want to be there for that. But talkin' with you, Peter, well, it's helped." He stood up to leave, shook Peter's hand, and said, "Thank you for feeding me. I'm talkin' more than just hamburgers."

"God bless you, Nate. You're going to be okay. God's got his hand on you."

"I think the devil does too," Nate said smiling.

Peter pulled out a business card and handed it to him. "Call me, man, when you get home. I want to hear about the rest of the trip."

"I will."

"And don't forget . . ."

Nate raised his eyebrows.

"The devil? He's God's devil."

Nate grinned. It was a quote from Martin Luther, one he'd used many times with Jess and Scott and others. The devil is just a created being, a fallen angel, subject to the providence of God. "Right. I'll be in touch."

Nate turned toward the other workers who were in the process of packing up. "Thank y'all!" he said, waving goodbye. "C'mon, Ember," and then he walked up the hill and back into the woods.

Peter Brenner had given Nate plenty to think about on the trail. A couple of nights later, Nate set up camp, then climbed to a cliff to watch the sunset. Ember laid down at his side. Peter had reminded him that God could not, would not abandon him. That nothing the devil could throw at him was outside God's control. That God could deliver him from the grip of his anger. That even right then, Jesus was advocating for Nate with the Father and guiding him day by day, like a shepherd, that even then he and Laura were connected in their mutual love of Christ.

"God, you know I miss her," he whispered. But talking to Peter Brenner, his heart had turned a corner. Someday he'd see her. Someday he'd see *Jesus.*

Nate stroked Ember's black coat and relished the peace he felt inside. The sun's light blazed yellow, then golden as the sun dropped toward the mountains in the west. Ember rested her head on his leg. Crickets began to chirp, and a lazy hawk drifted on the thermals over the valley below. He heard a whippoorwill call.

The mountains looked blue in the declining light. When the sun dropped behind the ridges its rays angled upward, setting the whole sky ablaze. Oranges, yellows, reds, and purples colored the sky before him, above him, behind him, all around him, until it felt to Nate like he was a part of it, enveloped in it, baptized in Glory. He whispered "Holy. O Lord God, you are holy, holy, holy."

A cool breeze flowed over him. His breathing slowed. His body relaxed. He sat perfectly still, his hand on Ember. "Holy, holy . . ." The golden sky turned orange, then red, then purple, then successive shades of blue, each darker than the one before. As daylight faded, a single star popped out. Night fell. The sky grew dark. And Nathan Tanner realized he could see again.

38

Dragon's Tooth. McAfee Knob. Tinker Cliffs. Nate steadily clicked off Virginia's Triple Crown, three iconic sites on the trail. The hikes were challenging, the vistas spectacular, and it seemed to Nate that after each one he felt more alive.

After completing the Triple Crown, Nate took a day off in Daleville, where Jeff met him. "Hey," Jeff said as he checked Nate's stump, "you seem better. What happened?"

Nate grinned. "Trail magic."

"I thought maybe it was just the shower."

"That too." Nate laughed. "But I been dirty plenty times before. I hit upon a bunch of trail angels a week or so ago. Church group givin' out food."

"And serving up Jesus along with it."

"That, too."

"What a pain."

That stopped Nate short. He'd only started seeing Jeff a little while before Laura died. He guessed he hadn't talked to him about his faith. "You want to spend the night?" he asked.

"No. I'll drive back. I have patients tomorrow."

"How about dinner?"

Jeff checked his watch. "I guess I could do that."

"Good. My treat."

• • •

It was a start. That was the best he could say about his dinner conversation with Jeff. Just a start. Over steaks and baked potatoes and salad, Nate had explained how Peter had helped him see his anger, helped him begin to let go of it.

"That's crazy," Jeff had responded. "I sure wouldn't forgive that man. Ever."

I cain't either without Jesus, Nate thought.

Later that night, after Jeff had left, Nate took a look at his maps. He'd traveled about halfway through the Virginia part of the AT, but he'd have to step up his pace if he was going to make it through the rest of it by his target date, two weeks before Jess was due in mid-July. He had about a hundred and sixty miles to go before he got to Skyline Drive, where he knew the hiking would be easier. He'd get an early start the next day, he decided, and ramp up his speed. The days were longer now. Sun was going down later. He could do it.

Nate made ten miles a day for the next two days, up to the Blue Ridge Parkway and the Peaks of Otter area. He camped near shelters, found a great swimming hole, and experienced overlooks of Bedford, a small town known for the "Bedford boys," nineteen young men who died in the first wave on D-Day, June 6, 1944. Losing nineteen young men was a heavy sacrifice for Bedford, population 3,000.

Nate's next scheduled zero day would be in Glasgow. It would be the last time he'd see Jeff. Kathryn, Laura's daughter, would pick up the baton after that.

As he hiked, Nate thought about Kathryn. She was born out of wedlock when Laura was a teenager and given up immediately for adoption. This was Laura's great trauma. The shame she'd felt, the sorrow at losing her baby, was something she'd carried her whole life.

His relationship with Kathryn in the months following Laura's death grew. Kathryn volunteered to help him clean out Laura's clothes and settle the estate. She spent time with him, asking questions about her mother and looking through pictures, which helped Nate relive some sweet moments. When he decided to do this hike, Kathryn had volunteered to be his trail boss on the second half of his journey.

He wondered, now, as he hiked, could he call Kathryn his stepdaughter? His daughter? That's the way he felt about her. There was no blood relationship but, except for a half-brother she'd recently discovered, Kathryn had no blood relations. Her adoptive parents were dead.

To him, Kathryn felt like family. He guessed he'd have to wait and see if she felt the same.

His goal that day was to reach Matt's Creek, just this side of the long James River Foot Bridge and not far from Glasgow. It would be a thirteen-mile hike, his longest so far. The weather was good, clear and sunny with temperatures around seventy. Low humidity. Not bad for June.

There were more people on the trail now. The "bubble" of hikers who had begun at Springer Mountain Georgia had caught up with him, but they went past him pretty quickly. He had to "hike his own hike," and that meant going slower than everyone else.

At every shelter, Nate checked the log book, where hikers left trail notes for each other. Butterfly kept leaving notes for "Pops."

She's a free spirit, that one, he said to himself, after reading one of them.

That proved out when, at the next shelter, he found a message saying she was leaving the trail for a while "to go on a meditation retreat." He couldn't imagine her sitting still for long, much less meditating. He wondered if marijuana was involved. "Maybe I'll see you when I get back, Pops!" she'd written. "Look for me."

He read one disturbing note from a southbound hiker. A woman had been assaulted on the trail, about Mile Marker 900. That would be up on the Skyline Drive in Shenandoah National Park. He hated to read that.

As free as the trail seemed, it wasn't a perfect environment, Nate knew. He'd done enough searches up in Shenandoah to testify to that. Mostly lost hikers, but there had been a couple of murders, including two young women found bound and stabbed. That was years ago, but truth was, you could not escape human nature. There were bad guys everywhere.

And a lot of good people too. He hoped Butterfly was still with those young men, assuming they were good people. He hoped she was safe and would be safe when she got back on the trail.

Nate had lunch that day with an old guy from Tennessee. It was "Big Cat's" second thru-hike, and he was making good time. "Plan to be at Katahdin in September," he said, "before the snow flies." He told Nate he was sixty-five, retired, and planned to hike until he died. "Ain't nothin' like it," he said. "Out here, it's just you and the woods, no drama, no worries."

Big Cat gave Nate some tips for the road up ahead. "Shenandoah's cool—some of the best views and food's easy to come by. Hamburgers everywhere. You get tired of the woods you can hike Skyline Drive. Then you find out how hard asphalt is on the feet!" He squinted in the bright sun. "After that's the Roller Coaster. Up one steep rise and down another for miles. People call it PUPS, pointless ups and downs. But it don't bother me. It ain't nothin' compared to the rocks in Pennsylvania. That state kills boots!"

Nate laughed. "Thankfully, I'm not goin' that far."

"Section hiker, then."

"Right. Just Virginia."

"Well, you have a mind to go further, let me know. I'll hike it wi' you."

Nate didn't tell him about his leg or Laura. He just wished him well and watched him leave. He found out two days later that, five miles up the trail, Big Cat had had a massive heart attack and died. What irony.

Ember nudged his leg. "You ready to go?" Nate asked, ruffling her coat. "All right then." If he looped the leash through her collar instead of clipping it, it was better, he found out. She'd stay close, but if he fell it would slip free and he wouldn't drag her along with him. He hefted his pack and adjusted it, picked up his poles, and they were on their way.

39

Walking through the shady tunnel with Ember right next to him, Nate figured they had about six miles to go. Because of the terrain, though, they were making less than two miles an hour. He wanted to set up camp at the Matt's Creek shelter, preferably before dark.

Hiking was a simple way to live. Keep moving. Follow the white blazes. Filter water. Eat. Drink. Sleep.

Oh, and also think and feel.

Nate loved the way Laura was soft but strong, too. The way she cared about people. He loved her cooking and the little decorative touches she'd added to their home. He loved caring for her as he felt a husband should, fixing things and steadying her when she was unsure. He loved loving her.

When he'd expressed that to Peter Brenner, the man had suggested Nate imagine what Laura was experiencing now, with Jesus. No more pain, no sorrow, no guilt or shame or unmet needs. Perfect peace. Boundless joy. Immersed in beauty. "Think about where she is, and remember that, before too very long, you'll be there, too."

That had helped. That plus confessing his anger. Nate figured he'd probably never be free from grief, but he felt better, and he was grateful. God had drawn him up out of the miry bog and set his feet back on the Rock. "Thank you," he said.

Up ahead he could see that the trail narrowed and wound around a rock face. The sun would be down soon. About half an hour to go to get to the place he wanted to camp. Tomorrow, he'd see Jeff for the last time, have a shower and a night in a motel, then start again. Next stop: Shenandoah National Park.

If it weren't for the gear strapped all around him he might have noticed Ember's ears prick and her head come up. He might have seen her nose working.

But he didn't see any of that and so it came as a complete shock as he made the turn at the protruding rock to come face-to-face with a black bear not thirty feet ahead on the trail. His heart jumped. He stopped dead in his tracks. Held up his hands. Said in a low voice, "Whoa, bear. We ain't gonna hurt you."

A trickle of sweat ran down his back, right between his shoulder blades. Ember growled. "Steady, girl. Leave it," he said. "Steady." She held her position. "God, don't let her chase that bear!" He touched his dog. "Steady, Em. Stay."

Then he saw one, no two, cubs emerge from the woods behind the momma. His mouth went dry. His heart hammered in his chest. Any animal will protect its young.

What weapon did he have? A couple of hiking sticks. Rocks. His knife. In other words, nothing.

The momma bear advanced toward Nate. "Just stay cool," he said. He banged his poles together. Yelled. Tried to look big. She kept coming. He began backing up slowly. He hoped that he could disappear behind the protruding rock and the bear would leave. "Back, Emmy. Back."

That's when he fell. Tripped. Dropped his poles. Fell backward off the trail and tumbled twenty feet down the mountain before slamming into a tree. Stunned, he heard the bear roar. Ember began barking furiously. He turned over in time to see his dog, her leash free, charge forward, toward the bear, then stop. She put herself between him and the bear, barking and growling, her hackles raised.

But the bear wasn't giving up. She kept coming toward them, her prey drive triggered. Nate fought to shed his backpack, got one arm out, then the bear roared again. Slipping free of the remaining strap, he tried to stand, but the grade was too steep, and he had nothing to pull himself up on. "Hey, bear, git, git!" he yelled. He tried again to get up, and fell, yelling the whole time. The bear charged.

Helpless, he curled into the fetal position, knife in hand, braced to take the attack. Hot with adrenaline, nothing happened. He heard

Ember barking and the bear growling. When he looked again what he saw amazed him. Ember was rushing the bear, then backing away, then rushing again, staying just outside the bear's reach, turning the bear away from Nate. They were moving away, Ember charging and backing up, the bear focused on her.

Nate crawled back up to the trail, his heart pounding. Ember had lured the bear fifty feet away. The two of them were still going at it, Ember flashing forward, then dashing away, the bear chasing her. Nate saw the bear stand on her back legs, then drop down again and shuffle forward, toward Ember, away from him. He found his trekking poles and forced himself to his feet, pain racing down his right hip. "Hey, get gone!" He yelled, raising his arms. "Go!" The baby bears followed the momma, squealing, and they left. Soon, they were out of sight, deep in the darkening woods.

He tried moving his leg. "Ooof," he said, feeling the pain. "Bruised is all," he told himself. He had to find Ember. He whistled. Called. From far away, he heard Ember yelp. "Oh, God, no! No, no."

Nate needed his pack. Without it, he didn't have a headlamp, much less a cell phone or his first aid kit. He slid down the hill, retrieved it, and started working his way back up to the trail, half-crawling at an angle.

Out of breath, he finally made it. He got to his feet and stood there for a minute, trying to decide what to do, thoughts and fears whirling through his mind. He called for Ember again. Whistled. She didn't respond. "God, please. Help me find my dog."

Night comes quickly in the mountains. The sun was already down. The spectacular sunset he'd seen a few nights before had seemed like heaven's glory spilling over into this world. Now it was a distant memory.

Nate put on his headlamp. He got his wallet, his cell phone, two candy bars, and his water bottle out of his pack, plus his handheld GPS, his compass, and a map. He stowed his pack behind a rock next to the trail, marked the position on his GPS, and limped off into the woods. Thirty pounds lighter, he could move faster and cover more territory.

Twenty minutes into the thick woods, he heard a little bark. More like a yip. He followed the sound, and in the light of his headlamp, saw Ember army crawling through the dark woods toward him. "Ember! Ember, girl!" He moved toward her. Her tail wagged.

He looked her over. Why was she crawling? His headlamp illuminated the wounds—two bear claw slashes on her right haunch. His stomach turned. She was bloody, her skin ripped open. Panting, probably close to shock, she needed medical care, more than he could give her. Stitches. Antibiotics. Painkillers. Fluids.

This dog had saved his life. Now he needed to save hers.

40

Nate knew he'd have to carry Ember out of the woods. But how?

First things first. He took off his shirt. He wrapped it around Ember's leg and around her belly, encasing the wound as best he could. He tightened it to try to staunch the bleeding, knotting it right over the wound. He looked around for a fallen tree or a rock. Something to sit on.

A rock. Right behind him.

He glanced at his GPS and figured out which way he needed to walk to get back to the trail. He collapsed his trekking poles and stuck them in his belt.

"All right, girl, here we go." Ember wagged her tail in a weak response. "Hang on," he said. He put his hands under her. "This is going to hurt a little." He pulled her toward himself, backing up to the rock.

Nate sat down on the rock. "Let's go," he said, and he scooped her up in his arms. When he had her, he rose to his feet, staggering a little to get his balance, pain streaking through his hip. "Thank you, God," he breathed. "Please help me, please help." And he started off.

How he made it, or even how long it took, Nate

couldn't tell you. It was one step at a time, until, arms shaking, he made it to the trail and laid Ember gently down. Then he collapsed on the ground, exhausted. His body felt like rubber. He lay there, for ten or fifteen minutes, shirtless, first sweaty, then freezing, the stones from the trail pressing into his back. And then he heard voices.

Nate sat up just as three men came down the trail, headlamps bobbing. "You okay, man?" one of them asked.

Nate shook his head. "No, I ain't." He held up his hand. "Can you help me up?" The man, who looked like a football player, pulled Nate to his feet. "Ran into a bear. My dog is hurt. I need to get her to a vet."

The man stared as his headlamp illuminated the thick burn scars on Nate's chest and arm. He met Nate's eyes.

"Afghanistan," Nate said.

The man gave a slight nod and said to the others, "C'mon. We need to help this brother."

Vets? "Thank you," Nate said. "We can use my tarp. Two of us can carry her."

"Have you called 911?"

"No."

"I'll do that," one of the other guys said.

Another one dug in his pack and handed Nate a T-shirt. "Keep it," he said.

The men insisted on carrying Ember themselves. Within minutes, they had the dog on a makeshift sling. They traded off, carrying their own packs plus Ember. Nate followed them, limping and exhausted.

A ranger driving a Gator-type ATV met them down the trail. "A K-9 officer is going to meet us at the road," he told Nate. "He's called the vet they use, and she's agreed to meet you at her office."

"Thank you," Nate said. "I'm mighty grateful," he looked around, "to all of you." He shook hands with the men, checked on Ember in the back, climbed into the ATV, and they bounced down to the road.

Twenty minutes later, Nate stood in the sparkling clean exam room at the practice of Dr. Victoria Lansing, DVM. Such a contrast to where he'd been for the last weeks. For the fourth time that night, he told the story of how Ember had protected him, how she'd drawn off the bear. This time, he felt a little faint as he recalled it.

That could have gone so wrong.

"I'm not sure which is more astonishing," Dr. Lansing said. "Ember being so smart and brave or you hiking with one leg."

"Yes, ma'am," Nate said. "How bad is she?"

"I think she was very lucky," the vet said, her head bent over Ember's hindquarters. "It was a glancing blow. Still, the wounds are deep. I'll clean them out and stitch her up. She'll need fluids and antibiotics, so I'd like to keep her overnight. But I think she'll be up and hiking again in no time."

"Thank you, ma'am!" Nate said, relief flooding through him. He wiped his hand over his face.

"Where are you staying tonight?"

"I got no idea," Nate said. "I ain't even sure where I'm at." He shook his head.

"I can help with that." The K-9 officer who'd brought Nate there had stayed with him. "I can take you to a motel or there's a hostel."

Nate looked at the doc. "How long before we can travel again?"

"I'd like you to give her a week off. She's lost a lot of blood."

"Okay. Motel, then."

"Fancy or cheap?" the officer asked.

"A place with grass where I can walk her and where I can get food easily since I ain't got a car."

"I'll see what I can do."

Ninety minutes later, Nate, too tired to shower and too dirty to sleep in a bed, lay on a sheet on the floor of a room at Mountain View Inn thanking God for all he'd provided that night. He was safe. Ember would recover. He'd had help when he needed it. Those men, veterans maybe? A ranger. A helpful cop. A kind vet. This room. Food. "Mor'n I could ask or imagine," Nate said. Exhausted, sleep came quickly.

• • •

Nate hung out in the small town for the next week. He wasn't that far from home. He could have asked Jeff or Kathryn to pick him up and take him back to his house. But he was afraid if he went home, he wouldn't come back on the trail. And something told him he wasn't done yet.

The K-9 officer who'd helped him initially, Tom Carter, drove Nate back to the vet's office to pick up Ember. He'd shown him where to find things around town, what food was available, and where the post office was.

Nate had Jeff ship the next supply of food, including Ember's food, to Buena Vista, saving him the trip. With time to kill, he walked around the small town, investigating what few shops there were. He washed his clothes. Took a shower every day just because he could. He tried watching TV but was instantly bored. Instead, he mapped out the rest of his trip, figuring as best he was able just where he'd camp and how far he'd walk every day. And he read the Gospel of John. Several times.

When Nate was ready to check out of the motel, Tom Carter picked him and Ember up and drove them to the James River Foot Bridge. "Thank you, Tom," Nate said, shaking the deputy's hand. "I appreciate all you done, and I wish you well."

"You, too, sir," Tom said. "I bought you something." He held a bag out to Nate, who took it, looked in it, and laughed. Bear spray.

"I'm hopin' not to need that," Nate said, "but I'll feel a lot better walkin' through the woods knowin' I have it."

"Take this, too." Tom handed him a bell. "It's a bear bell, for the dog."

Nate nodded. "Thank you. Very kind."

The James River Foot Bridge, built on the pilings of an old railroad bridge, stretched before him. Beneath it, the blue waters of the James River flowed. Beyond it, stood beautiful green mountains.

Nate breathed deeply. Fresh air.

All he had to do was walk, eat, sleep—and think—for the next three or four weeks. Simple. Then he could go home, to his friends, to Sprite, and to a new little baby. He was looking forward to it.

"Lord," he said out loud, "it's just like Satan to try to knock me back down with a bear attack just as I was beginnin' to see you again. I ain't gonna let him stop me from doin' this hike. You had my back. You provided all I needed. And I'm gonna keep walkin' with you until I know it's time to stop. I love you, God, and I thank you. Now, Ember, let's go!"

The weather grew hot and sticky as he walked. So much for all those showers. Ember seemed fine. He wanted her close, not sure what she'd do if she saw another bear. She seemed to naturally want that, too.

After his week off, the trail seemed more crowded. People were passing him right and left. Most thru-hikers did the trail northbound, but he was seeing a few SOBOs, southbound hikers, too. His plan was to hike just a few miles to the next shelter. But when he got there, he didn't feel like quitting. Ember seemed fine, so they kept going.

So much for plans.

That first night he set up his hammock near a shelter where there was a bear box. He fed Ember, then himself, and put everything that could smell even faintly of food, including a candy bar wrapper and his toothbrush, in a stuff sack. Then he stowed the sack in the bear box.

There were other people around, some using the shelter, others in tents. One group had a small campfire going. They were cooking something. He could smell it.

He was tired enough that he opted out of socializing. He told Ember to go to bed and climbed into his hammock. But as he started to zip up the mosquito netting, he had second thoughts. Ember was lying on her mat beneath him as usual. But what if a bear came nosing around looking for leftover food? How would she react?

Those thoughts bothered him enough he knew he wasn't going to be able to sleep. So he unzipped his hammock. Sat up. And invited Ember to join him.

Seventy pounds of shepherd. Plus his hundred and fifty pounds. And the hammock held. He angled his body to give her room. Zipped the mosquito netting closed. She curled up where the rest of his left leg should be. And together they slept.

In a week, he'd meet Kathryn along the trail. In less than two weeks he'd be at Rockfish Gap, Shenandoah National Park.

Almost home.

41

Two weeks and two days before my due date. The Fourth of July. Scott stood over the grill, spatula in hand, cooking non-traditional steaks and salmon. Hot dogs had too much sodium, he declared. So we upgraded.

He was also grilling corn on the cob and asparagus. There was a green salad already made in a bowl, and I sat in a chaise longue sipping decaffeinated iced tea.

We'd graduated from childbirth classes. Picked a pediatrician. My hospital bag was packed. And my mother kept calling with nervous questions.

"What hospital are you going to use?"

"How long will you be in there?"

"Do visitors have to wear masks?

"Are you having the baby with or without anesthesia?

"Will you be breastfeeding?"

"I think you have a ways to go," the doctor had said last time I was in. I was one centimeter dilated, but he said I could stay that way for a while. "Babies come when they want to," he told me.

I was ready for it to be over. Why wouldn't I be? No one ever told me the last month of pregnancy is like ten months long. An eternity.

Most nights I slept in the recliner. That's the only way I could breathe and the only way my dinner didn't ride up into my throat all night. I was achy all over, my ankles were fat, my face puffy. I had to take my wedding and engagement rings off because my hands were swollen. And all the work of the household, almost of all it, fell to poor Scott.

Kathryn came down frequently to help exercise the horses. She usually brought dinner for the three of us and stayed overnight. We both enjoyed her company.

I thought it was remarkable how well she related to Laura's horse, Abby. Abby became really grouchy after Laura's death, bullying Chief, Nate's horse. Scott said she was grieving. I didn't know horses could grieve, but he said they're more sensitive than I realize.

Once Kathryn started working with her, though, the mare gradually settled down. I wondered, did Kathryn smell like Laura? Was that possible? Could Abby detect that?

Because of my awkward body, I mostly had to watch everybody else play. Scott had rehabbed his shoulder and was riding again. Kathryn and even Amanda joined him.

But I didn't feel sorry for myself. Luke was the one I felt bad for. We hadn't been out on a search in weeks. I could walk him around our property. Throw the ball for him. Scott could take him when he went riding. But that was about it.

One day when I came home from a doctor's appointment, I found my SAR pack, which I had carelessly left out, had a big hole chewed in it. I was holding it in my hand, looking at it, stunned, when Scott walked into the room. Teasing, I asked, "Did you do this?" and I handed him the pack.

Behind Scott, I saw Luke slink away. I nodded his direction so Scott would turn around and look. But instead, he frowned. He unzipped the pack and reached inside. "Jess . . ." he said, pulling out my handgun.

It was my turn to slink away, mentally anyway. I knew better, way better, than to leave a gun unsecured. "I'm sorry! I forgot it was in there." *Pregnancy brain.*

He opened the front hall closet door and he put the gun on the high shelf.

I could tell Scott was annoyed, but he gave me grace. "I'll buy a small gun safe and put it up there. And we need to start using trigger locks."

"Okay."

"We might as well get in the habit now. As far as Luke goes," he said after securing the gun, "don't worry about him. He's got Sprite to play with."

Thankful for the change of subject, I said, "It's not the same. Searching is like working out a puzzle to him. Playing with Sprite is, well, like roughhousing. He misses the challenge." I shook my head. "Chewing the pack is like saying, 'I miss SAR' which the pack represents."

Scott thought about it for a minute. "Yeah, I get it. How about if I run him over that agility equipment you have set up? Would that help?"

"He'd enjoy that," I said, "but I hate laying one more thing on you."

He shrugged. "It might be fun."

It apparently was fun. Soon, not only was Scott doing agility with Luke, but he was making up games that involved scent discrimination, hide-and-seek, and complex puzzle-solving. I was maybe a little jealous, but I loved watching them play.

42

"Kathryn!" Nate said as Laura's daughter stepped out of her blue Subaru. "Oh, girl, it's good to see you!" He'd taken a swim in a deep creek the day before so he could give her a big hug. "How are you?"

"Nate, I barely recognize you!" She pushed back to arm's length, then embraced him again. "My gosh."

"Welcome to my home," he said, gesturing toward the trees around them. They met where the AT crossed a small, two-lane state road, not far from Wintergreen Resort.

"And Ember!" she said, bending down to greet the wagging dog. "Are you having fun?" She straightened back up. "Where can we go for lunch?"

"I could use some barbeque. How 'bout you?"

"Sounds great."

"Some place we can eat outside. My treat."

Kathryn had looked up places ahead of time, which was a good thing because there wasn't any cell phone service where they were. Nate put his pack and the dog in the cargo area of her Forester, then climbed in the passenger seat. "I hope I don't stink up your car. I get pretty rank, hiking."

"You're fine," she said, laughing. "I brought the clean clothes you packed. You can give me those and I'll wash them."

Sitting outside at a picnic table outside a small restaurant, for the next two hours they ate, talked, laughed, and just enjoyed each other's company. Kathryn ordered barbequed chicken salad. Nate's go-to was a pulled pork sandwich with slaw. He ate two. Plus he ordered pulled chicken for Ember.

"I can see why you said you'd pay," Kathryn said, laughing.

"Amazing how many calories you burn off walkin' all day," Nate said. "I'm thinkin' when I get back I got to watch it, or I'll put it all back on."

She told him about Amanda's baby.

"I did read Jess's text about that," he said. "You don't think too much about losing babies that far along in the pregnancy," he said. "Not these days. How is she?"

"She was devastated at first. She's better now."

"How's Jess dealin' with it?"

"She's trying to keep the focus on Amanda, and Scott, too. He was looking forward to that baby."

Nate gave a shake of his head. "It's a loss, for sure."

"But there's good news, too." Kathryn went on, filling him in on Scott's graduation, Amanda's progress, Ethan beginning the police academy.

"Jess is feeling fine, but she's not doing SAR right now."

"Too strenuous."

"Yes. Scott's being great. He's picked up most of the work around the house. I'm going down to help with the horses now and then. In fact, I'm headed there now, after I leave you wherever you want me to."

"You can take me back to where you picked me up," he said.

"And when do we meet again?"

"I'm figurin' eight days. Swift Run Gap. That's where 33 goes over the mountains."

"You realize I could drive you there in an hour."

"That'd be cheatin'." He grinned at her. "Besides, the point ain't gettin' there. It's the journey."

43

People told me about nesting, about how I'd feel the urge to make everything right at home before the baby came. I'd given up long ago on my whiteboard projects. We'd done the important things—the nursery and some deep cleaning. I'd actually moved out, to my mother's of all places, for two days while Scott painted downstairs. Something about being pregnant made me very sensitive to odor. I couldn't stand the smell of paint, any cleaning agent that wasn't lemon, and cigarettes. Weird.

Scott had a contractor building a laundry room downstairs, basically taking over the back porch. A large room, it would include a bathroom with a shower. I'd resisted that. It seemed like overkill. But as my pregnancy progressed and going up and down stairs was more of a problem, I could see the advantage. So I told him to go ahead. With any luck, it would be done before the baby came.

Fixing things for me included relationships. I'd enjoyed Kathryn's frequent visits once her school was over. But there was still an issue that was bugging me.

One day when Kathryn was at our house, I

decided I needed to clear the air. "Hey, Kathryn, can I ask you something?"

"Sure!"

"Why did you agree to help Nate with this hike?"

She smiled. "I was wondering when you were going to ask that." She placed another dish in the dishwasher. Then she sat down with me at the farm table. "Everybody grieves differently. When my parents died, I moved back home. I wanted to be there, around familiar things. I didn't even get rid of their clothes for six months. I used to go into their bedroom and walk into their closet and just look at the suits and dresses and shirts hanging there.

"Maybe I was pretending they were going to walk back in at any moment, that I'd been having a nightmare and that soon I'd wake up. I don't know. But having those clothes there was a comfort to me in those first six months. Nate grieved differently. Seeing Laura's things made him feel guilty."

"Guilty?"

"He felt like he'd failed to protect her," Kathryn said.

I blinked. I had no idea he felt that way. "Failed to protect her?" I protested. "He didn't have anything to do with her death."

"He thinks he shouldn't have let her buy that little car. And he feels bad he didn't go with her that day."

"Why, so he could be killed, too?" I grimaced. "First of all," I retorted, "he told her the car was a bad idea. She bought it anyway. Secondly, she wanted to go into town alone. And even if he'd been with her, he couldn't have kept that truck from hitting them." I tapped the table like I had to convince her.

Kathryn patiently waited for me to finish. "I never said grief was logical." She went on. "When he told me about this hike, I thought it was a crazy idea. But over time, I saw the possibility of it. Nate needed to get out of that house. He needed to break the pattern of despair he felt. He grew up in the mountains, so he knows that environment. He has this new leg. And he's pretty tough, physically. He was in a deep hole, Jess. He needed to make a change."

Her words had not convinced me, but I let her continue.

"Furthermore, I could tell that I could not talk him out of it. That man was determined to go." She shrugged. "So I figured I'd volunteer to help. That way, I had a chance of keeping an eye on him."

I sat quietly absorbing her words. "What about his faith?" I asked. "What happened to that?"

"He just got overwhelmed," Kathryn said, gently. "He really loved my mom."

I knew that was true. I saw it every time I was with them. "I didn't know most of this," I said, "what he was feeling." My heart felt sad, heavy.

"Of course you didn't. He hid it from you. Do you know why?"

"My pregnancy?"

"That was part of it. He didn't want to upset you and risk your pregnancy. The other part is he feels really close to you. Which made him feel vulnerable."

I frowned.

"This is what he said." She straightened up in her chair as she conjured up his accent. She lowered her voice. "If I start talkin' to her, I'm 'fraid my chest'll split wide open, and my guts'll be all over the floor. I'll fall apart completely. I cain't do that," she said.

Jess smiled. "Not a bad rendition."

"That's exactly what he said."

"So he was protecting himself."

"Yes, but also protecting you." Kathryn paused. "Jess," she reached over and put her hand on mine, "Nate's human like the rest of us. He doesn't always make the right choices."

Only Jesus does the right thing every time. "So you've seen him?"

"Yes."

"And how is he?" I didn't want to ask. I wanted to see for myself! I wanted to see him and run to him and hug him and see that he was still Nate.

"His beard is long, his hair is shaggy, and he's lost weight. He looks rough, but he's happier,

Jess, happier than when I saw him last. His eyes . . . his eyes aren't dull anymore. The light is back."

Those searchlight blue eyes. I took a deep breath and nodded. "I'm really glad."

44

Rockfish Gap. Nate stopped at a roadside area just to celebrate the achievement. To the left was Waynesboro. To the right, Charlottesville. He was right near the place Amanda had been kidnapped, near where Scott had been shot in the hip, near where he almost died. And Charlottesville? Home to the UVA Medical Center, where he and his friends were frequent flyers. Where he'd been med-evaced when he lost his leg. Where Scott had been taken, twice. Where Laura had died.

Home. Sort of. Almost.

So far, he'd hiked nearly four hundred miles. A hundred and fifty to go. He was already starting to think about cutting it short. The baby was due soon.

Nate shouldered his pack, grabbed Emmy's leash, and hiked to the entrance of Shenandoah National Park. He registered, as required. While he was doing that, a couple of guys headed southbound asked if he was The Dog Man. Surprised, he said yes. "Got a message for you," they said. "Butterfly's looking for you. She's about five miles north."

What could Butterfly want?

"Thank you. I'll step it up," Nate said. He began to hike. The first part was straight uphill.

"Not long now, Emmy," he told his dog, his breath coming hard. "We'll be seein' Sprite soon." *And Scott and Jess and Amanda and Ethan,* he thought. Now that he'd seen Kathryn, he missed them even more.

He'd thought about their conversation quite a lot on the trail up from Reed's Gap. Amanda losing her baby was sad. That girl had had more trouble. It made his heart hurt. Scott's friend Mike still being gone. Why'd he leave just when Kathryn might need him the most, right after Laura died?

But then, who was he to wonder. He'd taken off, too.

What would Butterfly want with him?

He and Emmy saw a couple of black bears as they hiked that day. Emmy alerted, but held steady, and Nate praised her for that. They got to Calf Shelter. There was a message in the logbook. *Hey, Pops. See you ahead. BF*

Curious.

He set up his hammock a little off from the shelter area. Fixed dinner. Fed Ember. Hung the food bag up on the bear pole. Used the privy. Took his leg off. Cleaned his stump. And went to bed.

By this time, both he and Ember were used to having her sleep in the hammock with him. She stayed quiet. They were fine.

Kathryn had asked if he felt vulnerable, sleeping

outside in a hammock. A little, he admitted. But then, how secure was a tent? Especially the ultralight backpacking tents people were using.

Around three in the morning, he heard a noise. He opened his eyes and listened. Heard a soft snuffling sound. Sticks breaking. He glanced down. Emmy had lifted her head too.

The noise seemed to move away. And then, screams!

Emmy stood. The hammock swayed.

"Bear! Bear!" a woman yelled. More voices joined in.

Nate grabbed the zipper and pulled it open. Too fast. He and Emmy tumbled out. He hit the ground, hard. "Em! Ember!" he said as she took off, barking.

He didn't have his leg on. He scrambled up on his one foot, hanging on to the tree. "Ember!" he bellowed, his heart thudding. He grabbed the bear spray off the side of his pack, then tried to balance, to pull his leg out of his clothes bag, to put it on, all while fearfully listening for a dog's yelp.

He just had managed to attach his leg when the yelling diminished. He stood still. He heard rustling in the woods. And then, out of the dark, Ember showed up, panting like mad and wagging her tail. "Ember!" he said. "You crazy dog!" He grabbed her leash, attached it, and collapsed on the ground.

"Ember." Nate ran his hands all over her, checking for wounds. Couldn't find anything. "So now you're a bear dog?" he said. She licked his face.

"Hey, man, you okay?" Two young men came over.

"Help me up, would you?" Nate held up his hand and they pulled him up. "Thanks. She scared me to death, running off like that."

"Some weekend campers left food outside their tent," the second young man said. "Over there." He gestured beyond the shelter. "Bear got it and ripped open their tent looking for more. They were the ones screaming."

"Ruining it for everyone. Now the park will close camping in the area for a while."

"Is that right?" Nate asked.

"That's what they've done in the past. They just closed camping at Matt's Creek because a bear caused problems."

"Did they now."

That was the end of sleep for that night. Nate packed up his gear. He wanted to wait for dawn to begin hiking. Everything looks like a bear at night when you're on edge. So he walked over to the firepit, rekindled the fire, and sat silently watching the yellow flames, Ember at his side.

Soon others from the shelter site joined him. "I heard dogs attract bears," one young woman said.

"Not as much as food left outside a tent," a young man snorted. "That dog, she ran that bear off."

Nate ruffled Ember's neck. He let their comments lay for a while, then he told them his bear story from Matt's Creek. Someone swore softly.

"Weren't you scared?" someone asked.

"Sure. Especially when I heard my dog yelp. But the Lord provided everything I needed. Those young folks who carried the dog. The ATV. The K-9 cop. The vet. A place to stay. Food. Everything."

"Did he provide the bear?"

Everyone laughed.

"Maybe. Ember and me, we took a week off to recover. I was bruised up. But then, we got back to it."

"I can't believe you got back on the trail after that," one of them said.

"I got a ways to go. Nothing to it but to do it."

The young people didn't respond.

The sky grew light. When Nate felt like it was safe, he put on his pack and left, Ember walking beside him. "From now on," he told Ember, "we got to camp only within shouting distance of shelters." That meant longer hikes. But he didn't want to deal with bears on his own. "And one more thing," he said, "I got to sleep with my leg on. So you'll have to scoot over. We'll make it work, don't worry."

They were getting an early start, but that was a good thing. Their target was Blackrock Hut, thirteen miles away, a hike that left him sore and aching. The following day he'd do another eight to ten miles and get to Loft Mountain, where he could get food, food he didn't have to cook himself.

He had to admit, between the bears and missing his friends, he was ready to be done with this hike.

Loft Mountain was where he found Butterfly. "What's going on? Why aren't you up north by now?" he asked her while inhaling a hot hamburger. Ember lay under the picnic table, her head on his foot, a subtle reminder of her presence in case he had extra food.

"The guys, they left me, you know? Went on ahead."

"Okay." That was not unusual. Lots of times people who were hiking together split up for a short time. "Where'd you plan to meet up? You were going to, right?"

She looked tired to Nate. Trail weary. He guessed he did, too. "No. I just told them to go. But then," she looked around nervously, "this creepy guy found me. And I can't shake him! If I speed up, so does he, and if I slow down, next thing I know, he's back."

"Does he try to talk to you?"

"Some. But mostly he's just lurking around, you know?" She paused. "He scares me."

Nate picked up his second burger. "What's he look like?"

She raised her eyebrows. "Kinda like you! Middle-aged, shaggy hair, beard. Taller than you. And brown eyes, not blue." She frowned. "Come to think of it, a lot of guys on the trail look like you."

Nate laughed.

Then Butterfly thought of something else. "I heard him talking to somebody, bragging about how he basically is living out of hiker boxes. Like he's homeless or something. Bumming off of other people."

"Is this man the reason you were leaving messages for me?"

She nodded. "The last few, anyway."

"Why me? Why not tell a ranger?"

"I trust you. I don't know why. And I don't have a good feeling about cops."

"Well," Nate said, "I'll tell you what. Why don't we travel together, at least 'til Swift Run Gap. That's where I'm meetin' my friend to resupply. I may go back on the trail after that, I may not. If you want to get off, and if I can help you in some way, I will. I can put you on a bus, drive you back home, find you a place to stay, or whatever." He gestured toward the trail. "If you want to keep goin', well, I'd suggest you find someone to hike with. Your instincts are tellin' you something, and there's no sense doin' this if you don't feel safe." He passed the rest of his burger to Ember under the table. "This guy have a trail name?"

She nodded. "Bear."

Nate paused, his third burger in midair, as a cold chill coursed through his body.

Butterfly pitched her tent right next to Nate's hammock that night. They filtered water together, and he walked her to the privy before they went to bed. "Now, you need to get up at night for any reason, you wake me, hear?" Nate said before climbing into his hammock.

Butterfly nodded.

"And we leave at first light. We got fourteen miles to cover, and I go slow."

"Okay," she said.

"The next day we'll have just four or five miles to where I meet my friend. Have you thought of what you might want to do?"

"I . . . I think I want to go home." Her voice quavered.

"Where's home?"

"Ohio. Dayton."

"Why'd you leave?"

Butterfly ducked her head. "Too many rules."

"You live at home?"

She nodded.

Nate rubbed his beard. "How old are you?"

"Twenty-four!"

He raised his eyebrows. "Really?"

She rolled her eyes. "Okay. Nineteen."

"And you thought you'd be free on the AT."

She nodded. "Right."

"How's that workin' out?"

She looked away. The light of his headlamp caught the tears in her eyes.

Nate took a deep breath. "What's your real name?" he asked.

She looked back. "Lacey. Lacey Brooks."

"Pleased to meet you Miss Brooks. I'm Nathan Tanner. I'm old enough to be your father. I'll see you through this. But for now, let's get to bed. We got a long way to go tomorrow, Lord willin'."

Apparently, the Lord was not willing. Tomorrow did not work out as Nate had planned. First light brought with it rain, a gentle rain at first, that became steadier as Nate and Lacey hiked. Steep elevation changes made the trail slippery. And just over six miles in, Lacey fell, twisting her ankle.

"I kin tape it," Nate said. She sat down on the rock and Nate took her shoe off, but when he removed her sock the ankle was already swelling.

They were near a stream. Nate had Lacey take her pack off and he helped her get to the stream.

"Put your foot in there," he said. Even in July, the water was icy cold. Then he went back and got both of their packs. "We're near Pinefield Hut," he said, checking his map. We'll stay here tonight. I'll tape it up good in the mornin' and we'll hope for the best. I'm meetin' my friend at seven tomorra evenin'. I want to make that if we can."

"I think I can walk on it," Lacey suggested.

"You'll do better if you just keep icin' it in that stream. Twenty minutes on, twenty minutes off. I'll go set us up at the shelter." Before Nate left, he dug out a tarp. "Here, use this as a raincover."

The rain continued all afternoon. Being forced to stop, Nate realized, was probably a good thing. He would have had trouble with the slippery, steep path eventually.

He played with Ember, cooked for himself and Lacey. But it was a random find in the privy that captured most of his attention. It was a local newspaper, an old issue stuffed in the corner, reporting on a young woman who'd been missing from James Madison University. Her body had been found recently. This was a follow-up story, an interview with her parents. In it, the young woman's father mentioned that the private investigator he'd hired cracked the case: Jessica Cooper.

Jess! What was she doing still working?

Nate checked the date of the paper. He broke out in a sweat. The paper was a couple weeks old and she'd found the body some time before. Was this the search Kathryn had told him about? No—police found that young woman alive. He walked back to the hut, the newspaper stuffed under his raingear.

Back at the hut, Nate dug in his pack and pulled out his phone. Yes, he had a signal! He went online to that newspaper's website, hit a paywall, retreated to Google, and searched until he found the whole story. Two missing young women, the second one found alive, and then after that, Jess finding the body of the first one.

Wow, he'd missed a lot while he'd been gone. Then he noticed the description the second young woman gave of the man who'd tried to abduct her. Bearded. Shaggy hair. Older. Heavyset. Scar. "And he smelled really bad," she said.

How far away from the AT did all this take place? He quickly did a map search. Not that far. Could the guy Lacey was talking about be the guy who abducted these women?

That's a big leap, Tanner, he told himself. After all a lot of guys had shaggy hair and beards. If he was on the trail, where was his car? How'd he get those girls? Unless he was local on the trail pretending to be a hiker.

He texted Scott. *Ending hike. Meeting Kathryn tomorrow 7:00 p.m. Swift Run Gap. May have a young woman with me. May need help. Your house possible?*

He got an answer back right away. *Absolutely. Can't wait to see you.*

Lacey was still at the creek. He didn't want to alarm her, talking about the abductions, but he also didn't want her alone. He walked down there and hung out like he enjoyed being soaked to the skin.

They went to bed early. Heard coyotes at night but rested undisturbed by bears or other hikers. When Nate evaluated Lacey's foot the next day, he thought it looked much better. "I kin tape it and I think you'll be able to walk on it," he said.

"Thank you."

Nate taped it up, then told her to sit while he packed up his stuff and hers. Then he shouldered his pack. "I cain't carry both packs," he said, "but I'll give you my trekking poles so you won't fall again."

"What about you?"

"I'm gonna find me a hiking stick."

While he searched the nearby woods, she gamely put on her pack. "I'm going to be slow, I'm sorry," she said, gingerly trying her ankle as he reappeared.

"I'm slow already. It's okay. We just need to be steady."

Eleven miles by 7:00 p.m., that was their goal. Under normal circumstances that was entirely doable. But these were not normal circumstances. The rain had stopped, but the trail was still wet, especially where it was rocky. Going down was harder than climbing. They had to do both. He found a spot with a cell signal and texted Kathryn. *On track to meet you at seven, Swift Run Gap Registration Area. If delayed, DO NOT wait there alone in the dark. Updates to follow.*

By lunchtime they had made four miles. By 2:00 p.m., they'd racked up another three. Four miles in four hours. "We can crawl that fast," Lacey joked.

"Maybe you can." He told her about his leg.

"What? I had no idea. I just thought you were old," she responded.

"I oughta leave you right here," Nate said, teasing. But, of course, he wouldn't, couldn't, not knowing what he knew now.

The afternoon wore on. *On track for seven Swift Run Gap,* he texted Kathryn. The humidity seemed particularly high. They saw more hikers as they approached the hut that was just a couple miles from their goal. Most were northbound. One group, though, was southbound.

Lacey punched Nate, her face fixed on that group.

He looked, trying not to stare, and then he saw a man, taller than he was, with shaggy hair and a beard, his brown eyes focused on Lacey, a scar near his eye.

"If he follows us," Nate said in a low voice after the group was past, "I'll keep him occupied. You go off, maybe to use the woods. Just slip away. Hide 'til we're out of sight. I'll keep him with me. Follow the signs down to Swift Run Gap registration area. Look for a blue Subaru Forester. My friend's name is Kathryn. Tell her what happened and wait for me there in her car. Oh, and call a ranger. Do you understand?"

Lacey nodded.

Ten minutes later, a northbound group came up behind them. Bear was among them.

"Remember what I said," Nate whispered.

"Okay."

"Hey, Butterfly, who's your boyfriend?" Bear joined them on her side.

"I'm the Dog Man," Nate said, keeping his voice cheerful. "Who're you?"

"I'm Bear. Where you headed?"

"Big Meadows," Nate responded, "where my car is at. You?" *His pack.* His pack was wrong. Not nearly big enough for backpacking.

"Oh, I'm goin' on through. Got big plans up ahead."

"Is that right?" Nate carefully navigated down an incline. "Say, you remind me of someone. You ever been to Harrisonburg?" The man shot Nate a look. "I seen a man at the shop where I take my car looks something like you," Nate said.

"Never been there."

Nate shook his head. "I don't know. I been a little crazy since I got out."

"Got out? Of what?"

"Jail." Out of the corner of his eye, Nate saw Lacey's eyes widen. "Got nailed for burglary. I didn't do it, man. Another guy did it. But they tapped me instead of him. Ever been in a jail? I'm tellin' you, it ain't fun. That's why I come out here. Walked out from that place and I ain't never goin' back. How 'bout you?"

"I gotta pee," Lacey said suddenly, and before the men could say anything, she was off in the woods.

Bear stopped. "We waitin' for her?"

"She'll catch up. Me, I'm ready for a beer."

"You're goin' slow enough."

"Got shot in the leg," Nate said. "It's givin' me trouble."

They walked on, talking. Bear started asking him questions, probing to see if Nate was for real. His answers must have been okay, because Bear began opening up, telling prison stories.

"When did you get out?" Nate asked.

"Few months ago. January."

"Cool."

"Didn't 'get out,' I escaped."

"Escaped?"

"They were taking me to Maryland. Prison van crashed. I ran. Been around here for a while, but I decided it's time to move on. Look," Bear said, "I gotta take a leak."

"Good idea! I'll come, too." Nate didn't like the idea of being alone in the woods with this man, but he couldn't risk him crossing paths with Lacey. So he followed him, making a lot of noise, crashing through the underbrush so Lacey could avoid them. He let Ember off leash so she could do her business.

Bear did what he needed to do and started walking back up to the trail. Nate followed him. The thicket of rhododendron and the ground runners were making it hard. He had to watch where he was walking, use his hiking stick. He lost track of Bear. Out of breath, he paused. Where was Bear?

Then a hard blow struck the back of his head. He saw a flash. Felt searing pain. And everything went black.

45

"Bear," aka Albert M. Russo, fifty-seven, of no fixed address, had a mission. Get a car. Get outta Dodge. That article in the paper had made him hot property. There was a reward out for him. As easy as the hunting grounds were here, he had to leave.

He wasn't going back to prison. Not now, not ever. As soon as Dog Man said he had a car up at Big Meadows, he chose him as his next target. He'd thought it would be the girl, but she was flighty, hard to catch, and he realized getting gone was more important than getting the girl. Girls were a dime a dozen.

He'd forgotten about the dog. The black German shepherd came out of the bush just as Russo raised the rock to hit the guy again. Instead, he had to defend himself. He threw it at the dog, who dodged it. When she charged him, barking, Russo landed a hard kick on the dog's ribcage, sending it tumbling down the hill.

Russo wasn't up for a fight with a dog.

He quickly went through Dog Man's pockets looking for car keys. He couldn't find any. But he found something better, an iPhone, open to a text message. The Dog Man was meeting a girl just off the trail. And the girl no doubt had a car, because he'd told her to park. A girl and a car. Ha! Lucky!

He could hear the dog coming back. He had to go. The phone was all he needed. He ripped the Dog Man's backcountry registration off his pack and took it with him.

Russo climbed up to the trail and ran north, hoping the dog would stay with its person. Then he stopped to make a plan.

He checked his watch. Dog Man had set their meeting time at seven at Swift Run Gap. Where was that? Somewhere up ahead? Russo didn't want to show up until dark, at least nine, because he wanted her to let him in that car. Would she wait that long?

Maybe if Dog Man told her to. So Russo, pretending to be Nate, texted her. *Ran into snag. Gonna be late. Like 8. Wait for me.*

46

"Hey, Scott. It's Kathryn." She was sitting in her Subaru near the Swift Run Gap Registration Station where she was scheduled to meet Nate. The rain from the day before had washed away the haze giving her a clear view of the lush, green Shenandoah Valley, highlighted in gold now as the sun dropped in the west.

She'd arrived at 6:30, just as planned, ready to pick up her . . . what? Stepfather? Friend? Her mother's husband? Nate was all of that and more to her now.

She was thrilled he was ending this hike. Like Jess, she'd thought it a little crazy. But the difference in his mood the last time she saw him was remarkable. He was alive again, and she couldn't wait until he was home.

Still, something seemed a little off, and who better to talk it out with than Scott.

"You know I'm picking up Nate at the place where the AT crosses 33," she said.

"Right."

"The original pickup time was six. He moved that to seven, which is fine. Then I got a text saying he's been delayed, and he'll be here at eight. Just now, I got another one moving it to nine."

"And . . ."

"It seems off."

"Why?" Scott asked. "I imagine it's difficult to keep to a hard-and-fast timeline when you're on the trail, especially with his leg and all."

Kathryn hesitated. Maybe she was being paranoid. "He was right on time the last time I met him. Earlier today, at noon, he sent me a message saying we should meet at seven. He told me if he got delayed not to wait alone in the dark. He emphasized that. Now, he's saying he'll be here at nine. It's almost dark then. So it seems contradictory."

She could tell Scott was listening to her by the pause.

"Well," he said, continuing, "do you think it's all that dark at that time? What's his concern?"

"I don't know."

"Are there people around where you are?"

"Not many. I've seen a couple of hikers pass through."

"Rangers?"

"No."

Silence followed. Scott was thinking.

"There's more to it, Scott. Let me read you the noon text: *On track to meet you at seven, Swift Run Gap Registration Area. If delayed, DO NOT wait there alone in the dark. Updates to follow.* The words 'do not' are in all caps."

"Hmmm," Scott said.

"Something else. Have you ever noticed that even though Nate talks like a hick, he doesn't write that way? His texts are perfect, almost like somebody rapped him across the knuckles in school when he messed up the grammar while writing, but nobody thought to correct his speech. So here's the text I got delaying the pickup until eight: *Ran into snag. Gonna be late. Like 8. Wait.*

"In the first text, he spells out 'seven.' In the second, 'eight' is a number. And 'gonna'? That's unusual. Now, here's the last text, delaying 'til nine: *Ain't gonna make 8. More like 9.* "The numbers are numbers and he wrote 'ain't.' "

"What are you suggesting?" Scott's voice was deadly serious.

"Somebody else has Nate's phone."

47

I could hear the change in Scott's voice. He was talking to Kathryn, that's all I knew.

With less than two weeks to go to my due date, I felt like a hippo and probably looked like one, too. My mother had been out to inspect the nursery that day. "Oh, you're carrying big!" she'd said *again*. Was that supposed to be encouraging? Whatever. I just wanted it to be over.

Scott walked back in the room. I literally saw his face change from concerned to relaxed. He wasn't fooling me one bit. "Hey, do you mind if I go out for a bit?" he asked.

"Nope. I'm going to bed as soon as I think I can fall asleep. Where are you going?" To be honest, I didn't care. I just wanted to be able to relax and go to bed. *Stay up on your sleep,* Dr. Browning had said. *You could go into labor at any time, and you want to be rested.* As if I needed the reminder, the Braxton-Hicks contractions had been hard that day.

"Kathryn's supposed to meet Nate this evening, right up there where 33 crosses the trail."

I knew it well.

"Anyway, she's having a little trouble figuring out the connection, and I thought, since it's so close, I'd go and help her."

"Maybe I should go with you," I said, starting to get up.

"No. Stay here. Please."

I frowned, questioning.

"We're so close to having this baby," Scott said. "I just want you here, safe at home." He bent down and kissed me. "I don't expect any trouble, but you know. Traffic."

I eyed him skeptically. But to be honest, right then all I cared about was getting some sleep. So if he wanted to go out driving an hour at this time of night, he could have at it. "Sure, fine. Promise me you'll bring Nate here, so I can see him in the morning."

"I'll invite him and encourage him to come." He kissed me. "I'm going to take Luke, if that's okay."

"Luke? Why? I haven't taught him to drive and he's not very good at reading the map."

Scott laughed. "I don't know what we're going to need but if something's confusing about the instructions about where exactly Nate will be, I figure Luke could find him regardless."

"Now that you're an expert with one search under your belt." I smiled at him. "Go. I'll be fine."

"No unusual contractions?"

"Just the Braxton-Hicks I've been having for a month. If that changes, I'll text you. You won't be that far away. First babies take a long time coming." I saw him look toward the kitchen. I followed his glance. He usually did the dishes after dinner. He hadn't done them yet. "I'll take care of that," I said.

"You sure?"

"Take off, go! I'll see you when you get back."

48

Kathryn found herself growing more nervous as the evening progressed. *This can't be right,* she thought. But she'd texted Nate. He assured her he was coming. And Scott was on the way, too. By her calculations, he should be there in fifteen minutes, if he'd left right away.

To distract herself, she put on an audiobook she'd been listening to, a novel about a Victorian-era lady detective in London. Funny, charming, and suspenseful. Maybe she should recommend it for her book club.

Outside, the sky changed from blue to pink to deep blue and then to black. She could see stars pop out. She tried not to notice. She was waiting. Alone. In the dark. Exactly what Nate had said not to do.

5 minutes, the new text read.

Finally she saw Nate approaching in her rear view mirror. Thank God. He tapped on the rear liftgate. She unlocked the doors and pressed "open." He threw his pack in the back, then closed the gate. She was removing her ear pods and putting them away when he opened the front passenger side door and got in. She looked over, smiling.

But her smile vanished. She jerked open her

door and jumped out, then she ran, ran as fast as she could down the hill and into the forest, ran until her heart was pounding and her lungs were screaming for air. Ran and ran and ran, until she collapsed.

49

When Scott arrived at the Swift Run Gap Registration Station no one was there. Not Kathryn. Not Nate. Not Kathryn's car. Confused, he checked his directions. He reread Kathryn's texts. He got out and was about to call the park's emergency number when he heard his name.

"Scott?"

He looked up. "Kathryn!"

"Oh, Scott!" She fell into his arms, her heart pounding a thousand miles an hour.

"What's going on? What happened?"

"I got carjacked," she said, her voice interrupted as she tried to breathe. "Someone has his phone. He took my car."

"Then where's Nate?"

"I don't know!"

"Here, sit down in the Jeep." He helped her into the passenger seat, then called 911. That operator transferred him to the park's emergency dispatcher. He identified himself as an armed off-duty FBI agent. Twelve minutes later, rangers arrived in two vehicles.

Kathryn was remarkably calm, Scott thought, as she gave her statement. "We've never had a carjacking," one of them said to Scott. "Not that I know of anyway."

"Call the state police. They'll issue a BOLO. That guy can't be too far away," Scott said. His adrenaline was pumping. "Meanwhile, we need to find the hiker Kathryn was coming to pick up."

"Can you give us a description?" a ranger asked.

Kathryn described Nate.

"Shaggy hair and beard covers about 60 percent of hikers," the second ranger said, sarcasm dripping.

"Black German shepherd should help," the first ranger suggested.

"We can do even better," Scott said. "I've got a search and rescue dog who knows him and will find him. If Nate's anywhere near the trail, this dog will find him. If you'll take me to the trail, we can do this."

"Which way was he going?" the first ranger asked.

"Northbound."

"Should we call for an ATV?" one ranger asked the other.

Scott interrupted. "It'll be better if I move on foot at dog speed," he said. "I know how he works."

"I think just one of us needs to go with him," the first ranger said.

"All right."

"I'm coming, too," Kathryn said.

Scott nodded, admiring her grit.

• • •

The path up the AT was quite a climb, Scott thought, wondering again just how Nate had hiked up and down all those mountains on one leg these last few months.

"This is it," the ranger said, stopping at a narrow path through the woods. "Follow the white blazes. You want to go south from here? Or north?"

"South. I'm assuming he wouldn't have gone past this turnoff."

"That way." The ranger pointed.

Scott focused, trying to remember all Jess did when she wanted Luke to search. "Luke, heel," he said, and the dog moved into position. *His vest. I forgot his vest.* Then Scott remembered this wasn't an actual search, a "find any human" air-scenting search. So he was going to have to improvise anyway. He unclipped Luke's leash.

"Okay, buddy, switch into Lassie-mode," he said to the dog, ruffling his coat. "You know Nate?" The dog's ears pricked up. "Can you find Nate? Luke, find Nate!" and he sent him off with his hand sweeping forward.

Luke took off down the trail, then began sweeping back and forth, the way he'd done with Jess. Quartering, she called it.

"What will he do if he comes across another dog?" the ranger asked.

"Nothing. Avoid it. He's used to distractions."

"How about a bear?"

"A bear?" Scott said. "I have no idea. I hadn't thought about a bear."

"Better think about a bear," the ranger said. "We have 'em."

Could his Glock stop a bear? Scott had no idea.

They followed Luke down the trail. At one point, he came back and looked at Scott like he was waiting for other directions. "Find Nate!" Scott repeated. "Where's Nate?"

The ranger's radio squawked. Scott, focused on Luke, couldn't understand it. "What's that?" he asked.

"Female hiker saying she was being stalked by a guy," the ranger said, shrugging. "Happens all the time. Girls flirt then complain when a guy tries to take her up on it."

"Wait." Scott stopped in his tracks. "Nate had texted me about a young woman who might need help. Could that be her?"

"Pretty vague."

Scott guessed that was true.

The radio squawked again. The ranger answered it. "The girl is ahead of us," he reported. "Says she's worried about another guy, the guy she was hiking with. She can't find him." He shook his head. "That happens all the time, too. Sometimes I think the guys are trying to shake somebody off. Well, we'll find out in about ten minutes."

That's when they heard barking. Big barks, then a second dog.

"I told you. He's getting into it with another dog."

"That's not fighting," Scott said.

Luke came running down the path. He jumped up on Scott, then took off again. "C'mon," Scott said. "Kathryn?"

"I'm right behind you."

They began running down the trail. They found Luke, barking, and followed him down through brambles and underbrush. They saw lights ahead, and then Ember, and then a blonde girl and a ranger bending over someone on the ground.

Nate.

50

What incredible luck, Albert Russo thought. Not only a car, but a good car. With a little cash in the console. He headed east toward the more populous area around Washington, DC where it would be harder to find him. As soon as he could, he'd switch the plates. Oh, and get food. The change and singles he'd found would be enough for fast food anyway.

He stopped at the first place he found. Bought a couple of burgers. He sat in the parking lot devouring them and started scrolling through the man's phone.

Cooper. The name jumped out at him like a red flag to a bull. Cooper. Wasn't her name Cooper? The broad who'd messed up his sweet deal?

He'd been living around Harrisonburg for months. Picking off girls whenever he wanted to. Eating out of dumpsters, stealing when he could. Yes, it was rough, but it wasn't rougher than prison. Wasn't rougher than being confined. He'd escaped that, thanks to the crash of a prison transport van. Escaped it and ran.

He'd learned about the AT and had followed it a long way, living on trail magic and hiker boxes. Stealing whatever he needed. His plan was to hike north. When he found Harrisonburg, and the easy pickings there, he stopped. Until that woman got nosey. Until she put two and two together and blew his cover.

They had his description. They'd found his prints, he was sure. Once they connected his real name to his trail name it would be game over.

It made him mad. He had to move, all because of her.

He tried to remember the rest of her name. It was in the paper, the one he'd lost. He could see the headline: "Cooper Cracks Case."

He looked down at the phone. Started scrolling through the contacts. Cooper . . . Cooper. Amanda. Jessica. Scott.

Jessica! Jessica was it. He was sure.

Address? He did a search.

What luck. He was headed that way. How sweet that would be!

51

After Scott left, I read until I couldn't keep my eyes open any longer. It was a good book, one Scott had recommended on trauma recovery. I was beginning to understand why he was so interested in using horses to help people, particularly children, overcome trauma.

But it was time for bed. I dropped the footrest of the recliner, stood up, and yawned. "C'mon, Sprite," I said to Nate's springer. "It's just you and me tonight."

I turned out the living room lights except for the little one in the front window we always left on. I'd found it in an antique shop one day. The base was a bronze figure of a cowboy on a bucking bronc. Scott loved it.

I padded upstairs, Sprite following me. I had to stop halfway. My hand touched my belly. I grabbed the banister. "Oh, baby!" I said. These Braxton-Hicks contractions were kicking me.

Once upstairs, I went into our bedroom. Sprite immediately went to her preferred corner and slumped down. I took off my watch and put it on the charger sitting on the night table, then did the same with my phone. I debated taking a shower, but I was too tired.

I started to unbutton my blouse, then realized

something—I hadn't done the dishes. "Oh, no." If Scott got home and they weren't done, I knew he wouldn't be upset. Are you kidding? He'd been coddling me. He'd just do them himself.

But I said I'd do them.

But I am pregnant.

But being pregnant is no excuse for being irresponsible.

Although even I had a hard time classifying "failing to do the dishes one night" as irresponsible.

Still.

I buttoned up my shirt. Told Sprite to stay put, that I'd be right back. Her arthritic joints didn't need a useless trip downstairs. I pulled the door mostly shut and went down the steps, yawning. Another contraction made me pause on the way.

Scott had been doing the dishes for so long, I'd almost forgotten how relaxing a sink full of warm, sudsy water could be, I thought as I prewashed the last plate. Oh, yes, we prewash. Despite what the experts said about giving your dishwasher detergent "something to chew on," Scott liked to prewash and so I did it as well. Also spoons. Scott said the spoons had to alternate the way they were placed in the silverware pockets, bowl up or bowl down, no two oriented the same in the same pocket. The spoons were not allowed to spoon.

Minor marital accommodations in my eyes.

Putting the last glass in the top rack, I reached down to close the dishwasher. As I did, I felt another contraction. Man! False labor seemed a lot like hard labor to me.

Then the lights went out. All the lights. What? I was plunged into complete darkness. I glanced at the microwave, the stove. The power was out. Why was the power out?

There was no storm, nothing had flickered. I looked out of the window toward the barn. The single small light was lit. So it was just the house? Why? Wouldn't the house and the barn get electricity from the same line coming in from the road?

Of course they would. It must be something with the house fuse box. I opened the kitchen drawer where the flashlight should be. Nothing.

Great. The fuse box was in the basement. I wasn't going down there without a flashlight.

I had a flashlight in my car. No, wait. Scott had my car.

Well, there should be one in my SAR pack.

That's when I heard a floorboard squeak. Fear jolted me, like a lightning bolt straight to my spine. Was someone in the house?

And then I smelled him.

52

"Is he breathing," Scott asked, sliding down the last five feet to where Nate lay on the ground. He could hear a ranger calling for medical assistance.

"Yes!" the young woman said. "But his head is bloody in the back."

"Who is he?" the other ranger asked examining his pack. "He doesn't have his backcountry camping permit displayed."

"Nate? Nate?" Scott said.

His eyes blinked open.

"Hey, man. It's Scott. Can you see me?"

"Where . . ."

"You're okay. Help is coming."

"It was that guy I'll bet," the young woman said.

"And your name is . . ." Scott asked.

"Bu . . . uh . . . Lacey. Lacey Brooks."

"Lacey, I'm Nate's friend, Scott. Do you know how this happened?"

She told Scott the whole story about the man who'd been stalking her. "Pops, that's what I call him, was protecting me. He told me to, like, sneak away and meet his friend Kathryn."

"That's me," Kathryn interrupted.

"But," Lacey said, continuing, "I was afraid, afraid to be out in the open. I called the rangers, like Nate told me to, and I told them a man was stalking me, but I don't think they believed me. So I just hid for a while, hoping he and Nate would move down the trail. After a while, I started moving forward, parallel to the trail. And then I saw Ember. She barked at me, so I went to her and found him. I really think that man did it. He was scary."

"When you found him, was he conscious?" Scott said.

"Pops? No. I called the rangers again and told them I'd found an injured hiker."

"That's how I got here," one ranger said. "I got help coming now. I'm going up to the trail to guide them in."

"How can I help?" Kathryn asked.

"Leash up both dogs so they don't interfere with the medics," Scott said.

"And maybe gather up the stuff from his pack?"

"Leave it. It's a crime scene," Scott said.

"Got it."

Nate groaned. He lifted his hand. "Help me," he said to Scott. He gestured that he wanted to sit up.

"No, Nate. You've got a head injury. Stay where you are."

Nate grimaced. He blinked a couple of times. "I'm gonna throw up."

"Go ahead. I've got you," Scott said, turning him on his side and holding him.

There was hardly anything in his stomach, but Nate leaned over and threw up what was there and then had dry heaves. "Oh, man," he said when he was done. "My phone." He held out his hand.

"A guy took your phone, Nate." Kathryn looked at Scott. "He was texting me."

Nate squeezed his eyes shut. He was obviously having problems processing what she was saying. "Who has my phone?"

"Bear," Lacey said. "They think Bear has your phone."

"He was texting me, pretending to be you," Kathryn said.

Nate groaned. "He's got your address, Scott."

"He's got a lot of addresses. Whatever's in your phone."

"No, no, listen." Nate gripped his scalp with one hand, like he was trying to stop the pain.

"It's all right, Nate," Scott said.

Nate's hand flew forward and he grabbed Scott's shirt. "No! Listen!" He took a deep breath. "That case Jess worked, the college girls?"

"From Harrisonburg. Right."

"This might be him."

Adrenaline shot through Scott. "What do you know about that?"

"I found a newspaper . . . read the description. A lot like him. Her name, Scott, her name was in the paper."

"Why would he go to my house?"

"To get her, to get Jess!" Nate cried out in agony. "Scott! Listen. That man is evil."

Scott's mouth went dry. "Describe him, Nate. Give me a description." Scott heard the medics coming down the hill. He pulled out his notebook and wrote down what Nate said. "Kathryn give me your license plate number again."

"Will you step back, sir?" the lead medic said.

"Nate, we'll catch up with you," Scott said. He turned to Kathryn. "If he's right, Jess could be in trouble. I've got to call for help."

"I'll go with Nate," Kathryn responded.

"Who are you?" a medic asked. "A friend?"

"Family. He's my stepfather," Kathryn said.

"I've got his dog. Lacey!" Scott called out. "You want to get off the trail?"

"Yes."

"Come with me. Take Ember. I'll take Luke."

Adrenaline powered Scott up to the trail. *Could Nate be right?* He tried Jess, no answer. Tried again. Still no answer. Out of breath, he stopped. "Hold on," he said to Lacey. He scrolled through his phone until he found the number for Sheriff Jim Turner.

"Jim," he said, once they connected. "Scott Cooper. I think my wife may be in danger at our house."

53

The smell turned my stomach. I thought I was going to throw up. I fought back panic. My adrenaline was pumping, my blood pressure soaring.

What could this person want? Guns. Money. Scott. Me.

Somehow, I knew it was me.

In my mind I saw that headline. "Cooper Cracks Case." I saw my name in print. My stomach clenched.

I prayed. *Lord God, the baby, the baby!* Another contraction.

I pictured my iPhone and watch charging in my bedroom. I could kick myself for taking them both off at once.

My hand closed around an eight-inch kitchen knife. I went over in my mind the most effective places to stab someone. Base of the skull. Jugular. His eyes. Carotids. I knew that in reality people usually didn't die quickly from knife wounds. It took time for them to bleed to death, time that he would still be a threat. A knife wasn't my best choice.

The best choice was to get away.

Silently I slipped toward the back door. Turned the knob. It didn't move. I felt for the double-cylinder deadbolt. The key was gone. There was no way to get out, not through the back door. *Jesus, help me!*

If he went upstairs, I could go out the front. I willed him to do that. He didn't. I could hear him near the front door.

If I went downstairs, into the basement, it might be harder to find me, but eventually, he would. I'd be trapped down there. I shivered. Was there a window I could crawl out of? A closet to hide in? A place I could barricade?

Then I thought about the Garmin inReach. Was it in my SAR pack? And where was that? Would it still have a charge?

Scott had moved the pack around because of the construction. Where'd he put it?

The man was in the living room. I could hear him manipulating the recliner.

The front hall closet. Scott had put my SAR pack in the front hall closet. Maybe I could find the Garmin in there. It would still take forever before help came. *Help me!*

I ditched my slippers. Barefoot, I walked across the kitchen, past the farm table, into the front hall. Could I make it out the door? No! He was coming my way. I heard little Sprite barking in my bedroom.

Silently, I made it to the closet door, opened the door, and slipped in, pulling the door shut behind me. I didn't dare move. He was right outside. I could smell him. I peered through the crack between the door and the doorjamb. His flashlight lit his face. I saw shaggy hair. Rough beard. Small eyes. A scar near his eye. I saw the man Julia Whitaker had described as her abductor.

My heart was pounding so hard I was afraid he'd hear it. I felt a contraction coming on. I bit my lip until I tasted blood to keep from crying out. My right hand gripped the knife.

I heard him walk back toward the kitchen. Quickly I bent down. Found my SAR pack. Quietly moved the zipper, tooth by tooth, until the top gaped open. Then I reached around inside. The Garmin, the Garmin. Where was the Garmin? Where was it?

Then I thought of something better.

54

"Hang on!" Scott said to Lacey, sitting in the passenger seat of the Jeep.

He'd gotten the police escort he'd asked for. They were racing down 33, lights and sirens blaring. His speedometer read 80. At this speed they'd be there in less than 20 minutes. The sheriff was sending deputies. Would they be too late?

Scott's phone rang. Mike. He almost didn't answer it. "Yeah, Mike, what's up?"

"Hey man, I wanted to surprise you. I'm at your house."

"You're what?" Scott's heart jumped.

"I'm at your house and all the lights are off. But it looks like Kathryn's here and you know, I feel kind of awkward, the way I left things."

"Mike, Mike! Listen man. It's not Kathryn!" He told Mike what was going on, what he was afraid was going on. "I think Jess is in danger. I think this guy is after her. I've got deputies on the way but . . ."

"I'm on it," Mike said, his voice serious. "I got this, brother!"

55

I wrapped my hand around the gun Scott had put on the high shelf in the closet. Thank God!

Another contraction. They were more frequent now. How frequent? I didn't know. I bit my lip against the pain, the metallic taste of blood in my mouth. And then . . . and then I felt a warm liquid run down my leg. *What? What was that? Blood? No! My water just broke!* I started trembling. *The baby, oh, God, the baby! He'll kill both of us!*

I heard the intruder run into something in the kitchen, heard dishes rattle. Heard him curse. I'd left the dishwasher open. Left my slippers in the middle of the floor. I heard him walk across the kitchen, past the farm table, toward the foyer. I peered through the crack. Saw it was him. The smell, the smell! I pressed myself back in the closet. I braced myself. I adopted a shooting stance.

When he flung the door open I fired, one, two, three, four, five shots.

A flashlight lit the room. "FBI, FBI!" a man yelled. "Get on the ground!"

I stumbled out of the closet and screamed bloody murder.

"Jess? It's me, Mike! Are you shot?"

Lights. More voices. More shouting. "Cuff him!" I heard someone say.

I cried out again.

Mike grabbed me. "Jess?"

"The baby. The baby's coming."

"No. Wait. You can't!" Mike said.

"Yes!" I said and then I screamed.

"She's having the baby!" Mike called out, his voice pitched higher than normal.

"Here! I can help," I heard a voice say.

Officer Hatchett, the deputy I'd saved on the side of the road months ago, had delivered babies before, his own included. He knew what to do. "Let's walk this way," he said. He wrapped his arm around my waist and led me to the living room. "I need light, towels, and warm water," he said, "and find me some sheets!"

"There's a quilt," I said, gesturing toward the couch.

Someone grabbed it and spread it on the floor. Gently Officer Hatchett helped me sit down. "You're doing fine," he said. "I want you to pant when you feel a contraction. Don't push." He looked up. "You," he said, "what's your name?"

"Mike. I'm FBI."

"Okay, Mike, get behind her and prop her up. Support her back. And hold her hand."

Mike sat down behind me. He took my hand. I felt a contraction and started to pant. Then I squeezed.

"Ow! You're killing me," Mike said.

"Shut up."

"Pant!" Deputy Hatchett said.

I panted.

"Sixty seconds. Two minutes apart."

I couldn't remember what that meant.

"Paramedic's here!"

"The suspect's dead. Take care of her," I heard someone say.

A young man with dark hair stood behind Deputy Hatchett. "Name's Tom, ma'am. I'm a paramedic. You're doing fine. Who's your doctor?"

I panted out the name.

"Call her," Tom told someone.

But there was no time. No time to call Dr. Palmer. No time to get me to the hospital. No time even to move me onto the stretcher.

"The baby's crowning," Hatch said. "Don't push, now. You're doing great. Don't push. We don't want him to come fast. Pant."

I panted, squeezing my eyes shut from the effort of holding back. I heard Mike say, "Ow!"

"Baby's head is out." A minute or two later. "We have a shoulder. Okay, now push!"

I pushed and yelled just as my husband rushed in and his son, our baby boy, slid into the world.

What an entrance.

56

Michael James Cooper. Named for both of his grandfathers. The most beautiful baby ever born except maybe Jesus. Perfect features. A wisp of blonde hair. Rosebud mouth. Big blue eyes. Two weeks old and already trying to hold his head up. So strong.

I couldn't take my eyes off of him. Still can't.

"They named him after me because I delivered him," I heard Mike Perez explaining.

"That is not true!" I called out, looking toward the foyer. I shifted my position on the couch in our living room, anticipating our guest.

Nate.

He'd spent a week in the hospital recovering from a severe concussion and another week at Kathryn's house trying to get over nausea and vertigo. Now he was finally here after all these months.

I rose to my feet when he came into the room, the baby in my arms, my eyes tearing up. He was thinner. Suntanned. Fresh haircut. Trimmed beard. Dressed in khaki cargo pants and a navy short-sleeved shirt, his anchor tattoo visible and his eyes bright and shining. "Nate," I breathed.

"Well, look at you," he said, grinning. He wrapped his arms around me, hugging me as best he could. He kissed my head. "And who is this?" He fingered the receiving blanket.

"Michael James Cooper," I said. "Your godson."

Behind him, Scott beamed.

We sat down on the couch, and I handed the baby to Nate. We took pictures. A lot of pictures. And little Mike fell asleep in Nate's arms.

Scott had told me early on that if we had a boy he wanted to name him for my father, Michael Chamberlain. "He was a hero of 9/11," Scott said, "and I want to honor him."

I countered with saying I wanted him to have Scott's father's name, too. "He was a good husband, a good father, nearly destroyed by tragedy. He deserves it too."

So we agreed. Michael James he would be.

We never did settle on a girl's name.

We all sat around our living room, a lot of small talk passing between us. We waded in shallow waters until we were ready to immerse ourselves in the deep. At some point, Little Mike woke up. I nursed him while everyone went to the kitchen to get food. Scott came back after twenty minutes, burped the baby and changed him before putting him down in the nearby bassinet.

Nate came back, bringing a mug of tea for me. He sat back down on the couch. Scott sat in the recliner. "First of all," Nate said, "I apologize for ignorin' you after Laura died." There was a catch in his voice. "I realize now it were wrong. I hurt you, and I'm sorry."

"Oh, Nate. I forgive you. You're back, that's what matters."

He held up his hand. "There's more. Second, I was wrong because I thought I needed to go off on my own. Fight this battle by myself. No. I shoulda stayed here with you all. You, Scott, Kathryn . . . you are family, Jesus' hands and heart. I shoulda stayed here and sorted things out with you. Reached out. Let you help."

I didn't respond.

"Instead, I reverted. Went way back to when I was a boy. I took to the woods. Alone is what felt right. It weren't." He took a deep breath. "I ain't sayin' God didn't bring good out of it. He did. But I was bein' wrong-headed still. You told me that. I couldn't hear it."

"You were deep in grief." I took his hand.

"Yep. Blind and deaf."

"And stubborn," I added, grinning.

Mike Perez and Kathryn came into the room and sat down. Nate did not stop talking.

"God was faithful, even when I weren't," he said. "The anchor held." He told us about the people he'd met, trail magic, Peter Brenner, the sunset. "And then, jus' when I was startin' to feel good, we met a bear."

I could hardly breathe as he told that story.

"Soon as you make a step toward God, the enemy will come after you. Most of you know that. But I'm here to say, God is faithful, despite what Satan throws at you. He'll carry you. He'll give you what you need."

"And if not," Perez said, "there's always the Glock in the closet." He winked at me.

Everyone laughed. Except Nate. From the way he was looking at Perez, I knew he'd just moved Mike to the top of his "most wanted" list. I'd been there once. So had Scott.

Then Nate turned to me. "I'm so proud of you. You knew what was right and you stuck to it, even when I fought you."

I felt a quiver in my gut. "I was so scared for you. Scared you were going to kill yourself, intentionally or not. But I found out I couldn't control you. All I could do was pray and trust God. And here you are." I looked directly at my husband. "Even Scott learned something." I said. " 'Safe at home' applies only to baseball." I grinned at him.

Scott shook his head. The thought of Albert Russo being in the house, stalking me, was still raw. He may have had the front room scrubbed cleaned of the man's blood, he may have had new locks placed on the doors, he may have ordered an alarm system, but he still couldn't stop thinking of the terror of that night.

Nate smiled. "Takes a lifetime to learn all this, don't it?"

"Yes," I said. "And I have a feeling we're not done yet."

ACKNOWLEDGMENTS

Story ideas emerge from all kinds of places. About five years ago a former neighbor, Jack Ledden, gave me a book, "Hiking Through" by Paul Stutzman, about a middle-aged guy who decides to thru-hike the Appalachian Trail. I put it on my groaning "to be read" shelf and forgot about it. A couple of years ago, I picked it up again.

That time, something about Paul Stutzman's story clicked. What a crazy idea, walking 2200 miles from Georgia to Maine in the mountains! There was something alluring about it. I bought more books by thru-hikers, then official trail guides and maps and how-to books. I started watching YouTube videos and reading online trail journals, and learning about gear and trail culture. Slowly a story began to form in my imagination.

As any writer knows, it's a long way from "seeing" a story in your head to transferring that story into words on a computer screen and then paper. It's a massive struggle, believe me, frustrating at times and an absolute joy at other times. It's hours and hours alone with your computer, working out dialogue and settings and scenes and character development and a logical story arc. It's checking spelling and grammar, commas and extra spaces until you're bleary eyed.

At that point, it's time, time to get feedback from friends and experts.

I am blessed with great help in that regard. My daughter, Becky Chappell, always a first reader, freely lets me know if the story will fly. Her daughter, Noelle, is following in her footsteps. Jessica Burnside and Sharon Johnson of DOGS-East Search & Rescue provide valuable insights into the hows and whys of SAR. Dru Wells freely shares her FBI expertise (and often catches mistakes in other aspects of the book). Debbie Robbins, Bonnie DelBalzo, and Janet Schutt all read early versions of this story and gave me great feedback and advice.

I'm thankful for Barbara Scott, who worked her magic editing, and June Padgett, who created the cover, and Janet Grant, my literary agent, who gave me the idea of an SAR series to begin with. I'm grateful to all of you for your help!

All to the Glory of God,

Linda

ABOUT THE AUTHOR

Linda J. White has loved dogs and a good dog story since early childhood. Family allergies kept her from having a dog as a child but seven dogs have enhanced her adult life. She lost her most recent buddy, a twelve-year-old Sheltie, Keira, while working on this book.

Linda has been a government worker, a mom at home, a Bible study teacher, a freelance writer, and the assistant editorial-page editor of a daily newspaper as well as being the author of award-winning, bestselling novels. Her late husband, Larry, a graduate of the American Film Institute, made training films for the FBI Academy for nearly thirty years. Linda has three grown children and five grandchildren and lives in Yorktown, Virginia, where she enjoys hiking and watching birds migrate and grandchildren grow.

For more about Linda see her website, www.lindajwhite.net

Center Point Large Print
600 Brooks Road / PO Box 1
Thorndike, ME 04986-0001 USA

(207) 568-3717

US & Canada:
1 800 929-9108
www.centerpointlargeprint.com